Twilight of War

Based on Historical Events

David Lee Corley

DEDICATION

Dedicated to all the men and women that fought and sacrificed for their country.

Table of Contents

Quote

"All War is a symptom of man's failure as a thinking animal."

– John Steinbeck

Prologue

The gloom of the monsoon season hung over Vietnam like a suffocating blanket. For over a decade, war had ravaged this land. Now, after years of bloodshed and loss, an uneasy quiet had settled across the battle-scarred countryside.

In the North, the armies of Hanoi scanned the horizons warily. A generation had grown up knowing little but war. Their meager rations and threadbare uniforms attested to the cost. Yet morale remained high. They were winning, inch by bloody inch, against the world's greatest superpower. They had already sent the French packing. Now the Americans too were leaving, tails between their legs. Victory, it seemed, was at hand.

In Saigon, fear and uncertainty gripped the capital. Refugees crowded the streets outside the US embassy, desperately seeking asylum before the final American pullout. President Thieu remained defiant, vowing to fight on, but his bravado rang increasingly hollow. His armies were exhausted, his generals plotting their own survival. Defeat, it was whispered, was inevitable.

The last US combat troops still in country were hollow-eyed ghosts packing up their bases. For over a decade they had fought and died here in this foreign land for reasons most no longer understood. Their numbers had dwindled as the US military withdrew, yet still they died - victims of stray shells, trigger-happy enemies, and occasional cruelty. Most counted down the days until their escape from this futile war.

Back home in America, the country remained bitterly divided even with peace seemingly at hand. Massive protests had finally pushed Nixon to end US involvement, yet many still believed in the mission to stop communist domination. For the families of the over 58,000 dead, the grief and pain did not end with the fading conflict. They wanted to know their sons and husbands had not died in vain. Others simply wanted to forget the war had ever happened.

Across the world, there was a collective sense of relief that America's Vietnam misadventure was finally ending. Yet there were also worries about the future. The failure of US power could embolden the communist revolution and Soviet adventurism elsewhere. But for now, the overriding emotion was thankfulness that the unspeakable brutality was coming to an end. North and South alike were exhausted and bankrupted, with hundreds of thousands of dead. Surely nothing more could be gained from continued fighting. The war had to end.

Yet as time marched on, the promised peace remained elusive. Both sides remained locked in obstinacy, with threats and intermittent attacks continuing. None could admit weakness, all clung to escalatory brinksmanship and propaganda. Pride, paranoia, and the lust for power placed any hope of reconciliation and healing out of reach. The guns had fallen momentarily silent, but in the hearts of men on all sides, the embers still smoldered. New sparks could yet cause the fires of war to rage again. The future yawned ahead, fraught with uncertainty. Any twilight, as all warriors knew, could quickly return to darkest night. And this troubled land had known more than its share of dark and bloody nights with no dawn.

The Agony of Victory

Borderlands, South Vietnam

Tom Coyle loved flying. He felt more at home behind the controls of an aircraft than sitting in an easy chair sipping a cold beer while watching football on the television. People were different that way and Coyle was more different than most. Flying came naturally. He felt the aircraft. He didn't fight it, at least most of the time. It was true, he held the record for having crashed his aircraft more times than any other pilot in Vietnam. It wasn't something he was particularly proud of, but he figured he had probably logged more flying hours than any other pilot, so crashing was just part of the mix.

The fact that he survived was more of a testament to his skill as a pilot than time behind the yolk. It took talent not to get killed when he crashed. He often thought it was because he didn't fight the aircraft as it headed for the ground. He just let it happen and tried to guide it in as best he could. It seemed to work. He was still alive, and he wasn't about to change the way he did things, especially when it came to crashing. If it ain't broke, don't fix it.

Coyle and his crew flew a Lockheed AC-130 Spectre modified by the CIA for a larger variety of missions deep in enemy territory. While the prop-driven aircraft was an easy target for the enemy's anti-aircraft batteries during the day, the Spectre owned the night. In addition to four 7.62mm MXU-470 miniguns, four 20mm GE M-61 Gatling guns, and two 40mm Bofors automatic cannons, the Spectre was equipped with infrared sensors, AN/AAD-4 FLIR and side-looking radars, low-light television cameras, and the "Black Crow" vehicle-detection system. With the belly of the Spectre painted black, the aircrew could see the enemy below, while the enemy only saw the dark sky above.

Their mission was to hunt the enemy and destroy them. Simple. And that is what they did night after night. When the sunset, their engines started. There were more targets than ever before. It used to be hard to find the enemy. Now, NVA and weapon shipments were pouring across the borders. Coyle often said there were so many communist caravans he could close his eyes, throw a rock, and still hit the enemy below. If it wasn't for the additional enemy anti-aircraft batteries that accompanied the caravans, the challenge of hunting would be completely gone. It was strange that battle had become redundant, but it was.

It would be another twenty minutes before they reached the most active enemy supply routes along the border, then the hunt would begin. Until then, Coyle could relax somewhat. He let his co-pilot fly the aircraft so he could conserve his strength for the coming battle.

He poured himself a cup of hot coffee from his thermos and sat back starring out at the outline of clouds through the windshield. It was a waxing crescent moon which was better than a full moon but still made the mission more dangerous than a moonless night. The moonlight outlined the gunship just as it outlined the clouds.

In the jungle below…

A thick canopy of jungle leaves blocked out the night sky, leaving NVA Corporal Tran drenched in darkness and sweat. The screech of cicadas was deafening in the tense stillness as he scanned the narrow dirt track slicing through the dense brush. The convoy would be passing soon to deliver men and munitions to the communist units in the South. It was his job and the job of his comrades to protect the trucks and their precious cargo.

Tran rubbed his gritty eyes, fighting exhaustion. Sleep brought dreams of the American gunship's terrifying apparition against the stars - the dragon that poured liquid fire from above. He glanced over at Sergeant Noh's silhouette, noting his partner's ramrod posture. They all knew discovery brought swift oblivion. They sat motionless, all light extinguished.

Distant engine rumbles announced the convoy's arrival. Tran froze, straining to discern direction in the pitch blackness. He felt more than saw. Noh melt into the undergrowth, a stealthy phantom when needed. Moments crawled by, before hulking truck shapes emerged from the void.

Tran squinted skyward as the vehicles lumbered past just meters away. The Americans owned the darkness with their electronic eyes that could peel back jungle cover. But the canopy here was thick. It would take a miracle or disaster for the gunships to glimpse them from 2,000 feet up. Still, Tran shivered imagining the dragon's electronic eyes turning his way. Few tempted the dragon and lived to tell about it… very few.

The passing trucks were the dragon's target. It loved to rip them apart with its streams of lava. If it saw them through the darkness, they would be annihilated within a few minutes. Of course, the NVA would fight back with their anti-aircraft guns hidden in the jungle along the convoy's route, but fighting the dragon meant giving away their position and turning their dragon's wrath on themselves, something even the bravest soldiers were hesitant to do. Nobody wanted to die, especially by a dragon. Most followed Mao's instructions and only attacked when they were sure they could win. It was good advice, especially when dealing with American gunships. Instead, most of the gun crews sat silent in shame until the danger passed. They would live to fight another night when the odds were better. They were not cowards, they just didn't want to waste their lives on an unwinnable battle.

The convoy passed without incident, leaving only silence. After five tense minutes, a barely audible bird call signified all clear. Tran whistled back his own coded response before sagging against a tree, pulse racing. Still unseen. But for how long?

A nearby snap of breaking undergrowth instantly jolted his nerves back taut. Tran whirled toward the sound, AK-47 leveled mid-stride as four slim shadows emerged from vegetation. The point man's gold tooth glinted in a fleeting shaft of moonlight filtering down -

Bao, veteran fighter, and Captain Thu's second.

Bao offered a grim smile and said, "Relax. The danger will not come from the ground. We haven't seen any ARVN patrols for months. Their troops stay tucked away in their fortified hamlets and cities. We own the jungle and they know it."

"They're foolish to give us free rein. I've never seen so many of our trucks and supplies. When the final offensive comes, our troops will be well prepared," said Tran.

"Let's hope it happens soon. My wife wants another child and I plan on give her one."

Both men laughed and spat betel nut juice into the rotting leaves on the ground. "Where are the VC that are supposed to be protecting your unit?" said Bao.

"Patrolling, I suppose," said Tran.

"That or napping. I've never seen troops that sleep so much," said Sgt. Noh.

"Saving their strength for when it is needed," said Bao with a smirk.

"What do you expect? They're mostly farmers. Once the day's work is done, there's not much to do but sleep or drink," said Tran.

"I'd drink," said Bao.

"Me too," said Noh.

In the distance, Bao saw two glowing orange dots on the truck route. Two VC soldiers, weapons slung approached. "What the hell do you think you're doing?" said Bao. "Put those cigarettes out before you give away our position!"

"Not even the Americans can see through the jungle canopy," said one of the VC.

"Really. Do you know a lot about infrared equipment?"

"What's infrared?"

"The thing that's gonna get us all killed if you don't put out those cigarettes. Now!"

The two VC put out their cigarettes crushing the burning butts on the ground with their sandals. "Ignorant fools," said Noh.

The distant thrum of aircraft engines caught everyone's attention as their eyes shifted nervously toward the black abyss above the jungle canopy.

In sky above…

Coyle starred out the windshield into the darkness in front of the gunship. His eyes squinted as if focusing. "Do you feel that?" he said.

"I don't see anything," said his co-pilot.

"I didn't ask what you see."

"Oh, for Christ's sake, Coyle. Are you going all Ouija board again? You know that kinda shit gives me the heebie-jeebies."

"They're down there. I can feel it. Chief, get the guns up."

The chief exchanged looks with his gunners, then gave the order to prepare to fire all weapons.

"What's the heading?" said the co-pilot.

"One more mile, then start your pylon turn."

"Now, you're just guessing, aren't you?"

"They'll let us know where they are."

"Who's they?"

Coyle stayed silent in response. The co-pilot obeyed his commander's orders.

In the jungle below…

Everyone watched and listened. The pitch of the aircraft engines changed as the gunship began its pylon turn, tilting its side-mounted guns toward the ground. "It's circling," said Bao.

"Do you see 'em?" said Tran.

"No, but I hear 'em. Get your battery ready, Sgt. Noh. But no sudden moves that will draw the dragon's attention."

The VC were more nervous than the NVA. As peasants, their culture was steeped in tradition with mythical beasts being at the top of the list. "It's coming to eat us, isn't it?" said a Viet Cong private.

"Shut up and keep watching. We can't fight what we don't see," said his comrade.

Sgt. Noh barked out commands to prepare the anti-aircraft guns, but to hold fire until he gave the order.

Bao's spine tingled, picturing the aircraft's lethal guns aligning on their position. He knew that the gunship could not see them as long as they did not move or give their position away below the thick jungle canopy. He glanced at the wide-eyed VC troops peering upward, muzzles wavering. "Steady, comrades," he urged. "It cannot see us yet. Ready positions but hold fire!" Rifles lowered slightly, sweating fingers poised on triggers.

In the sky above…

Coyle's gaze bored into the blackness revealed in the aircraft control room's eerie green glow. "Anything on the television cameras or infrared?"

"Nothing," said the technicians.

Coyle thought for a moment, then…"We need to flush them out. I'm taking control."

"You have control of the aircraft. But if we fire before they do won't we lose our advantage? We'll expose ourselves and become the target first," said the co-pilot.

"We can't fight what we can't see."

"Neither can they. You don't know if they're even down there, Coyle."

"Let's find out," said Coyle as he switched the weapon selector to the middle 7.62mm minigun and fired a short burst.

A fiery stream spewed forth from the side of the Spectre, slashing the abyss, revealing the ship's position.

On the ground…

Cries erupted below as the VC fighters scrambled backward from the jet of flames.

"There!" said Bao pointing skyward. "Hold fire. It's too far away. We wait until it gets closer."

The barrels of the anti-aircraft guns swung around and targeted the aircraft's last position. The gunship was gone once again, hidden in the ink black sky.

"I can't see it," said Sgt. Noh.

"It's circling back," Tran said, craning his neck to follow the faint engine noise from the sky above.

"Hold positions!" the commander said. "We strike when it's right above us, not before."

The anti-aircraft guns swiveled again realigning to the sky directly over them. The gunner's finger rested on the weapon's trigger, waiting for Bao's signal.

Bao scanned the darkness desperately as another minigun barrage erupted closer, scattering soil and pulverized trees. "Not yet. It is still out of range," said

Bao, but it was too late.

One of the Viet Cong was overcome by fear and fired his rifle at the dragon. "You fool," said Bao.

In the sky above…

The brief muzzle flash told Coyle all he needed. "There!" said Coyle as he banked the aircraft hard to the right, realigning its guns directly over the muzzle flash as he flipped the weapon switches to activate all the miniguns. In seconds, the Spectre unleashed, racing tracer rounds illuminating the ground a satanic red.

On the ground below…

With both fighting positions revealed, it was a matter of moments before one side was dead. There would be no in between in the battle. "Fire!" screamed Bao.

The gunner discharged the anti-aircraft guns, four barrels blazing in sequence, tracer round racing skyward. The assistant gunners loaded new rounds into the feeders as fast as possible. Their lives and the lives of their comrades depended on keeping the guns firing without pause.

In the sky above…

Tracer rounds surrounded the gunship illuminating the aircraft's fuselage and wings.

Coyle didn't let up. He and his crew needed to put as much lead on the ground as possible if they were to survive. Two of the enemy's anti-aircraft rounds punched holes in the starboard wing. They had found their mark. It would only be a few seconds before more enemy rounds tore his ship apart. Coyle sharpened his aim through the reticle on the side widow. With a slight change in angle he placed the crosshairs on the four blazing muzzles below.

On ground below…

"We've got them. We've got them!" yelled Bao as he felt something stab through his shoulder ripping off his arm. He glanced down at his arm on the ground as several more rounds punched through his neck and chest. He slumped and fell, dead.

Two thousand feet away, the Spectre's three miniguns were all aimed at the same point on the ground. It was a tight pattern only a few yards square. As the bullets' path moved around the anti-aircraft battery's position, the communists were torn to shreds. Tran jerked like a ragdoll as the barrage tore him apart. Shrapnel spewed from one of the gun's chambers as several damaged rounds exploded. Sgt. Noh was the last to die as the battery fell silent. The entire team and their VC guards were dead. Only explosions from rounds cooking off broke the silence. Not even a groan from the wounded. There were none.

In the sky above…

The crew cheered as anti-aircraft gunfire stopped. "That was some shooting, Coyle. I thought they had us for sure," said the weapon specialist.

"Wait…" said the operator of the Black Crow vehicle identification system. "I've got multiple vehicles one half mile to the North."

"You've got control," said Coyle jumping out of the

pilot's seat.

"I have control of the aircraft," said the co-pilot.

Coyle moved to the operator's side to view the scope and said, "How many?"

"A lot of them. Maybe sixty or seventy. It's hard to tell through the jungle canopy. Whatever it is, it's big."

"Anti-aircraft guns?"

"I've identified three truck-mounted ZPU-4s dispersed through the column. There may be more that I don't see."

"What about armor?"

"Three Panhard armored cars dispersed throughout the column and two BTR-60s near the front of the column."

"Juicy."

"Deadly."

Coyle turned to his weapon's chief, "How much ammo do we have for the miniguns?"

"We used most of it. I'm guess twenty to thirty percent remains," said the chief.

"Alright, here is what we are going to do. We're going to fly a long pylon turn parallel to the length of the entire convoy. After we open fire, we'll drop a series of parachute flares to light up the column. We'll fire at the trucks first and kill as many of the soldiers as possible while they're still figuring out they're under attack. When our ammunition for the miniguns runs out, we switch to Bofors Autocannons and switch targets to the armor and the anti-aircraft batteries. When the Bofors run out of ammo, we switch to the Vulcan Cannons and pound anything still moving. Once the Vulcans runout, we call it a night and head for home."

"Assuming we're still alive," said one of the

assistant gunners.

"We'll make it through as long as everyone stays focused on their jobs."

"You promise?"

"I promise to buy the first two rounds from the top shelf at the officer's club when we return. But you have to be alive to order your drinks."

"Deal," said everyone in unison.

"Do you really think it's a good idea to go after the troop trucks before taking out the anti-aircraft batteries?" said the co-pilot as Coyle climbed back into the pilot's seat and took control of the gunship once again.

"Look, it'll take 'em time to get their guns ready and fire their first shots. We just need to be done with our first run before they're ready. With luck everything will be blocked in and their vehicles will be unable to maneuver."

Coyle turned back to the Black Crow operator and said, "I'm gonna need you to guide me into the head of the column, then point out the armor and anti-aircraft on the return run."

"You got it," said the operator.

"Chief, you and your men need to be ready with those flares."

"We're already on it," said the chief.

Following the Black Crow operator's instructions, Coyle lined up the gunship with images on the screen of the convoy.

Coyle doubted that the NVA would hear the aircraft's engines over their own vehicle engines. He was counting on a surprise attack to give them the edge. With a column this size there would usually be a lot more aircraft attacking from different angles to keep the enemy off balance. But most of the American aircraft had been redeployed or given to the South Vietnamese Air Force.

The South Vietnamese commanders did not want to endanger their precious aircraft by sending them North. Instead, they would conserve their pilots and planes for the communist offensive they knew was coming. The South Vietnamese air force would be held in reserve to fend off the enemy when they attacked the major population centers like Saigon, Hue, and Da Nang. ARVN commanders had little hope of stopping the NVA in the northern jungles. They were unwilling to sacrifice their troops for territory that was sparsely populated and hard to defend. And while there was some logic to their thinking, the lack of defense gave the NVA a free hand to build up supplies and troops in their border camps and supply depots. Once the NVA commanders had installed their anti-aircraft systems below the jungle canopies, they no longer feared the South Vietnamese or even the remaining American aircraft.

Without American ground forces threatening to attack their troops, the NVA felt confident they could easily defend themselves against the ARVN ground forces. It had the effect of turning the camps and depots into sanctuaries where their troops could relax and prepare for the coming offensive. The only time the NVA and Viet Cong feared the enemy's aircraft was when they were traveling to the south. Even with their mobile anti-aircraft systems, their troops and trucks were exposed and could be destroyed.

In the jungle below…

A North Vietnamese truck's worn shocks groaned as they hit another crater in the dirt road. Lam fought the steering wheel as he pressed forward into the darkness. The ragged jungle encroached from both sides, branches scraping the truck's canvas hide. His guard Dung took a long drag on a cigarette, the brief orange glow barely penetrating the blackness of their unlit cabin. "You shouldn't smoke while we are moving," said Lam.

"You would rather stop?" said Dung.

"I would rather you didn't smoke until our rest stop."

"I'll keep it low, below the windshield."

"Fine. We're almost there anyway."

"Home to Ha Giang after this run," Dung said over the truck's strained gears and loose panels.

"Going back to that pretty wife you keep talking about?" Lam laughed hoarsely. "If she hasn't already taken a richer husband! Maybe you'll take her little sister as your second wife." Their laughter petered out as the truck lurched over the uneven road, tires slipping in the mud tracks.

Up ahead, the faintest glow marked another NVA position secured in the undergrowth. A checkpoint. Dung pulled a flask from his jacket, the sharp tang of rice wine cutting through the humid air a moment before Lam waved it off.

The checkpoint guards waved them through silently, Kalashnikovs gripped tight across their chests. Their route was highly secret, used only under cover of darkness to deliver men and supplies to the South.

Chunks of muddy earth pelted the truck's undercarriage from another water-filled crater. Lam winced, imagining his commander's reaction to any damage. Of course, a damaged truck was better than a missing one. He'd heard gunship stories from other drivers. Aircraft that could see men on the ground and strike them dead where they walked before they even knew what was happening. Lam focused on the rhythmic rattling of the gear shift to quiet his nerves. Almost through the most dangerous sector.

Dung cracked his window, letting in a rush of thick jungle air that did little to cut the stuffy heat. He jabbed his cigarette cherry toward a gap in the canopy. "Little moon tonight at least," he said. Lam nodded. Total darkness was both a blessing and curse. No menacing shadows up high, but more risk of crashing headlong into an unseen ditch.

A bolt shook loose inside the engine block, setting up an arrhythmic clanking like a clock missing cogs. Lam frowned. Something else for the mechanic to complain about once he got back to camp. The old Soviet trucks kept running by sheer determination it seemed. A few muttered curses signaled Dung's flask had found bottom. Soon they'd reach the resupply point and could wet their parched throats before turning in for a few hours sleep.

Dung fumbled with the truck's creaking radio, static hissing through tiny speakers before he shut it off with a grunt. Lam fixed his gaze westward. Less than twenty kilometers to go now. Then sweet respite from this rattling metal coffin if only for a few hours.

The first 7.65mm rounds impacted the road six feet ahead without warning. Lam had only a split second to process the eruption of dirt and fractured trees before slashing red streams of tracer bullets converged on the truck cabin like a deadly hailstorm. Lam and Dung's world disappeared in pain and fire as the unseen dragon unleashed its fury.

In the sky above…

The miniguns continued their assault, whirling with a high-pitched whine mixed with a series syncopated hammer blows as the bullets left the rotating barrels. The loadmaster set the timer on a Mark 24 magnesium flare and handed the flare to the assistant gunner who stepped across the deck toward the open cargo door. The metal flare tube was three feet long and weighed about twenty-five pounds. The gunner hooked up a ripcord to the flare's safety ring, then tossed the flare out the doorway.

The flare fell until the ripcord yanked the pull ring attached to the safety pin releasing the flare's parachute and activating the fuse. After a few more seconds, the parachute was fully deployed and the magnesium inside the flare ignited creating two million candlepower. The flare illuminated the convoy below allowing Coyle to target the vehicles as he flew down the line. The flare burned for two and a half minutes before going out.

While the flares illuminated the battlefield as they dropped, they also lit the Spectre making it a target for the anti-aircraft guns coming online. The miniguns continued their rain of fire on the convoy.

On ground below…

Troops sitting in the trucks heard the explosions up ahead. They had heard the stories of the dragon and knew what was happening. They piled out of the back of the truck and dove into the jungle beside the road.

The first three made it out, the fourth did not. As he reached the open back, bullets ripped through the canvas top striking his comrades multiple times within a blink of an eye, sending a red mist into the air. As he tried to climb out, he too was engulfed in the barrage from above. He died with one foot out of the truck.

Troops that made it out of the trucks before the Spectre destroyed their vehicles and their passengers, scrambled into the jungle and searching for any cover they could find. For some that meant safety, while others were caught in the explosions from supply trucks carrying ammunition, especially mortar shells.

The NVA anti-aircraft gun crews struggled to ready their weapons and aim the four 14.5mm machine gun barrels skyward. The individual gun's feeding system only housed 150-round belts. The gunners would conserve ammunition until the enemy aircraft was in their sights and range. They would need every bullet to take down the dragon before it consumed them.

In sky above…

"Minigun ammo is down to ten percent," said the weapon master.

"We stick to the plan. Prepare to switch to the Bofors Autocannons," said Coyle. "We need to take out their anti-aircraft systems before they take us out. And keep dropping those flares."

Even while barking out orders, Coyle did not take his eye off the aircraft's sight positioned over the side window. It was a simple system maneuvering the aircraft to position the target below in the sight's crosshairs. In addition to aiming the aircraft's weapons, Coyle controlled which guns fired and when. He was the gunner and pilot. The weapon's chief and assistant gunners supported the pilot, reloading ammunition and clearing any weapon jams.

The loadmaster prepared another flare and handed if off to an assistant gunner. As the assistant gunner approached the open doorway, the gunship came to the end of the convoy and banked hard to turn the ship around for another run. The deck suddenly pitched to thirty degrees and the assistant gunner lost his balance. He fell dropping the flare onto the deck. He looked at his hand and saw the flare's safety ring on one of his fingers. It would only be a matter of seconds before the flare rolling across the deck would ignite. "Live flare," he shouted.

Everyone knew the dire situation, especially the loadmaster. The flares were his responsibility. If the flare's magnesium ignited inside the aircraft it could easily detonate the ammunition waiting to be loaded into the weapons sitting in open crates on the deck. The explosions would be catastrophic. And if that wasn't enough, the magnesium would most likely burn through the metal deck in a few seconds and land on the aircraft's control cables directly beneath. Either way, it meant the death of the gunship and all aboard.

Coyle kept his wits and let his crew handle the emergency. He had enough problems of his own. As he looked out the side window, he saw the anti-aircraft gun at the far end of the convoy open fire at his gunship. Tracer rounds surrounded the aircraft. Coyle maneuvered the aircraft as best he could to sight the anti-aircraft gun in the side window's crosshairs, but it wasn't easy – he was still turning the aircraft for the return run and he didn't want to shift the direction of the deck which could cause the flare to roll in the opposite direction and out of the hands of the crew.

The loadmaster shuffled across the pitched deck keeping his balance. The flare's fuse was already smoking as it prepared to ignite. He only had a few moments. He made the best of them by picking up the flare, cradling it in his arms, and moving toward the open doorway. If it ignited in his arms, he was a deadman. Reaching the doorway, he swung back the flare in his arms to launch it out the door. Just as he started his swing forward a string of anti-aircraft bullets pierced the deck a few feet in front of him. He watched wide-eyed as the bullets moved toward him. Two .50 Cal bullets hit him in the thigh and crotch splitting him in half. The assistant gunners were splattered with the loadmaster's blood and flesh. The momentum of his swing carried the smoking flare out the doorway along with both halves of his body.

One moment later, the flare ignited with a blinding light and fell to the earth tumbling end over end along with the loadmaster's body parts.

Inside the weapon's hold, the crew was in shock, unmoving. Coyle knew that would all die if they did not fight the enemy below. "Stay focused on your jobs! We'll mourn later," he shouted.

It was harsh but enough to get the crew moving again.

Coyle opened fire at the anti-aircraft gun that had killed the loadmaster. He wasn't seeking revenge. He wanted to save his crew and destroy the remains of the convoy. He struggled to keep his emotions out of it and to stay focused at the task at hand. The Bofors autocannons fired 40mm shells at 140 rounds per minute. Even at the slower rate of fire, the autocannons using armor-piercing shells were deadly against armored vehicles. The side-by-side autocannons boomed as they fired one at a time. The air inside the hold contracted and expanded as the guns' breaches opened and closed.

On ground below…

The anti-aircraft gun crew watched in horror as the 40mm rounds pounded the ground and split trees around the weapon site before finally finding their mark. The crew and their weapon were completely demolished. Only blood-stained bent metal remained as burning ammunition crates cooked off unused rounds.

In sky above…

Seeing the anti-aircraft weapon destroyed, Coyle released the trigger to conserve ammunition. Each Bofors autocannon had 256 rounds which provide two minutes of continuous fire. It took time for the pilot to sight the enemy which wasted precious ammunition before destroying the target. Coyle scanned the convoy for the two remaining anti-aircraft guns. When one opened fire, he quickly targeted it and snuffed it out like the first one. When he destroyed the final anti-aircraft gun, he knew the crew was safe. At two thousand feet none of the enemy's small arms could reach them. The armored cars and armored personnel carriers had machine guns, but the angle was too steep to be effective.

When the ammunition for the Bofors ran out, Coyle switch the weapons select control panel to the Vulcan Gatling guns. Like the Bofors autocannons the

Vulcans 20mm rounds could easily penetrate the thinner armor on top of the enemy's armored vehicles. But unlike the Bofers, the Vulcans had an incredible rate of fire at 6,000 rounds per minute. Coyle fired the Vulcans in short bursts until he homed in on his target, then fired a long burst until the armored vehicle was destroyed.

Coyle made two passes along the convoys route before he ran out of targets. Everything below the aircraft was burning. There was no movement that he could detect. While he was sure that many of the troops were hiding in the jungle, he had no way of detecting them unless they moved or fired their rifles. The infrared sensors were useless with so many vehicles burning. With fuel and ammunition running low, Coyle turned the aircraft away from the battlefield and headed for home. The victorious crew didn't celebrate, but instead remained silent out of respect for their lost comrade that had saved their lives.

The Growing Tide

June 5, 1973 - Saigon, South Vietnam

The soft clink of glasses and polite laughter echoed through the lush garden reception at President Thieu's Saigon palace - a reticent farewell for longtime American Ambassador Ellsworth Bunker now returning stateside. President Thieu circulated among the dignitaries, stoic as ever despite brewing unease at shifting currents back in Washington. "Mister Ambassador, a poignant, if premature, sendoff in my view," Thieu remarked, catching Bunker alone admiring the bonsai sculpted by imperial ancestors. "I have relied much on your wise counsel these last years. And with President Nixon's rather untimely resignation, I admit concerns grow about continuity regarding our accords."

Bunker smiled politely. "You and me both, Mr. President. But matters proceed apace. I have full faith in Graham Martin assuming the post of ambassador, and in President Ford's ability to steer Congress straight on our prior commitments here."

"You believe President Ford will keep Nixon's commitments to punish the North Vietnamese if they break the Paris Peace agreement?"

"I believe he will, but Congress may be another matter."

"Yes, I've read the proposed Case-Church Amendment. Strong words coming from an ally. That of course assumes that the United States is still our ally."

"Of course, it is, Mr. President. Our most important ally."

"Then why are you cutting our military and financial aid in half next year? You expect us to fight the communists with broomsticks?"

"Perhaps the matter of budgets is better discussed with Graham Martin when he arrives?"

"I don't know him. I know and trust you, Ambassador Bunker."

"I appreciate that, Mr. President. Look, nothing is set in stone, especially with budgets. It's a negotiation between politicians. We want more money to fight the communists, they want money for the pet projects in their respective states. I imagine the give and take will put us somewhere in between."

"In-between would still be a drastic cut in our funding at a time when we are left alone to defend our nation against the North and their allies."

"It's difficult time for everyone, Mr. President. The oil crisis is causing inflation to spiral out of control in America, just as it is in South Vietnam."

"And yet we will be asked to stretch our funding beyond reason. Did you know that ninety percent of ARVN troops no longer make enough to support their families?"

"Yes. It's an issue that should be addressed as soon as possible when your new ambassador arrives in a few weeks."

"I am not sure we can wait that long. Morale in the military is at an all-time low. How can we ask our troops to choose between defending their country and feeding their families?"

"I'm not sure you have a choice, Mr. President. While President Ford wishes to help, Congress has his hands tied and they are in no mood to offer Vietnam more aid when Americans are suffering at home. They believe Americans have sacrificed enough. They want the rest of the world to step up and take over the burden of fighting communism in Southeast Asia."

"And you think this is reasonable?"

"Mr. President, it longer matters what I think or even say. No one in America wants to listen."

"Including the president?"

"He still listens, but I can tell his patience is wearing thin. He wants the war to be over, so he can move on to more pressing matters in Europe and South America."

"More pressing matters…? So, we really are alone in this fight?"

"As a friend? Yes. That's the reality you must face."

"You offer little hope."

"Believe me when I say it's not what I want. But we must all be realistic if South Vietnam is to survive."

Bunker sighed, the sun casting premature shadows across the lush garden. "American memories run short, old friend. But South Vietnam has many stalwart champions still. We must trust our system while reinforcing your vital importance to containing communism."

Thieu knew that Bunker was on his side and telling the truth. It wasn't what he wanted to hear, but as

Bunder said "It is the reality of the situation."

Bunker appraised the towering palace defenses, symbolic of the nation's withdrawing posture. "Our generals inform me ARVN forces are now garrisons inside cities awaiting assault rather than contesting borders. Ceding terrain risks morale...and invites Northern seizure of more territory."

Thieu bristled subtly at the criticism as servants refilled glasses. "You've appraised the reports yourself, Ambassador. When we committed major forces to highlands defense previously, the outcome proved grievous. This strategy acknowledges realities - we marshal steel across urban redoubts while husbanding manpower for the enemy's final gambit."

Bunker frowned, worry lines etching deeper. "And if that gambit requires no final battle? If they continue nibbling periphery while you feed forces piecemeal into the grinder?" He stepped nearer, voice lowering. "Vietnamization cannot sustain against inexorable application of will. Better to sting and slow the beast beyond frontiers than resign to consuming the nation's heart."

"Military strategist? Your new career?"

"I hear what I hear, Mr. President."

Thieu mulled Bunker's words as dancers swirled gracefully across palace floors soon perhaps overrun by less gracious guests. The Ambassador's departure heralded the ebbing sway America held over South Vietnam's dwindling options. But Thieu could not easily abandon fortifying the Mekong bastion, whatever breaches opened in the highlands. The Mekong Delta was the nations breadbasket. No matter what, he needed to feed his people if there was to be any hope of keeping their support in the coming offensive. The NVA and VC had compelling arguments to switch sides at the point of their bayonets.

Border between South and North Vietnam

The pale dawn light barely penetrated the dense tangle of jungle surrounding the six mud-caked soldiers. Granier paused where the faint trail disappeared into thick undergrowth. Behind him, the South Vietnamese recon team waited silently in their defensive positions, alert eyes scanning for any sign of movement among the vines and ancient tree trunks. Somewhere north, past this sea of vegetation, the NVA lurked.

Deep into contested terrain, Granier's team represented Saigon's only reliable eyes on gathering enemy movements. Aerial reconnaissance gave the NVA too much warning to hide swelling ranks. And the promised intelligence from American controllers at Nakhon Phanom was distracted as focus shifted from Vietnam to newer global fronts. For now, with the last US combat boots gone by early 1973, Saigon saw only what these experienced scouts discovered in bloody inch-by-inch slogs across the fire-scarred DMZ valleys. Granier, a CIA officer and veteran scout, was asked to head many of the recon missions. Washington wouldn't refuse. They still wanted to know what was happening in Vietnam but did little to stop the onslaught from the North everyone knew was coming.

Granier had handpicked his team from the Nung hill tribes. ARVN commanders in Saigon doubted the Nungs' value, but Granier knew their lethal skills traversing this land as lifelong jungle dwellers made them perfect for covert missions that conventional forces bungled. Their sinewy forms could flow soundlessly through foliage like the Viet Cong - and kill just as quickly with their rifles and machetes. Wars and the land itself forged them tough as old teak roots polished to iron.

Blindness meant annihilation if the expected NVA invasion came crashing down on the South without warning. Granier shoved away the echo of abandoning South Vietnamese forces to their fate. Many of the American commanders wanted to forget Vietnam and move on to other hotspots where the communists were trying to expand their revolution. The republic would endure, if enough dedicated ARVN soldiers remained to staff long-range patrols and report back on ground truth. He glanced back at Lieutenant Kinh gently parting broad leaves aside to reveal the path forward. *Always into peril*, thought Granier. *But never lightly without cause.*

Granier checked the Schmidt & Bender scope mounted on his Remington M40 bolt-action sniper rifle for the third time since setting out from Firebase Bastone two nights before. Moving through dense jungle, it was easy for a scope to get misaligned or damaged. Satisfied his equipment was functioning properly, he gestured forward and resumed point position alone. The others maintained ten-meter separation, ghosts drifting through diffused sunlight and swirling mist.

Progress was steady but heavy going. Vegetation clawing at their fatigues and boots was the least of their worries. Every step risked ambush. Any rustle of leaves could be an NVA patrol or just foraging wildlife. There was no way to tell, except experience in the bush. For this reason Granier, even though the commander of the team, took the lead. He was the most experienced long-range scout remaining in Vietnam even over the natives that accompanied him.

As the sweltering humidity soared by mid-morning, Granier allowed himself a grim smile. Already more appealing than another endless hour cleaning weapons back at the bunker. Out here with danger as their guide, survival counted solely on their wits and training. While he wouldn't admit it to anyone, he loved it. He felt alive in the jungle, his senses heightened, his mind sharp.

While not big in stature like the American that led them, the Nung were born in jungle foliage, deadly with their British L1A1 rifles, a weapon similar to the enemy's AK47 know to reliably operate even in the harshest environments. The Nung were familiar with every inch of terrain near the border region. Ong, their radio operator built like a pipe-cleaner, boasted encyclopedic knowledge of this area's concealed tunnels and caves for emergency concealment. Together they represented the scrappy few skilled enough to track their enemy's secrets without being seen.

Kneeling beside a small stream, Granier used his machete to harvest some shrub stems. He cut each at an angle, nodding in satisfaction at their seeping white liquid. Poison squirted into the water supply could slow any large unit movement. If war had taught him one lesson in the nearly thirty years since storming ashore the Pacific islands, it was that asymmetric engagement remained the outmanned force's advantage. Granier would use every trick in the book to survive and win.

The trail began to rise as the jungle parted partially. Granier felt tense muscles loosen slightly despite the added visibility. Satellite aerial imaging suggested this whole area remained firmly in ARVN control. Granier almost laughed out load at the futility of such fallacy. Out here beyond the worried diplomats and wine-sipping generals in Saigon, the NVA controlled whatever earth they currently walked on, and most they couldn't physically occupy. Another hundred meters gained. Granier remained alert. Complacency killed, a lesson many Americans had failed to understand.

The faint trail became slick mud underfoot as the reconnaissance team pushed uphill into thickening vegetation. In the distance, ominous rumbles echoed, signaling another squall rolling through the jungle folds. Granier quickened the pace, eager to clear the exposed ridge crest before the pending deluge. No way to avoid getting drenched, but the high ground offered better visibility to chart their next leg of their journey.

The triple canopy shuddered as fat raindrops began pelting down on the leaves. Within seconds, rivulets streamed down the slope, carving ragged channels in the loose topsoil. Granier waved the patrol to a small grove of trees halfway up the ridge. They huddled beneath the dense foliage, donning rain capes that did little to staunch the torrents.

It was coming down in relentless sheets, hammering every surface and threatening to overwhelm even the ground beneath them. Granier edged to the fringe, squinting toward the higher ridge. A curtain of water barred the path where the trail had been. He cursed. Another delay.

He glanced back to ensure the team was fortifying their position when a panicked cry snapped him around in time to see a section of sodden earth cleaving away, carrying their radio operator with it.

"Hold fast to any branch or root!" Granier bellowed over the storm. In seconds the landslide's remnants pooled twenty yards downhill, a swirling morass of liquid dirt that clung to everything it touched. Desperate splashing marked where Ong, his radio equipment weighing him down struggled half-submerged like a prey animal trapped in the mud of a Savannah watering hole.

Granier anchored his boot on a stunted tree and leapt downward, skidding badly but stopping short of the quicksoil froth. He shouted for rope as Ong's head dipped below the opaque surface. Private Tranh tossed him one end of a rope which he wrapped around his waist. Running out of time, Granier plunged into the chest-high muck feet first then dove forward under the surface. He had to find Ong before paralysis set in from pressure…

Visibility was nil. He grasped only slick tendrils of vines and loose stones as he swept his arms wide feeling for Ong's slim form. No purchase to clutch Ong's uniform or belt. Granier's lungs burned for air, but he groped further out, probing what felt like a sunken log. Wait - the log moved! Granier latched onto Ong's muddy field pack and pulled with all his strength toward the surface. Already unconscious, Ong was dead weight.

They broke through the surface, Granier clutching Ong. Granier coughed violently as Tranh and Kinh dragged them onto solid ground. Ong was limp in Granier's arms, face caked in viscous clay. Granier brushed just enough mud aside to detect shallow breathing as the medic took over, clearing airways for precious oxygen. As the medic worked on Ong, Granier hacked up the remaining mud in his lungs and throat.

Although they stayed silent, the team was in awe of what Granier had done. It was selfless action that created loyalty, especially among the tribesmen.

"I've got the radio working. Should I call for an evac?" said Tranh.

"No chopper," Granier ordered. "We'd show our hand. Ong's just going to have to gut it out. Patch up and police your gear."

He scanned north where rain-cleared views hinted at smudged shapes in the far valley. If his instinct proved right, Saigon might depend on what was hidden there.

Kinh took first watch while they snatched thin sleep. Granier allowed just ninety minutes before they moved out. No fire. No rice. The risk of detection was too great. Empty bellies would sap strength, but the mission took priority. Before moving out, Granier approached Ong. The radio operator sat grimacing as he re-tied off a crude splint of jungle wood around his swollen knee with ugly shades of violet and red.

"A rescue team from Bastone can fetch you tomorrow if needed," Granier offered neutrally. "No shame for an injury bad as this."

Ong didn't hesitate, almost spitting his response. "They stitch me up so I cannot walk ever again instead. My place remains with you all."

He hauled himself up smoothly if leaning heavier on his right side. Ong would endure - his mettle outshone the petty brass who discounted him.

Granier nodded then roused the rest of the team. They resumed their cloaked climb toward the passes in silence and without complaint. Less than ideal but expected for their service.

Dusk bled shadows across the valley as Granier's team approached the ridge. He bellied up to the edge, rifle scope searching for signs of jungle movement. Ong moved up beside him with the radio, antenna outstretched, ready to transmit. For long minutes Granier saw nothing through crosshairs quartering the expanse. Then filtered moonlight glinted off steel – rifle barrels and helmets topping a platoon navigating the valley spine.

Granier instinctively traced avenues parallel, finding more platoons fanning out. Boldly clustered, the enemy's spacing invited ambush, yet they pressed directly southward, as if unconcerned of being discovered. The Americans and their aircraft were gone. Only the South Vietnamese remained, and the ARVN and Air Force were busy defending the cities and major population centers. The border was left unguarded except a few outposts and air bases defended by the South Vietnamese. With the Americans gone, it was like the South Vietnamese had already conceded much of their territory to the North without even a fight. The government didn't seem to care about anything beyond the cities except for the Mekong Delta and its rice. It was a terrible strategy and Granier knew it. It allowed the NVA and VC to store endless amounts of weapons and supplies and concentrate their forces wherever they wished.

Before resuming his vigil, Granier muttered the coordinates to Ong who scratched them out with a pencil on a small notebook. Granier spotted an entire company churning up mud behind heavy trucks. No caution around aerial eyes now; they moved openly, oblivious to jeopardy.

Unease swelled in Granier's gut with each new sighting. The NVA hadn't deployed such strength here in years. Each fresh platoon embroidered an operational tapestry almost arrogant in its coordination. As if oblivious to the Republic's defenses looming beyond. When Granier's scope locked onto the Battalion commander pacing confidently, clearly positioned to direct the entire orchestra below, Granier understood.

These were no scattered insurgent bands, but a deliberate sledgehammer of crack units unleashed to crush South Vietnam for good. The officer's uniform with assorted insignia marked him unmistakably as the battalion commander. Granier kept both eyes open, transitioning from detached spotter to hunter with finger resting just outside the trigger guard. One round would pierce that officer's chest before he knew what ripped his life away. A collapsing figure would seed chaos among the ranks and delay their deployment. It would also create a distraction for Granier's team to slip away. Angry at what he discovered, Granier really wanted to kill someone.

He blinked, forcibly lowering his barrel. The mission directive echoed back clearly - intelligence gathering took priority over individual kills. Their duty was to reveal the enemy's plan, not thwart it alone. There would be a time and target for precise shots. But for now, he must remain unseen so as not to expose what he knew. Granier relayed another encoded grid square to Ong lying on the ground next to him.

Granier refocused his role - complete the vital sketch work; others must handle the coming fight. Ong looked up expectantly as Granier pressed the transmit switch. "Raven One to Firebird. We have urgent intelligence..."

"...tally estimated two infantry battalions reinforced with artillery battalions heading 218 degrees toward border, break."

Granier kept his voice low but crisp for the radio mic as Ong scribbled shorthand into coded logs. Even burst transmissions risked SIGINT triangulation this close to the DMZ.

"Possible regimental operations center spotted at grid Golf-Sierra-3-2-niner based on staff activity and communications vehicles, break. Expect division-level offensive imminent, over."

He clicked the mic off without waiting for confirmation. Saigon either acknowledged the coming onslaught or they didn't. Either way, Granier's patrol just became priority hunt targets for the enemy. He tapped Ong's shoulder, signaling the frail radio operator to collapse the antenna and prepare to withdraw under darkness's shroud.

They descended carefully from the elevated ridge, boots silencing cracked branches while senses strained for any sound of NVA sweeps. The valley continued its hidden purpose - stockpiling assault assets stage by stage. As Granier slipped between the gnarled trunks of old-growth canopy, he glimpsed vehicles cutting fresh track and off-loading supplies, no longer concealing intense buildup.

The injection of men and materiel from the North was accelerating. And Saigon still slumbered, refusing to read the signs or act on them.

Colonel Khuong stared grimly at the detailed map, listening to coded updates from forward units taking risky radio checks rather than rely on runners up the mountain trails. The concentration of forces was accelerating beyond Hanoi's most optimistic projections for dry season operations. Such an opportunity might dislodge the flailing republic once and for all. His internal musing was interrupted by the crackling speakers overhead – a scrambled message, but recognizable as originating from an American military radio.

Everybody in the command post froze at those squawks and hisses. Khuong's expression hardened like granite. ARVN long range scouts - it had to be. Scrambling their best pathfinders just for this precious intel.

He locked eyes with Major Bui, both hands slicing perpendicular - blanket this valley, find whoever spoke! The intelligence chief barked into field radios positioned nearby. In seconds, confirmation returned - a brief broadcast intercept, coordinates triangulated within two kilometers...then silence.

Khuong scowled, envisioning skilled commandos vanishing into untamed ravines and mile-high thickets. "They're already gone, but every man leaves a trail. Take your best platoon at speed. Once you pinpoint their location we will reinforce and trap them."

He jabbed stiff fingers at the map where the radio spike erupted. Bui gathered a platoon commander with a curt order - bring their heads at all cost! Soldiers raced from the headquarters perimeter toward idling trucks. Khuong inhaled slowly, mind cycling back to operational tempos. A pinprick vulnerability, but it forewarned Saigon's map keepers. He must accelerate advance units beyond possible ambush zones. Concealment evaporated; now speed and numbers became essential above all...

Sergeant Tan peered through night lenses, his platoon readying weapons with bloodlust as their trucks bounded up the mountain access point. These pathfinders were elite scouts, but Tan's trackers could run a mountain goat to ground in harsh monsoons.

Exiting the trucks, Tan and his platoon made their way toward the location of the coded broadcast and fanned out. One of scouts found something. The shredded camouflage snagged on brush clinched it - they'd seized the right trail. Half of Tan's men poured forward, ready to flush their prey into the clearing kill zone ahead. The other half stayed in their trucks and charged forward to cutoff the enemy's escape.

Meanwhile, Granier's exhausted team wove between sagging boughs and monstrous roots, making for high plateau where the tree cover ended. The odds of losing skilled trackers shrank by the hour. They must risk a last coded warning to Saigon before going dark to survive.

Granier clicked his radio once to confirm battery while Ong hastily rigged his pencil antenna. Behind Granier, Lieutenant Kinh swung left, rifle leveled - the scouts heard it too. Muffled diesel rumble carrying along ridge stone meant one thing: a mechanized unit, heading straight for them.

There was no more time. Granier gave Ong the go-ahead to transmit the message himself. Rifle fire suddenly split the night as Kinh's men engaged the oncoming threat. Granier dropped prone, sighting into the darkness, buying precious seconds for Ong's scratched plea.

The frantic firefight would draw every NVA unit

from miles around. But prayerfully Saigon now had coordinates for the North's jugular. Granier wondered if he should have taken that commander's life when he peered through crosshairs into the valley after all. Kinh's men directed disciplined fire at the oncoming headlights, strafing the attacking platoon's leading edge. Granier sighted down his Remington's scope, sharp mind calculating angles and ranges as the enemy soldiers jumped from their vehicles to engage on foot.

The first viscous zip of enemy rounds ripping foliage sent Granier's team diving behind thick trunks. Blind return volleys bought a few seconds before one of his men toppled, riddled by a concealed machine gun they failed to mark. Perhaps a second enemy column higher up attacking their flank. The scout was screaming in pain as he died.

Granier blocked the screams from his mind, stabilizing his breathing as he drew a bead on the distant muzzle flare perforating their perimeter. He led his target one meter, squeezed gently. The NVA soldier went dark mid-burst.

Another squatter shape maneuvering closer lost its stealth to confidence, backlit by pursuing truck headlights for a bare instant. Granier waited no longer than the next frantic heartbeat - a squeeze sent a hot rifle crack echoing as intended through the valley. The soldier crumpled into ferns without further sound, buying a precious distraction to waver the siege. Granier took advantage of the pause to give a hand signal to his men.

In wordless sync, the team's survivors broke from cover, rallying behind Granier's rearguard rifle shots targeting known threats with lethality even NVA marksmen must reluctantly praise. A new target emerged higher on the ridge's slope, firing down on the team with a machine gun, clip after clip, unceasing.

Granier marked the working machine gun's cyclic rate and mental timers - seconds until the overheated Kalashnikov barrel warped. He squeezed between thunderous volleys, dropping the new gunner as he reloaded. After each rifle shot, Granier moved to a new position. Like a chess master, he always plotted his next move before firing his weapon.

Granier ordered his men to fall back while he alone kept the enemy at bay. Their withdrawal window was already closing as pursuing trucks carrying reinforcements skidded into the scene, disgorging more vengeful infantry. Their numbers increased by the minute. Granier marked every NVA attempt to coordinate new units with oil-drum rifle retorts splitting the night. Behind each shot, a man fell.

Yet the incoming rush refused to back down for any single rifle, even Granier's. Green tracer streams slashed closer while his surviving band evaporated into the wilderness. Only Ong remained cramming radio parts into his ruck before Granier roughly sent him to follow the others.

The signal for retreat reached even stubborn men by necessity this night. No final stands to blood the enemy. Disciplined fighters. Granier broke from his position and ran downhill after his men, muzzle flashes still chasing their backs for endless minutes until even the northern fury exhausted itself.

Only after descending mile upon mile into the soupy jungle basin did Granier wave halt beside where a swollen tributary met the river yawning south towards contested freedom. For now, swollen waters shielded their position. The staccato rumble of trucks began withdrawing back upslope having lost the scent. They were invisible again. But for how long?

Granier posted Tranh on overwatch upstream as the remaining scouts inventoried gear and ammunition in the gully. They still had rucks and arms - but the firefight had depleted half their ammunition. Even with the team hungry and exhausted, Granier ordered no fire for tea or rice. The risk was too great.

The medic finished binding Ong's leg and turned to Granier. "He won't manage further on this terrain."

Granier's jaw tightened. More precarious time bleeding off evasion. But abandoning Ong guaranteed interrogation or death if NVA patrols canvassed nearby.

"Lash stretcher poles. We alternate two carriers." The order cost two rifles from action if confronted. But loyalty to comrades trumped additional risk.

In minutes they rigged a makeshift litter from cut branches, rain ponchos, and rope. Granier secured Ong's radio/antenna and studied his map for a safe route, then glanced south weighing odds. Odds cared nothing for desperate souls. Granier whistled Tranh in from overwatch. The team was on the move once again.

Haggard days and nights blurred as Granier's team snaked onward. Brief squalls turned earth to mud Granier denied the use of trails lest tripwires or bounty hunters awaited their betrayed passage. Sleep scratched in desperate moments propped sitting against soggy trunks, weapons across laps. The enemy was tough, but they too needed sleep. The question was how much? Falling within the enemy's reach meant sure death.

Granier led his battered team through endless rain. Ong worsened despite tight binds and became delirious from fever, crying out from the makeshift pole stretcher despite attempts to muzzle him.

As much as Granier and the rest of the team hated to admit it, Ong's death would give the others a fighting chance. Without clean surgical intervention, sepsis would claim the operator before human trackers hunted the team down. There was little they could do to save Ong except keep moving in hopes of reaching help and anti-biotics that could battle the disease.

Granier blamed himself. He never should have let Ong travel on his knee once wounded. He never asked those under his command to do what he could not do, but that didn't mean that they could keep up with him. Granier was not normal and could withstand far more pain and fatigue than the average soldier. At times, he forgot that simple reality.

When Ong's brittle voice cracked across the dawn mists like gunfire, Granier shot awake. He wondered how long he had slept and how close the enemy had moved toward their position. He glanced at his watch and figured he had slept almost an hour. He cursed himself for being careless but knew the sleep would do him good. Like the other team members, his strength was at the end of its rope. He woke everyone and got them moving once again. This time, he carried one end of Ong's litter.

After several hours of trudging through rain-soaked mud and grass, the winding gorge they had been traveling in finally opened onto a broad valley where Granier halted their slog. While the medic treated Ong, Granier stood watch. The medic changed Ong's dressing, worry creasing his eyes. The wounded operator's skin seemed almost translucent, blue veins stark beneath. Granier conferred privately with the medic. "Without medicine, we'll lose him," whispered the ashen medic.

"How long does he have?" said Granier.

"A day at most unless he gets some rest, food, and most of all… anti-biotics."

Granier considered the bleak equation. He gazed southward where endless ridges promised no swift deliverance. "Alright, light a small fire, but use dry wood to cut down on smoke. Cook up the last of the rice and make a poultice. We rest two hours. No more."

"That should help."

Granier grabbed the radio gear and his rifle, then headed for the ridge to their West. "Where are you going?" said the medic.

"To buy time," said Granier.

Unburdened, Granier moved fast. He trekked over two ridges, then halfway down into a valley. He needed to make his broadcast as realistic as possible. He extended the aerial and powered on the radio. He turned off the encryption and broadcast in the clear. "Sugar Alpha 3, this is Raven 11 on swing route to Buffalo. Request Blue Star delivery at grid Iron Mike 34-21, over."

There was no response, but he didn't expect one. The broadcast was meant for the enemy. With luck they would triangulate the broadcast's location and relocate their search effects to the valley he was now in and away from the team. Although there was always a chance it could be picked up by the American's monitoring broadcasts. Only the Americans would understand the references to American football he used to describe their location and route. At least that's what he hoped. He broadcast the message a second time, then packed up the gear and headed back to the team two valley's over.

As Granier descended the final ridge, he looked out at the valley they had entered. The valley folded into emerald hills decorated with cloud-laced granite outcrops. It was beautiful like much of Vietnam. He spotted smoke rising from the mist in the distance to the South. He doubted it was the enemy. It was something else. A village perhaps.

On his return, the team quickly broke camp and continued their journey South. Ong was quiet. The rest had done him some good.

As the team pressed forward, they entered the mist and found a lake hidden beneath. On one side of the lake were the charred remains of a village, a recent battle evident. The surviving villagers were cooking rice and smoking fish. Granier and the medic approached what they thought was the village elder. The medic explained that they needed medicine for one of their comrades. Granier offered South Vietnamese money, then American dollars in exchange. The elder wasn't interested in either, but saw French piastres in Granier's billfold and regained interest. They traded for food and medicine until Granier ran out of the French money.

As the medic treated Ong with the medicine they had purchased, Granier studied the lake. It didn't show on his map which meant it was possible the NVA didn't have it on their maps either. Using the medic to interpret once again, Granier discussed the lake with the elder and found it was confluence of several rivers, not a lake. A single river continued on the opposite side of the confluence. While Granier had no more money, he traded Ong's rifle and some ammunition for help constructing two rafts. His team was exhausted from carrying Ong at such a brisk pace. The rafts would keep them moving while giving everyone a chance to rest. With luck, they would stay ahead of the NVA chasing them.

Made from bamboo and vines, the two rafts were finished in less than two hours. Granier thanked the elder and set out with his team across the fog-covered confluence searching for the mouth of the river that would carry them Southward. They found it.

Once they entered the mouth of the river, their speed picked up considerably. Granier was relieved to put distance between his team and their pursuers. They continued downstream until nightfall. It was too dangerous to navigate the river in the darkness. Unseen rocks and logs could easily destroy the rafts. The team guided their rafts to shore and made camp. Granier knew it was risky but figured they had put a good deal of distance between the team and the NVA.

The medic treated Ong who surprisingly was doing better. His fever had been reduced and the delirium was gone. Ong had no idea what had happened the last few days and started to get up to rejoin the team. Granier ordered him to stay down and rest. The team had two guards throughout the night. Granier wasn't taking any unnecessary chances.

Sunrise filtered through the morning mist shrouding the river. Granier woke sore, his muscles stiff. Like most pain he shrugged it off. He knew that once he got moving the pain would recede. To Granier, pain was good. It was nature's way of telling him that he was still alive. It kept him sharp. He walked the camp to check on everyone. It wasn't much of a walk.

He saw the medic kneeling on one of the rafts preparing Ong's resting place with a lean-to for shade for the journey down river. He waved good morning. Granier nodded back. Everyone seemed more relaxed, their ordeal almost over as long as their luck held out. It didn't.

Mortar fire shattered the fog. Everyone scrambled for cover. Granier waved the medic off the raft which had no cover. The medic crossed the bamboo lashed together as he stepped toward shore. A mortar round crashed into the raft. A direct hit. The medic disappeared in a cascade of water and broken bamboo. He was gone.

Tracer rounds from across the river revealed the enemy hiding behind the reeds. Machine guns split the air. Another team member was hit in the side of the head. He fell motionless… dead.

The team fired back, but they were clearly outgunned and outnumbered twenty to one. Grabbing the medic's rifle, Ong joined the fight. They needed every man they had which wasn't much – just three soldiers plus Granier.

The 81mm mortar rounds crashing down were part of a NVA company's heavy weapons squad. The NVA didn't need to risk attack. Their mortar rounds would soon pulverize the recon team. It seemed that all was lost, but Granier wouldn't give up and neither would his team. They had little doubt they would be tortured then killed if captured. It would be a fight to the death as more mortar rounds landed on their positions.

Then, appearing over the jungle, a lone Huey strafed the enemy's position with rockets and machine guns. Enemy gunfire was diverted toward the new threat. The Huey was moving fast and flying low making it hard to hit. The door gunner was firing a minigun spewing out 3,000 rounds per minute. As the helicopter banked for another run, the gunner switched sides grabbing another minigun mounted in the opposite doorway.

Granier and his team did what they could to help the attack helicopter's aircrew. Granier took down any enemy visible with deadly accurate fire from his sniper rifle. He saw what he thought was the company commander and put a bullet in his forehead. He went down into the long grass and didn't appear again.

A rocket from the Huey found its mark and detonated a stack of mortar rounds next to one of the mortars destroying it and its crew. The explosions rocked the earth. The enemy mortar crews had enough and broke for the safety of the jungle leaving their hot tubes behind.

Not missing a beat, the Huey's pilot shifted focus to the machine gun positions along the shore behind the reeds. Flying at top speed and allowing the minigun to do its worst, the door gunner decimated the enemy gun crews on shore cutting the reeds and soldiers down like a sickle. Before the Huey could complete its second pass, the enemy had disappeared into the jungle. The battle was over.

After a few minutes needed to ensure that the enemy was indeed gone, the Huey set down next to the camp. Granier was surprised to see Scott Dickson, Tom Coyle's son climb out of the pilot's seat. "What are you doing here, Scott?," said Granier.

"Got your message. Nice football metaphors," said Scott.

"So, it worked?"

"You could have done a better job selecting the

football teams. My door gunner's from Alabama."

"Good to know."

"We should go. No telling if the enemy will return. How many you got?"

"Three, not counting me."

"I was told you started with six."

"We did. We paid for the intel."

"I hope it was worth it."

"We'll see."

Granier and his team climbed onboard. The Huey took off, banked hard and headed back to base. The mission was over. Nobody was celebrating.

A Bold Plan

Saigon, South Vietnam

The rotor wash from the Huey whipped across the tarmac as Tom Coyle disembarked, duffle bag in hand, his bent frame unfolding from the cramped passenger bay. Despite the early hour, the Saigon heat was already oppressive, mirroring the uneasy pangs in his gut.

It had been a long week flying interdiction missions to stem the endless flow of enemy forces along the border between North and South Vietnam. What he had seen chilled him more than the jungle humidity. Truck after truck streaming down across the border, unworried about US air power now that American forces had exited. He and his CIA aircrew had lit up the night sky to blow those columns straight to Hell, but the hollow pit in his stomach knew many more would keep coming.

Coyle crossed the tarmac, each weary step carrying the weight of his ambivalence. In his guts, he knew the South would falter without the full might of American firepower. The hollow eyes of the Saigon locals told that bitter truth.

Part of him desired to board the next Freedom Bird

lifting skyward, return to the small town where he once tossed footballs in autumn leaves without a care. Back to a normalcy he vaguely recalled - cold beers at the VFW with old friends, Fourth of July sparklers with nieces and nephews, clipping coupons on a Sunday morning.

But a relentless spark inside refused him that comfort. After every airman lost, village burned, and child orphaned - he couldn't casually abandon the people of the South to the communist steamroller. He'd seen too many vibrant lives offered up on the blood-soaked altar of this war to simply walk away while flames of hope still flickered. Like his daddy taught him as a boy - you finish what you start with all your might, through Hell or high water. And that was it. He'd fight for these people's freedom until his dying breath if that's what duty required.

A jeep from the embassy awaited to pick up Coyle, his ride already confirmed before landing. The familiar smells and humidity enveloped him as he stepped across the tarmac to another transient war-time homecoming. But the silence reminded him this was no longer the American Saigon of old. Just a few jets remained, most aircraft now flown by ARVN pilots of varying questionable skill. The empty hangars and barracks were just echoes of the magnificent US military machine now departed after so many years of bloody toil.

As the jeep passed the embassy gates, he spotted a familiar grizzled figure standing on the veranda, arms crossed, staring out at the city. It was Granier. Coyle let out a weary smile - after so many years at war, somehow their paths still crossed at just the right times.

As Coyle stepped from the jeep, Granier descended

the steps wordlessly. The raw exhaustion in his gait said enough after weeks ranging deep along the DMZ and across enemy lines. Granier had been running CIA reconnaissance missions to track NVA divisions since the American pullout. Dark circles under his flinty eyes whispered of the toll it had taken, matching the grave developments he'd spied. "How was the shit show up North?" said Coyle.

"Shitty," said Granier.

"Same here. I lost my loadmaster. You?"

"More."

"Was it worth it?"

"Let's find out. The brass are waiting."

Coyle followed Granier toward the embassy's front doors. "We should have a beer after this. I think we're gonna need it," said Coyle.

"Alright."

The men strode towards the entrance, embassy staff scurrying about in a state of tense pressure as rumors spread. The expandable manila envelope Coyle carried felt like a lead weight being handed over - more photographic evidence of the coming storm soon to be unleashed.

The Marine guard directed them to the situation room downstairs without a word, faces even more dour than usual around this dying soon-to-be tomb should the dominoes fall unchecked. As they descended, Coyle steeled his gut. Just straight truth about what he witnessed. The brass wanted honest intel without whitewash, they'd get it served raw from the front lines.

Granier just scowled ahead as always. He didn't need to convince himself to tell the truth to his commanders. He wouldn't soften the blow, not for anyone.

They entered the situation room to find Thomas Polgar already standing at the head of the map-covered table, furrowed brow considering the latest bleak markers. The CIA station chief carried an air of fatal resolve as his agency took on a holding action while diplomats whispered of evacuation plans as a last resort.

Major General Murray rose from a chair facing Polgar with an acknowledging nod to the warriors just back from the fray. The defense attaché had replaced MACV command ever since US ground forces departed, left coordinating fractured advisory roles.

"Gentlemen, please...sit and fill us in," Murray implored, his Alabama drawl softened by years abroad. "Any tin, tricks, and trails you gathered...we need it first-hand now, raw and honest."

Coyle took a hard seat, grateful to unload his rucksack. He placed the manila envelope on the table not deigning to open it further, his stare conveying the import of its content - hard aerial proof of communist ambitions unchecked.

"Officer Coyle, why don't you go first?" said Polgar.

"Very well," said Coyle, then recounted his mission and what he observed.

As Coyle concluded his report, Murray asked, "Were the crossing points limited or occurring over a broad front along the border? Were there any geographic chokepoints we could target to disrupt flows?"

"Crossing points were over a broad front along the DMZ. It was like they didn't need the Ho Chi Minh trail anymore. They were just dropping down from the North wherever they wanted. They have no fear of their convoys being attacked, except by gunships like ours. But even then, there are so few left that are being used to interdict weapons and supplies. We destroyed well over fifty trucks and vehicles and I honestly don't think we even make a dent in the flow of arms and troops across the border."

"So, what would you suggest?"

"Resume the bombing and bring back the ARVN ground forces. While they weren't great, at least they had some effect. What is happening now is pure mayhem. We're asking for disaster when their weapons and troops reach the cities."

"You understand that we can only recommend at this point."

"Nixon promised that America would retaliate if Hanoi broke the peace agreement. Sending vast quantities of weapons, supplies, and troops across the border to the South is a clear violation. So, retaliate. We have aircraft carriers off the coast that do plenty of damage if they are unleashed."

"Nixon's gone. Retaliation is off the table. At least not from us," said Polgar. "Nobody in Washington or the Pentagon wants to extend the war."

"Even if it means losing?" said Granier.

"We are no longer the ones that will determine if the war is won or lost. That's up to Saigon and Hanoi.

"Officer Granier, you can give your report now," said Polgar.

Granier gave a detailed account of what happened during the recon mission and what he observed. When he was finished, Murray asked, "Were some units breaking off at forward staging points just north of the DMZ or were entire regiments pushing straight towards interior South Vietnam?"

"Except for the units that chased us, the regiments were staying together. These were not reinforcements. These were elite troops that had trained together and were meant to fight together."

"And their battle preparedness and morale?"

"They didn't seem overly concerned when they went after us like hounds on a hunt. Those of us that survived were lucky to make it out of there alive."

"Alright. Thank you, Officer Granier and Coyle. We recognize that both of you are the most experienced officers remaining in Vietnam. Officer Granier, you fought alongside Ho Chi Minh and General Giap when they were our allies in World War II. Do you have any insight that might help us now in deciphering General Giap's next move?"

"The only insight I can offer you is that Giap thinks of everything down to the last detail. The man is brilliant."

"And yet, he got his ass kicked during the Tet Offensive," said Polgar.

"Giap didn't plan the Tet Offensive."

"You're sure about that?"

"Real sure. He's not stupid. He may have offered advice. Whoever planned the Tet Offensive lacked patience, something Giap has plenty of. He wouldn't have wasted troops like that."

"So, who was it?"

"I don't know. But if I had to bet, I'd say Le Duan was behind it. He's ambitious and willing to gamble. End the war with a bold move like Tet was right up Le Duan's alley."

"And you think that's what he is doing now? Preparing for another bold move?"

"Yeah. Except this time the Americans won't be

there to stop him."

"Our intelligence believes Giap is back in charge of the military."

"He probably is. That's a two-edged sword. He'll be cautious and take his time before the final assault. But when he strikes, it will be like thunder."

"Thank you for your input, Officers. You can go."

"Before we go can I have permission to speak freely?"

"Sure. Go ahead."

"You heard Coyle, and you heard me. Elite units and more weapons and supplies than ever before are pouring across the border with little to no resistance. Where in the hell are the ARVN? We are all experienced practitioners of war and we know that ceding territory along the border is a terrible strategy. Don't the generals in Saigon realize their error?"

Polgar and Murray exchange a knowing look before Polgar answered Granier, "The ARVN commanders had decided not to defend the border."

"Why?"

"They're focusing their resources on the population centers and the Mekong Delta in the South. The Mekong is Saigon's rice basket. As long as they hold it, they can feed their people indefinitely."

"Those cities and rice fields won't mean jack when the whole country is overrun. What's our endgame here if the ARVN collapses? An evacuation under fire - is that what we're reduced to planning while the North conquers the South uncontested?" said Coyle.

"And what about the hill tribes in the North?" said Granier. "They've fought by our side defending the South for over a decade."

"Saigon will continue to supply them with weapons and ammunition to defend themselves against the communists."

"And the outposts along the border?"

"Most are being abandoned as we speak. ARVN forces are consolidating in the large outpost in and around air bases where they can call on air power to defend themselves."

"The ARVN have been decimated every time they tried to stand toe-to-toe with the NVA in the highlands over the past few years. Their tactical incompetence is mind-boggling - they still bunch up in columns on the roads just begging for ambush. The NVA will chew them up again if they leave their defensive bunkers," said Polgar.

"What about the South Vietnamese Air Force?" said Coyle.

"The feeling in Saigon is that they should conserve their aircraft and pilots until the NVA and VC attack the cities or the Mekong. The terrain around an urban environment is usually open and allows the aircraft to attack the enemy more easily than the jungle. In addition, the enemy anti-aircraft weapons cannot hide beneath the jungle canopy and must fight out in the open."

"So, basically the South Vietnamese want perfect conditions before they fight?" said Granier.

"Something like that… yes. There is a feeling that if they lose any aircraft or pilots before the big push by the North Vietnamese, they will not be able to have them replaced."

"Is that true?"

"Somewhat, yes. The Pentagon is not anxious to send any more advanced weapons to Vietnam when there are other countries in the world that need to be defended against communism."

"Why have the ARVN commanders become so timid?" said Coyle

"They're cowards," said Granier.

"No, not really," said Polgar. "They're disillusioned. And can you blame them? They've been fighting this war longer than we have and their biggest ally just pulled up stakes and abandoned them."

"They outnumber the enemy three to one. The ARVN have over one million troops in the field," said Granier.

"On paper maybe. But almost a third of the soldiers pay their commanders their entire salary to show them present during roll call so they can work at another job. It's disheartening for those troops that are willing to fight to see their comrades dodge their service."

"They have the best equipped military in the world besides the United States," said Coyle.

"Yes, they do. But it takes more than weapons and ammunition to win wars. They have to be willing to stand their ground which is something the South Vietnamese are unwilling to do at the moment."

"Even if they did, I'm not sure it would make a difference," said Murray. "The last time the ARVN went on the defensive with a major force, they were almost wiped out. You remember, Coyle. You were there in Laos."

"That doesn't mean you stop trying," said Coyle.

"I don't disagree, but getting the ARVN military

commanders to believe that is not easy or even possible at this point. They fear that their forces will be decimated if they defend the frontiers, then there is nothing to stop the communists from taking over the entire country."

"You keep saying that 'at this point.' Is there some point where things are going to change?" said Granier.

"It's possible. Situations change. That's what we're hoping for anyway. We all know the consequences if South Vietnam falls. The communists are not going to stop. Laos has already been lost. Cambodia is hanging on by its fingernails. Malaysia or Thailand could next."

"You've got to convince the ARVN commanders to fight or all will be lost," said Granier.

"Honestly, we don't have much clout with the generals in Saigon once we pulled our troops out."

"We're still giving them money, aren't we?"

"Yes, but it seems to be disappearing at an alarming rate now that our overwatch is gone."

"The generals are preparing for the departure before the tsunami hits."

"I imagine so."

"So, what about bribing them directly to fight?"

"We've considered that, but is seems too little, too late. Plus, I doubt they would have much success. An army that fights for money will only risk their lives so far and then desert. The NVA know this and will take advantage."

"I can't believe the ARVN fought for all these years and now they are just going to let it slip away without a fight," said Coyle.

"The ARVN will fight before the end comes. They won't have a choice. I am also sure some units will win battles in spite of their leaders."

"And what are we supposed to do?"

"Help them however we can, whenever we can."

"And hope the attitude in Washington changes," said Polgar. "It's a long shot but it could happen. One last thing… it may be that the best way to look forward is to remember that the longer we keep South Vietnam out of the hands of the communist, the more time we buy for other nations to prepare to meet the revolution. America's strategy was never about just one nation… it was about the world. Keep the faith and fight on. In the end, it will be worth it," said Polgar.

After the briefing, Granier led Coyle on foot to one of his favorite haunts - the Bushman's Bar tucked in a back alley off Tu Do Street. They pushed through the bead-curtained entrance into the cavernous, smoky watering hole. Ceiling fans stirred the humidity and strands of cigarette smoke over the worn wooden tables. The place catered to off-duty pilots, spec ops vets, and CIA spooks too weary for glitzy hotel bars and high-priced hookers. Just stools, chairs, and a long oak counter with liquor bottles glinting in muted light.

In the corner, a three-piece combo rattled out bawdy versions of pop hits while scantily-clad country girls swayed and dipped on a makeshift stage, garish makeup shining under the purple lights. Some of the dancers doubled as servers, dropping beers and bantering with the grim clientele in exchange for greasy bundles of piastres.

Granier and Coyle saddled up to the bar, exchanging silent nods with the bartender as two tumblers of bourbon arrived wordlessly. The searing liquor matched their mood after the dire intel updates. They carried their drinks to a corner table near the back stage, cobra gunship propellers and battalion flags hanging from the beams completed the war-weary decor.

"So, that's it? We fight until we lose?" said Coyle. "That's one hell of a strategy."

"What do you want… a gold star on your forehead?" said Granier. "We're warriors. We fight because we're good at it… and we're expendable."

"Maybe that's why you fight, but I like to think I fight for a higher cause."

Granier grunted, taking a long pull of bourbon. "And what cause might that be at this stage, Coyle? Bringing our beloved democracy to the poor peasants wading in rice fields? Tell me, what has your higher cause won here besides stacks of body bags shipped back home."

Coyle bristled, his jaw tensing. "It wasn't supposed to end like this. The ARVN were making progress - you saw those battalions in action same as me. Fearless fighters when led properly. Now their leaders are stacking gold bars waiting for the end. Everything we bled for washes away while the South gets sold down the river."

"What did you expect?" Granier rasped, signaling for two more shots. "You heard the embassy report. ARVN colonels collecting pay vouchers for ghost soldiers. Generals hoarding the best weapons for personal protection squads." He shook his head bitterly. "When the master loses the spirit to fight, the hound doesn't defend the family farm. The South's soul was hallowed out years before the last Hueys took off."

Coyle stared into his glass, the shapes of old battles flashing before him. Faces of the loyal fighters now abandoned to fate. He lifted red-rimmed eyes to meet Granier's stony gaze. "I can't just walk away. The war's not yet lost. We owe it to stand tall beside those who still believe."

Granier leaned forward, voice dropping low. "Let me tell you what our beloved allies believe in. Care to guess the going rate an ARVN captain pays his major for a transfer back to Saigon? Fifty grams of gold. That's belief you can measure by the kilo."

Coyle gripped his glass tightly to keep composure. "There's always been corruption greasing the South. But they turned back the Tet Offensive when we stood together. Back when commanders weren't beholden to geomancy and horoscopes before moving battalions. Back when colonels were too scared of US advisers to bail out from the bush."

Granier slowly spun his shot glass on the scarred table. "And where was our esteemed leadership when the line cracked at Pleiku and Kontum? Busy measuring peace table corner angles. Or whispering about the secret mining of harbors and bombing dikes like punishing peasants might bring Old Uncle Ho to beg forgiveness."

He slammed back the shot then stared Coyle down with coal-cinder eyes. "This Saigon parade float you want to rescue never existed, Coyle. It's time the generals in Saigon pay the devil his due."

Granier's eyes bore across the table with grim finality after his diatribe. Coyle sat back, letting harsh truths sink in as smoke curled in the tawdry lights. He needed to confront the truth of the situation. There was too much at risk to avoid reality. Maybe this Saigon they dreamt worth saving never existed outside fabricated dispatches and campaign speeches.

Coyle sighed, rolling a cocktail napkin into abstraction as he gathered his thoughts. "You've always had cold eyes for this crusade." He straightened up to meet his friend's hardened gaze. "But what's your endgame here, Granier? Watch fixed-wings get overrun on the tarmac? Play last croupier at the Continental before the Reds roll in with their tanks?"

Granier softened by degrees, sensing his friend wrestled with disenchantment. He rubbed his weathered knuckles, mind sifting through options. "I'm not as convinced of defeat as you think, Coyle. Old wolves bite deepest when backed into the corner. But we're gonna need a plan. A good one if there is any hope of turning this thing around."

"Do you have something in mind, Granier?"

"No more waiting for orders or permission. There's no time for that. We do what the rest cannot. The giants have departed over the oceans. So, the wolves will hunt while prey remains."

Granier's callused grip on Coyle's arm underscored the moment between battle-tested allies. What others abandoned to fate, they still might save through stubborn will. "Okay, but what do we hunt? What will make a difference?" said Coyle.

"If remaining ARVN regiments continue to withdraw inside enclaves to await siege, then millions will be left defenseless when Northern armor rolls south unopposed."

"I agree. But how do we get ARVN to engage the NVA?"

"We show them that they can win."

"And how do we do that?"

"Bold, well-planned assaults that demoralize the enemy. If the ARVN commanders see victories that really make a difference, they will find their courage and join the fight."

"I like it. The targets will need to be daring. Something nobody thought was possible."

"Exactly."

"Do you have ideas?"

"Some. But not enough. And we're gonna need more than just you and I to pull this off. We need the best of the best – well-armed, elite teams."

Coyle waved over the dancer who'd been eyeing their table. The pretty farm girl glanced warily at the intense Americans.

Coyle gently touched her arm, softening his tone. "My apologies, Miss. Could I trouble you for paper, pen, and a pot of strong coffee? My colleague and I have work to do tonight."

She looked confused. Coyle made it easier to understand by making hand gestures to match his words. "Write. Coffee."

She nodded her understanding, then swayed towards the bar as Granier watched his friend with an amused snort...

The Lost

Quang Tri province in northern South Vietnam had seen some of the most intense fighting early in the Vietnam War. Given its strategic position along the DMZ border, it was a constant battleground between ARVN and communist forces. Now, NVA divisions were assailing the capital city itself in overwhelming force. Outgunned and outmanned, the remaining ARVN defenders fought desperately to stall the communist onslaught so refugees could escape.

Fierce urban warfare raged across contested streets and strong points while civilians packed belongings and fled in panic before the inevitable collapse. As mortars and rockets pounded the shrinking perimeter, ARVN Rangers and Marines mounted tenacious but futile counterattacks. Buying time with their blood against hopeless odds. This was their final post. Their final duty.

News of the city's impending fall reached the outskirts, sending waves of displaced villagers rushing toward rumors of evacuation. After years enduring the see-saw battles nearby, these peasant farmers knew occupation meant more suffering at communist hands. Food and shelter grew scarcer by the day as most fled south or took refuge in the countryside. The roads were clogged with civilians pushing handcarts, bicycles, and exhausted pedestrians carrying everything they owned of value on bundles lashed to their backs.

A lucky few heard of the departing buses to carry some civilians to safety before the final enemy push. After being turned away elsewhere, this convoy was their last gasp hope. Just miles away, their would-be protectors fought room-to-room knowing each bullet only prolonged the inevitable defeat. The ARVN would soon share the fate of other provincial capitals already toppled since the American withdrawal, their sacrifices erased in history's painful sweep.

Karen first caught word of Quang Tri city's plight from an AP wire report while in Saigon covering student demonstrations. Determined to document the human impact as fronts collapsed across the northern provinces, she dispatched immediate plans to embed within the swelling exodus. Her editor strongly advised avoiding risky combat zones with the American contingent gone, but she insisted no other photographers remained willing to reveal the refugee tragedy.

Scrambling passage on a Cessna courier flight, she endured four stomach-churning hours buffeted by monsoon headwinds up Vietnam's spine. All for a brief, dizzying glimpse of the panicked aftermath. She had witnessed too many sieges unravel in numbingly similar viciousness. The chance of escape always pitifully small for those unable or unwilling to flee until the last possible moments.

Peering through rain-streaked windows, Karen's guts twisted seeing columns of smoke smudging the horizon. The aerial scope multiplied as they neared the beleaguered capital. Below, a choked rural artery clogged with humanity desperate to stay ahead of communist forces momentarily held at bay in the east.

Bracing for landing, Karen swallowed back bile taking in the maelstrom consuming Quang Tri. She had embedded in fallen enclaves before, but the scale of human suffering and frantic despair choked her like acrid smoke. It seemed the entire province compressed into miles of packed ox-carts, overladen motorbikes, and fearful families shepherding the elderly and infants. All desperate for momentum if not actual escape. She steeled herself as the Cessna struts settled into the muddy runway. The cargo door creaked open.

As soon as Karen exited the plane, she was buffeted by waves of refugees pressing across the single runway. Choking diesel exhaust and cries for rescue collided with her senses. She scanned the logjammed perimeter for any vehicle heading inward rather than escaping. There were none. Everyone wanted out. Nobody wanted in.

Fifty yards away, an enterprising young Vietnamese man yelled "Motobike! Motobike!" above the din, trying to hawk outbound passage. Karen barged through the sweating scrum, cash in hand. She pressed two hundred dollars into his palm while commandeering the motorbike keys. "I buy," she said wondering if he understood. His protests evaporated upon glimpsing her sheaf of US greenbacks. Hard currency outweighed odds of driving back into the cauldron.

Kickstarting the sputtering Honda Trail 90 to life, Karen squeezed the throttle and muscled through the human current. Refueling stalls became her slalom gates as she gained speed past security teams guarding evacuation convoys. Heavily laden trucks and jeeps threatened to pin her against the runway fences, but she managed ragged clearances while navigating for side roads toward the city center.

Weaving between backstreets clogged with abandoned war machinery, she alternated using the horn and swerving around burned-out armored personnel carriers. Tenacious families seeking lost relatives blocked her path only to dive clear at the last moment seeing that the crazy American would not stop. She tasted both their desperation and her own adrenaline-soaked mortality. Gritting through near spills, Karen hurtled nearer the desperate city.

Karen throttled the straining Honda to its limits, swerving through alleyways clogged with vehicles destroyed by mortar barrages. She laid off the horn to conserve momentum against pleading encampments clinging to final safe haven promises before enemy forces overran the city center.

She knew NVA infiltration teams already filtered behind crumbling defenses to isolate escape routes. Drawing too much attention risked her one free pass of mobility getting impounded or disabled.

Rounding a final shattered statue marking the city gates, Karen squeezed the protesting brake levers and hopped off her rickety transport. She walked the bike into a narrow storefront, stuffing folded bills into the manager's relieved hands to safeguard the Honda. She knew he would not leave his store even with the communists coming. It was all he owned and he was too old to start again.

Steeling her nerves, Karen stepped into the larger boulevard thronged by desperate thousands seeking transit out of the firestorm. She donned press credentials prominently and hefted her trusted Canon AE-1 to frame the exodus composition. Facing the human tidal wave meant keeping composed amidst the swirling anguish as a solo observer sworn to document their collective fate.

She focused down to F8 aperture and slowly tracked individual frames of loss and raw panic intersecting before her lens. Stoic elders in strained limbo, stunned children clinging to overwhelmed parents. All knew escape routes were overwhelmed, fate now a game of numbers and counteroffensive gambits. Karen swallowed bitter fury and photographed on, determined to memorialize their struggles beyond the official record's sanitized body counts.

The wails of the desperate refugees cut straight through to Karen's core as she snapped photos, documenting their exodus from Quang Tri. Elderly hobbling along, mothers clutching wide-eyed toddlers, young boys struggling under the weight of sacks holding their only possessions. Entire lives uprooted once again by the cruel fortunes of war.

Her camera clicked in rapid succession, capturing the pain and loss etched on their faces. This is what the world needed to see - the human toll inflicted by both sides of this endless conflict. Her role was to observe, record, and reveal uncomfortable truths without interference. Even if that truth was the anguish of the innocent caught in the ideological crossfire.

A tiny girl tripped on the muddy path, spilling the

contents of her bag. Karen instinctively started toward her before stopping short, her journalistic instincts dueling with compassion. The girl's tear-filled eyes pierced Karen as she refocused her lens to document the moment rather than intervene. Years immersed in war's hardest edges had taught Karen not to penetrate the invisible barrier separating observer from participant. The mere act of helping could influence events and violate the photojournalist's directive pounded into her during journalism school - report the truth without ever altering the scene.

Yet seeing the little girl desperately stuffing moldy clothes back into her torn satchel ignited Karen's memories of comforting Vietnamese children orphaned by battlefields. Her camera felt heavier than usual this morning, weighted by the images of humanity's suffering across its film. She glanced around furtively before sighing, peeling the camera strap off her neck and crossing over to the ragged girl.

Karen gently helped the stunned child replace the last spilled items before hoisting the bag. They continued toward the swelling crowd at the evacuation point where buses idled to ferry the displaced masses south. A temporary waystation on the road to diminishing hopes and further sorrow if this war continued its abusive trajectory. Karen swallowed back shame at her small failure of discipline - a single ethical compromise that might taint the entire chronicle she aimed to construct for audiences half a world away.

Yet leaving a child abandoned and crying in the dirt also severed her conscience, no matter journalism's professed rules. This war left no unsullied moral absolutes as guideposts, only degrees of anguish weighed and recorded through her camera's scratched lenses under omnipresent clouds of red dust.

After delivering the little girl into her grandfather's care, Karen pushed through the anxious throng toward the idling buses spewing black diesel fumes. She raised her camera just as two ARVN guards began lashing the crowd with canes, sending panicked mothers and confused children scrambling back from the vehicles' open doors. Cries of pain accompanied their blows as an officer shouted harsh commands for order. Reflexively, Karen photographed the unstable scene, wincing as a teenage boy took a cane across his shoulders when briefly leaving the crowd to collect an elder's spilled bag.

The ethical dilemma intensified, almost overwhelming. Every instinct compelled her to intervene, to use her status as an American journalist to halt the guards' indiscriminate punishment. Instead, she forced herself to keep photographing, documenting callous injustice even as her stomach knotted at passively observing cruelty. This was her duty - reveal uncomfortable truths and human rights violations from all sides. The world must see and judge for itself no matter how the images cut against her conscience.

When a weeping mother cradling an infant took an errant cane blow, Karen could stand no more. She broke from her observer's code and rushed forward waving her credentials, shouting in crude Vietnamese for the guards to stop. Like a threat, she snapped the guards' photos. Evidence of their cruelty. Her sudden appearance shocked them into hesitation as she placed her body between violent authorities and their victims. For a long minute, the standoff held, before the guards reluctantly withdrew, leaving Karen shielding the now silent refugees.

She had shattered every rule drilled into her by editors and mentors over the years of covering the war's greatest anguish and most ambiguous heroes. Yet the feeling of guardianship swelled her heart as villagers touched her foreign hair like an angel of mercy. Despite knowing the wider world might revile her for interrupting the impartial record, Karen vowed to safeguard these people, come what may. The rest could judge her choices, but inaction had become impossible. The war had stolen too much, from too many. If just one child made it onto those buses who otherwise faced blows and bullets, then whatever professional sacrifices awaited seemed worthwhile burdens to bear witness.

Karen photographed for hours, grimly cataloging the refugees' despair as overcrowded buses and trucks gradually transported the lucky few south. She kept her distance, camera vision framing vignettes of loss and sporadic kindness in the disorder.

Reeling children passed into strangers' care when sorely tested parents reached their limits through the endless waiting. Some white-clad nuns tended the injured despite lacking triage supplies. Karen noticed but chose not to join in, even as her photographer's cloak felt more a burden than shield that day.

Finally, the unlucky remainder massed outside the ARVN perimeter as dusk approached, pleading their case or offer what little they still retained for passage on one of the remaining buses. Karen's film roll neared its final frames when a worn captain emerged to confer with his guards. His unit manned the last intact bunkers covering this route just inside the war-scarred ramparts.

The officer exhaled, then met Karen's eye and beckoned her closer. She crossed through the razor concertina wire to find vantage alongside the last sentinel of a shrinking enclave. His hoarse words acknowledged the inevitable climax at dawn. But hope of escape remained slim as ammunition stores dwindled. Resignation lined his face at the doomed fortress. "You get good pictures today? You show world what coming, yes?" Karen nodded in sullen confirmation.

"You must do more," he implored, pressing a dented flask into her palm. "My brother Tran Duc Hung waits in Saigon, 4th Artillery Battalion, Dong Du base. Please...if I cannot leave here, return this so he knows we fought to the end."

Karen clutched the flask bearing the weight of his hope. She had photographed refugees' makeshift memorials without fully grasping each's profound emotional gravity until now. This single vessel linked past and unknown futures.

The captain retreated to the bunker without looking back, his personal continuity now in her care just as her cameras preserved callous history. New sorrow and outrage joined the older pains etched inside her as Karen exited the cordon into night's uncertainty. She carried the flask as steadfastly as the film preserving stark, heartbreaking truths about duty and human bonds that transcended orders or rules.

Saigon, South Vietnam

The swirling Saigon street noises faded as Coyle followed Granier through the beaded curtain into the back room of the Binh Minh inn. Despite the late hour, Granier selected this safehouse rendezvous based on years cultivating assets across shadow fronts. With most intelligence ranks thinned, they dared not meet openly even under embassy auspices.

Granier checked sight lines from the room's barred window before lowering rice paper screens. He then ran an electronic sweep for bugs while Coyle secured the weathered teak door behind them. They sat at a rustic table and kept their voices low regardless, knowing these days even friends became commodities easily bartered.

"I've confirmed the specs on airfield security up North," muttered Coyle, unrolling target photos across the table's scarred surface. "SAM coverage remains top notch, but we've gamed penetrations before when necessary."

“Maybe we go in on the ground,” said Granier studying the photos.

“Maybe. But that takes time. Something we’re running short on.”

Granier grunted his agreement. Coyle thought for a moment, then said, “Maybe we do both. We insert a team to clear a path. Take out the air defenses, then attack the airbase by air.”

Granier nodded and said, “Give me a day to think about it and study the intel. I’ll see what I can come up with.”

"Alright."

"And the trucking transit reports? Any choke points emerge that buys us leverage?"

Coyle passed stained dossiers bound with fraying twine. "Main conduits still channel through Lang Son given the rail links. But the enemy's redundancy keeps supplies flowing even when facing interdiction."

Granier weighed the factors. "If we sever key command links, their offensive coordination shatters," Granier said. "A viper becomes a worm when sightless." He withdrew a coded list of infiltration contacts still positioned behind changing lines. "Although their numbers have been thinned, we still have operators behind enemy lines. They can help identify the commanders that need eliminating."

Coyle nodded, then leaned in. "The fuel depots remain the jugular for any enemy expedition." His finger circled installations arrayed to support armor and mobility assets surging south. "Here - Loc Ninh hub for the Saigon axis. Surgically removed, their tanks starve in the field regardless of commanders."

"And their strategic reserves around Thanh Hóa?" grunted Granier. "If we paralyze their airfields and vehicle parks as I propose, their army will be unable to gain momentum."

"Agreed." Coyle assented, calculating logistics strains across a calendared campaign deep into enemy territory. "So, I count eight operations. That's a lot for the time period we discussed. We're gonna need a big team."

"Teams. Specialists."

"We don't have a lot to choose from."

"More than you think. We can draw from my Phoenix recruits."

"You think they'd be up for something like this?"

"Some. I think I can still get access to their personnel files. That'll help. What about air teams?"

"On the fixed wing side, we can draw from the South Vietnamese teams I trained. Helicopters and jets are another matter."

"We need Scott."

"Leave my son out of this."

"Why? He can help with recruitment, plus he's one hell of a pilot."

"He's also my son and I don't want to put him in harm's way."

"You don't think he's in harm's way now? This is Scott we are talking about."

"You and I could go to jail for what we are planning. Maybe even be hanged for treason. I don't want Scott caught up in that."

"He's a big boy, Coyle. It should be his decision, not yours."

"Let me think about it."

"Think all you want, but if we wait much longer, the North's final offensive will catch us still playing armchair general."

"I'll think quick. Who else do you have in mind for the teams?"

"Lieutenant Khoi served beside MACV-SOG scouts before Tet. Fluent across tribal dialects - and a skilled parachutist. He's a good fighter as well as a good leader."

"Alright. What about demolition?"

"Sergeant Le from the combat engineers - expert with plastic charges. He has a light touch with timers."

"Good," said Coyle pleased with the way their plans were taking shape. They were bold. Very bold. Their conversation continued deep into the night. As dawn approached, Granier had the inn's cook prepare breakfast. He hoped the nourishment would give them more energy to continue their planning, but it just made them sleepy. Coyle ended the discussions with one last question, "How are we gonna keep this secret from the brass?"

"We need to complete our assigned missions so we don't raise suspicions."

"…and plan and execute the brashest covert missions ever contrived?"

"Sure."

"What about sleep?"

"Sleep when you're dead."

The Team

Saigon, South Vietnam

Coyle and Granier sat inside a vast, empty hangar on the air base. Their voices echoed off the corrugated metal walls and high rafter ceilings. Rows of bare fluorescent lights illuminated the concrete floor, showing years of oil stains and tread marks from the squadrons of fighters and transport aircraft that once occupied this space.

Now, only a single table with a map and scattered documents occupied the acre of space. Coyle and Granier sat across from each other, cognizant of their voices carrying but reasonably sure no one could eavesdrop on their discussion here.

Coyle let out a low whistle as he scanned the roster they assembled. "That's more operatives than I envisioned! Practically a small army."

Granier nodded, shifting in the uncomfortable metal folding chair. "Yeah, the roster has grown past our initial expectations. We set out to keep this tight and quiet."

Coyle rubbed his chin. "Makes me think we overreached, bit off more than we can handle."

Granier considered this, absently drumming his fingers on his bicep. "Perhaps, but if the intelligence is solid, I believe we can accomplish the missions. We needed a bold plan to shake things up. This is a bold plan."

"Yeah...but we both agree we need to move faster. This roster could take a year to fill out with the men we need. Plus, security is gonna be a bitch."

"Speaking of which, we should add security to the roster."

"I agree," said Coyle adding to the roster. "Let's go over the list again and see if there are skills that we can cut."

"Alright," said Granier grabbing the list and reading it off. "Helicopter pilots and aircrews, demolitions men, forward air controllers, combat medics, radio operators, scouts, snipers, interpreters, intelligence operatives, signals operatives, undercover Vietnamese, intelligence agents, and security. That makes...sixteen distinct roles."

"So, what if we found men that could fill multiple roles?"

Granier shook his head. "No time to cross-train operatives and finding men with multiple skills will take more time which we don't have. We need the most capable, specialized men we can get - true professionals. A sniper must focus on his craft, perfecting his skill. The pilot, the communicator, the scout - they must all concentrate their efforts on their roles."

Coyle nodded slowly. "Alright, you're right. We get the top operatives in each field and run lean, elite teams."

"If we drop redundancy in the teams it will decrease

the number of men we need but will increase our risks."

"I agree. We need to run as lean as possible. Drop redundancy and we'll deal with the additional risk."

"Even though this is a large roster, I don't think we are going to have an issue with finding volunteers. I think a lot of men feel the same way we do. This has to be done if Saigon is to survive."

"I hope that's the case. If so, we may be able to rely on the men we recruit recommending more men that fill out the roster faster."

"Let's go over the missions one more time and make sure we have everyone we need to succeed."

"Okay. Then it's time to start recruiting."

"Agreed. Things will never be perfect. It's war."

Pleiku, South Vietnam

Pleiku Air Base was surrounded by NVA in the nearby jungle. Yet, it still stood. But nobody knew for how long. There were substantial ARVN forces protecting it and many of the hill tribes relocated to the base as more and more NVA forces invaded the south and destroyed their villages and crops. Everyone knew that if the NVA decided they wanted Pleiku, there wasn't much the ARVN or the few American aircrews that remained could do to keep them away. As the guards kept watch on the perimeter, the soldiers and aircrews slept.

Scott stared at the slowly spinning overhead fan, watching the blades cut through the muggy air. Sleep eluded him, as it often did lately. Dark circles hung under his eyes, testament to the toll this endless war was taking. As he lay restless, his mind turned to the events of the last few days.

The ammunition run to the isolated ARVN outpost had been sobering. Scott knew in his gut that the outmanned and outgunned South Vietnamese troops there didn't stand a chance once the North Vietnamese Army decided to overrun them. But command kept insisting on resupply runs, so he and his Huey crew delivered pallet after pallet of ammo they feared would soon fall into enemy hands.

On the return leg, Scott spotted smoke rising in the distance - never a good sign. As they cautiously approached, the scene below made his breath catch in his throat. An entire hamlet razed, dozens of villagers lying dead on the ground, their simple thatched huts and wooden palisades burned to ash. Scott felt his hands tighten on the controls of the Huey, knuckles turning white-hot with anger and frustration. The NVA and VC attackers were still swarming the area, shouting with victorious bravado. Scott and his door gunner unleashed a barrage of rockets and bullets, but he knew they were too late - the killing was already done. After a few tense minutes of trading shots, he broke off the attack. *Another tragedy for the history books*, he thought bitterly. *How many more before this nightmare ended?*

As they turned toward base, movement on the ground below caught his eye. A family - mother, father, two young children - running in panic across a rice paddy dike as a squad of NVA soldiers closed in. Just ahead, a bridge spanned a wide river; if the family could make it across, they might yet survive. Scott banked the Huey hard right, lining up a shot for his door gunner. "Buy them some time!" he shouted over the aircraft's intercom. The gunner raked the dike with bursts of fire, slowing the advance of their pursuers. They fired back timidly. The enemy knew what a minigun could do and they wanted no part of it.

The family raced toward the bridge as Scott pushed the Huey to full throttle. Tracers arced past the cockpit in response - the NVA squad had them zeroed in now too. Just then, a series of muffled thumps echoed across the valley. Mortars. Seconds later, the bridge erupted into a cloud of smoke and fire, cutting off the family's escape. Scott watched helplessly as they skidded to a stop, huddling in what little cover the end of the bridge still provided. Wide eyes darted from the ruins of the bridge back to the dike where the NVA squad was closing ground.

"Hang on, I'm taking us down!" Scott barked. Putting the chopper between the family and the advancing troops, he flared hard and touched down on the rocky soil. "Cover me!" His door gunner rotated the smoking minigun toward the dike as Scott jumped out.

"Come on, let's move!" He waved frantically to the terrified family. As they stumbled toward him, clutching their children tight to their chests, his gunner unleashed hell on the NVA to keep their heads down. Scott hustled the family aboard and they lifted off just as the squad converged on their position. "Get us out of here!" he yelled to his co-pilot.

They turned back toward base, the trembling family safe for the moment, but their future as uncertain as ever in this doomed country. Scott felt a mix of relief at saving their lives and anger at the futility of it. How many refugees had they evacuated over the years, only to end up trapped in squalid, overcrowded camps with nowhere to go? When would it end?

When Scott returned from the debrief, he was surprised to see his father Tom Coyle and friend Rene Granier waiting at his barracks. Had word already reached them? Was he in trouble over the risky rescue operation? But instead, Coyle and Granier laid out an intriguing covert ops proposal which could change the direction of the war. They would run small teams carrying out unsanctioned missions designed to destroy the morale of the NVA and their leaders in Hanoi. If successful, the missions could demonstrate to the ARVN commanders that it was still possible to defeat the North if they leave the protection of the cities and attack the enemy as they crossed the border. The entire operation was filled with risk and if caught they could face charges of treason and spend the rest of their lives in prison.

Scott listened intently, his weariness lifting. Here was a chance to strike back, to directly attack NVA operations flooding weapons and troops across the border. A glimmer of hope pierced the clouds of despair that had been building in his heart. Even before they were finished explaining the entire operation, Scott met his father's gaze and nodded. "I'm in."

Central Highlands, South Vietnam

Granier marched up the winding jungle trail as the Montagnard village came into view, tucked on a plateau between towering limestone peaks. Rough timber and thatch huts blended into the tangled greens and browns of the surrounding rainforest. Wisps of cooking fire smoke rose lazily through the banana and bamboo groves that fed and concealed the remote settlement.

Two perimeter guards, wearing faded tiger-stripe fatigues and carrying worn but serviceable AK-47s, stepped silently from the underbrush to challenge Granier as he approached. His indigenous interpreter Xuan exchanged a few quick words, defusing the situation. The guards nodded respectfully to Granier before letting the unusual visitors pass.

Granier could feel dozens of eyes tracking them as they made their way through the village. Chickens and lean jungle dogs scattered before their boots. The people here lived hardscrabble lives, far removed from Saigon's palaces and politics. But the coming offensive threatened all Vietnamese, high and low. Granier needed these forgotten warriors for the covert campaign ahead.

Xuan indicated the carved facade of the longhouse directly ahead. Flowering vines curled around its timber pillars and wide roofline. Gray smoke issued from a central fire-pit within its cavernous interior visible as he approached.

Granier stepped into the longhouse, ducking under the low doorway. The smell of cooking fires and tobacco filled his nose. Across the hard-packed dirt floor, a group of Montagnard tribesmen eyed him with unreadable expressions.

Beside Granier, Xuan cleared his throat and spoke in the native language, "Chief Aran, Commander Granier requests an audience."

An older Montagnard, his leathery skin covered with faded blue tattoos, stood up from the group. Studying Granier for a long moment, Chief Aran finally gestured to the open floor before his men.

Xuan whispered, "You may speak, Commander."

Granier faced the chief, getting straight to business.

"Chief Aran, you and your people have fought bravely against the Viet Cong and their allies from the North. I have need of experienced warriors to join sensitive missions I am leading."

As Xuan translated, Aran listened silently, arms crossed over his broad chest. Several younger warriors watched Granier intently, while the elders kept their eyes downcast.

"The missions will strike NVA supply depots and troop camps near the borders. Swift, covert attacks and then disappear like ghosts back into jungle," Granier continued, encouraged by the spark of interest in a few men's eyes. "Skilled scouts to gather intelligence, and the strongest fighters to raid enemy camps. We leave no traces, inflict damage, capture supplies."

Again, Aran listened to the full translation, motionless. After several long moments contemplating, he finally met Granier's eyes and spoke directly to him in broken but understandable English.

"Your missions...very dangerous I think. NVA will search for your ghosts, punish our villages if they help you." He gestured to the families gathered on woven mats at the back of the longhouse. "If warriors leave, cannot protect people."

Granier chose his next words carefully, sensing the chief's reservations. "You speak the truth, Chief Aran. The missions do carry risks that could endanger your people. I will not lie."

Granier unslung his rifle and set it before the chief in a gesture of respect. "But the NVA tightens the noose on South Vietnam each day. My team aims to loosen it, any way we can. Any chance to buy more time before the end comes."

Aran stared at the rifle a moment before lifting his

eyes to meet Granier's intense gaze again. Granier pressed his plea further. "For your people to have any future, Chief Aran, we must slow the North's advance. I give you my word, these Ghost Warriors will haunt their steps."

A long silence hung in the air. Then, Aran turned and barked orders to the Montagnard warriors in their native dialect. Six men, sinewy and battle-hardened, grabbed gear and rifles before approaching Granier. They clapped fists over hearts and bowed their heads, ready to serve.

Granier was hoping for more but decided not to press the chief. The teams would make due with those warriors offered. He bowed his thanks to the chief.

Hue, South Vietnam

Hue, the ancient imperial capital of Vietnam, straddled the Perfume River in a timeless embrace. The city's graceful pagodas and crumbling palaces bore witness to centuries of history, now overshadowed by the scars of recent battles. Bullet-pocked walls and sandbag fortifications stood alongside traditional gardens and bustling markets, a jarring contrast of war and everyday life. The Citadel, once the seat of emperors, now served as a grim reminder of the Tet Offensive's savage fighting. Yet amidst the faded grandeur and battle debris, Hue's resilient spirit endured, its people determined to preserve their heritage against all odds.

On the outskirts of Hue, ARVN soldiers labored tirelessly to bolster the city's defenses against the looming threat of an NVA and Viet Cong assault. Under the relentless sun, they dug trenches and foxholes, filling sandbags to reinforce bunkers and defensive positions. The sound of shovels and pickaxes mingled with the distant thud of artillery, a constant reminder of the enemy's proximity.

Captain Nguyen, a battle-hardened veteran, oversaw the construction of a new pillbox overlooking a key bridge leading into the city. He knew that the NVA would attempt to seize this strategic entry point, just as they had during the Tet Offensive years before. The memory of those brutal street battles still haunted him, driving him to ensure that Hue would not fall again.

As the fortifications took shape, ARVN soldiers manning the perimeter scanned the surrounding countryside with wary eyes. They knew the enemy was out there, massing in the jungle-clad hills, preparing for the final push. Refugees fleeing the rural villages brought tales of NVA and Viet Cong units on the move, their numbers swelling with each passing day.

Despite the grim reports, the ARVN troops remained resolute. They fortified key buildings within the city, turning schools and government offices into makeshift strongpoints. Sandbags and barbed wire sprouted along streets once lined with colorful shophouses and bustling cafes. The people of Hue watched the preparations with a mix of fear and resignation, their lives once again upended by the tides of war.

As the sun crawled across the sky, Captain Nguyen gathered his men for a briefing. They huddled around a map of the city, marked with the latest intelligence on enemy movements. "We hold the line here," he said, his voice steady. "We fight for our families, our homes, our country. The enemy may come in waves, but we will stand firm. We are the defenders of Hue."

The ARVN soldiers nodded grimly, their faces etched with determination. They knew the odds were stacked against them, but they would not yield. They would fight house to house, street by street, until the last bullet was spent. For in the ancient city of Hue, steeped in the blood and glory of generations past, there could be no surrender. Only the final stand of the brave against the coming storm.

The staccato rhythm of Huey rotors echoed across the rooftops as Granier strode through the narrow alley, his destination a nondescript concrete building tucked between a noodle shop and a rundown apartment complex. He rapped twice on the steel door, then twice more. A slot at eye level slid open, two dark eyes peering out suspiciously.

"I'm here to see Dao Minh," Granier said in Vietnamese. "Tell him Granier is calling."

The eyes narrowed, then the slot snapped shut. Muffled voices argued behind the door before a series of locks disengaged. The door swung open, revealing a spartan room with a few chairs and a table strewn with maps and photographs.

Dao Minh leaned against the far wall, arms crossed, appraising Granier with a mix of wariness and respect. He had the wiry build and coiled intensity of a born fighter, honed by years of hard living and clandestine missions. "Granier. It's been a long time," Dao said, his voice flat.

"Too long," Granier replied, stepping inside as the door closed behind him.

“Give us the room,” said Dao to his men.

The men left leaving Dao and Granier alone. "I heard you're chief of Plan F-6 operations in Hue now.

Congratulations."

Dao shrugged. "Same work, different title. We do what needs to be done."

Granier nodded, taking a seat uninvited. He leaned forward, elbows on knees. "I have a proposition for you, Dao. One that could change the course of this war."

Dao's eyes flickered with interest as he pulled up a chair. "I'm listening."

"I'm putting together a team," Granier said. "Elite fighters, special skills. Operating outside official channels to hit the NVA where it hurts."

"You mean like Phoenix? Assassinations, sabotage?"

"Similar, but with a different goal. We aim to show that the North can be beaten, that their all-out offensive can be stopped cold." Granier's voice hardened. "But to do that, I need the best. I need you, Dao."

Dao leaned back, considering. "What exactly did you have in mind?"

Granier laid out the bones of the plan - lightning raids on NVA supply lines and depots, taking out key commanders, sewing chaos and fear. Each mission carefully selected to damage not just the enemy's capacity, but their confidence.

"You have a sniper's patience and a guerrilla's cunning, Dao. You can get close and strike hard. That's what this team needs."

Dao was silent for a long moment, gaze distant. Then he focused back on Granier with a wolf's hungry smile. "When do we start?"

Granier clasped Dao's hand, feeling the calluses of a man who'd spent a life at war. "We're already in motion. Welcome to the Ghost Warriors Team."

"Interesting name. I assume you need more men."

"You assume correctly. But only the best. Men with experience. Men you trust."

"I have six, maybe seven. Good fighters. Skilled."

"If you are recommending them, we'd feel honored to have them."

As they began to discuss specifics, Granier felt a flicker of hope. With fighters like Dao on his side, perhaps the tide could yet be turned. Or at least, they'd make the enemy bleed for every inch of ground. In a war with no front lines, that could be enough.

The roar of distant artillery made the walls shudder, a reminder of the urgency of their task. Granier and Dao bent over the maps, two soldiers planning one last campaign in a conflict that had already claimed too many lives. But this time, they would dictate the terms of battle. This time, the ghosts would strike back.

Bien Hoa Air Base, South Vietnam

The midday sun beat down mercilessly on the tarmac as Coyle strode towards the hangar, his boots kicking up puffs of dust with each step. Inside, the familiar scents of engine oil, sweat, and stale cigarette smoke assailed his nostrils. The AC-130 Spectre gunship loomed in the shadows, its black-painted belly bristling with an arsenal of weapons.

Around the aircraft, a crew of men worked on maintenance and repairs, their faces glistening with sweat in the oppressive heat. Coyle recognized them all - hardened veterans who had flown countless missions together, braving enemy fire and impossible odds.

"Gentlemen," Coyle called out, his voice cutting

through the din of tools and chatter. "A word, if you will."

The crew looked up, curiosity and wariness mingling on their faces as they gathered around Coyle. They knew him as a skilled pilot and a tough but fair commander, a man who would never ask them to undertake a mission he wouldn't fly himself.

"I know you're busy. So, I'll cut to the chase," Coyle said, meeting each man's gaze in turn. "I'm putting together a special operation. Off the books, high risk, high reward. We'll be hitting the enemy where it hurts, taking out their supply lines and command centers."

A murmur rippled through the group, a mix of excitement and apprehension. They were no strangers to dangerous missions, but this sounded like something else entirely.

"I won't lie to you," Coyle continued. "This won't be easy. We'll be flying low and fast, often in day, deep into enemy territory. But if we succeed, we could turn the tide of this war. Give ARVN on the ground the confidence they need for a fighting chance."

He paused, letting his words sink in. "I'm not ordering anyone to join me. This is strictly voluntary. But I need the best, and that's you men. So, what do you say? Will you fly with me one more time?"

For a long moment, silence hung heavily in the air, broken only by the distant roar of jet engines. Then, one by one, the crew members nodded their acceptance.

"I'm in, sir," said the new loadmaster, a wiry man with a salt-and-pepper mustache. "Been itching to give Charlie a taste of his own medicine."

"Count me in, too," chimed the sensor operator, a lanky Texan with a drawl as thick as honey. "I reckon we've got some scores to settle."

As the crew voiced their support for Coyle's daring mission, one man remained silent, his eyes downcast. Daniel "Doc" Sawyer, the Spectre's electronic warfare officer, shifted uncomfortably as the others turned to him expectantly.

Coyle approached Sawyer, placing a hand on his shoulder. "Doc, you've been with us through thick and thin. Your skills have saved our hides more times than I can count. Are you with us on this one?"

Sawyer looked up, his blue eyes filled with conflicting emotions. He took a deep breath before speaking, his voice heavy with regret. "Sir, I... I cannot join you this time."

A ripple of surprise passed through the assembled crew. Sawyer had always been reliable, fearless even in the face of enemy fire. Coyle frowned, concerned. "What's on your mind, Doc?"

"My family, sir," Sawyer replied, his voice cracking slightly. "My wife, Linh, and our children... they are still in Saigon. With the enemy closing in, I fear for their safety. I cannot risk leaving them, not now."

Coyle's expression softened, understanding dawning on his face. He knew the toll this war had taken on families, especially those with Vietnamese roots. Sawyer had met Linh while serving as a medic attached to an ARVN unit, their love blossoming amidst the chaos of war.

"I respect that, Doc," Coyle said, his tone sincere. "Family comes first, always. You've given more than enough to this war already."

Sawyer bowed his head, relief and gratitude etched on his face. "Thank you, sir. I am sorry I cannot be with you and the guys. But I will do everything in my power to ensure your success from the ground."

Coyle clasped Sawyer's hand firmly, a gesture of respect and camaraderie. "I know you will, Doc. Your knowledge and contacts have been invaluable. We couldn't have come this far without you."

As Sawyer stepped back, the crew looked on with a newfound understanding. They all had loved ones they longed to protect, regardless of nationality. Sawyer's decision was a poignant reminder of the human cost of the war, the sacrifices that transcended borders and allegiances.

Coyle turned back to his men, his resolve stronger than ever. "Alright, you heard the man. We've got a job to do, and we're going to do it right. For Doc, for all the families caught in the crossfire, we're going to give the enemy hell and then some."

The crew responded with a resounding "Hoorah!" their determination redoubled. As the men dispersed to their tasks, Coyle caught Sawyer's eye one last time, a silent promise passing between them. They would each fight this war in their own way - one in the skies, the other on the ground - but their goal remained the same. To bring peace and security to a land torn asunder, to give hope to the families caught in the midst of chaos.

And in that moment, as the Spectre loomed behind them, both men knew that their bond had been forged in the crucible of war, a friendship that would endure long after the last shots were fired.

Coyle felt a surge of pride and gratitude as he looked at his men, knowing that he could ask for no finer crew. "Alright then," he said, a fierce grin spreading across his face. "We've got a war to win."

As the crew dispersed to begin their preparations,

Coyle turned to gaze at the Spectre, its black hull gleaming in the shafts of harsh sunlight through the windows. *The enemy would never see them coming*, he thought, a grim satisfaction settling in his gut. The ghosts were about to take flight, and heaven help anyone who stood in their way.

Da Nang, South Vietnam

The salty tang of the South China Sea mingled with the pungent aromas of street food and motorbike exhaust as Granier wove through the crowded streets of Da Nang. The coastal city, once a bustling hub for American troops, now bore the scars of a war that refused to end. Bullet-riddled buildings on the verge of collapse were surrounded by colorful shophouses and makeshift market stalls, a jarring contrast of resilience and ruin.

Granier's destination lay in the heart of the city, a nondescript bar tucked away in a narrow alley off Bach Dang Street. As he navigated the labyrinth of side streets, he couldn't help but notice the wary eyes that followed his every move. The people of Da Nang had seen too much, endured too much to trust easily, even a familiar face like his own.

The bar itself was a relic of a bygone era, its faded sign proclaiming "Lucky's" in peeling paint. Inside, the air was thick with the haze of cigarette smoke and the clinking of glass against glass. Ceiling fans stirred the oppressive heat, providing little relief to the patrons who hunched over their drinks, lost in their own thoughts and memories.

In a corner booth, nursing a bottle of Jim Beam, sat Alex Harmon. His once sharp features were now etched with lines of grief and fatigue, his eyes haunted by the spirits of the fallen. Granier slid into the seat across from him, nodding a silent greeting to his friend and comrade-in-arms.

"I was wondering when you'd show up," Harmon said, his voice rough with disuse. "Heard through the grapevine that you were putting together a special ops team. Figured it was only a matter of time before you came knocking."

Granier signaled the bartender for a glass, then leaned in closer, his voice low and urgent. "You know me too well, Harmon. I need your help, your expertise. We're planning something big, something that could turn the tide of this whole damned war."

Harmon's eyes narrowed, a flicker of interest sparking behind the weariness. "I'm listening."

As Granier laid out the details of the covert operation, the daring raids and surgical strikes, Harmon's demeanor shifted, the old fire reigniting in his bones. He had been a key player in the Phoenix Program, his intelligence skills and network of informants second to none. If anyone could give them the edge they needed, it was him.

"I need you to lead our intelligence unit, Harmon," Granier said, his gaze unwavering. "Be our eyes and ears on the ground, keep us one step ahead of the enemy. With your knowledge and contacts, we can make this happen."

Harmon was silent for a long moment, the weight of the decision hanging heavy in the air between them. Outside, the sounds of the city swirled, a cacophony of life and desperation, hope and despair. Finally, he drained his glass and met Granier's eyes, a grim determination etched on his face. "You know this is treason. They could hang you… all of you."

"I am well aware," said Granier unflinching.

"I'm in," he said, his voice steady and sure. "If this is our last chance to make a difference, to give these people a fighting chance, then I'll be damned if I sit on the sidelines. Let's give 'em hell."

Granier clasped Harmon's hand, a surge of relief and gratitude washing over him. With Harmon watching his back, he knew they could face whatever challenges lay ahead, no matter how daunting. Together, they would forge a path through the darkness.

As they stepped out into the sweltering Da Nang night, the weight of their mission settled on their shoulders like a familiar burden. In the heart of the embattled city, amidst the ruins and the rubble, the seeds of resistance had been planted, and soon the enemy would feel the fury of the ghosts they had awakened.

Saigon, South Vietnam

The rooftop of the old French colonial building offered a stunning view of Saigon's skyline, a patchwork of ancient temples and modern high-rises stretching out to the horizon. The setting sun cast a warm glow over the city, the fading light reflecting off the winding Saigon River in the distance. It was here, far from the prying eyes and ears of the streets below, that Granier had chosen to meet with Scott Dickson.

Scott stepped out onto the rooftop, the warm breeze ruffling his hair as he scanned the area for Granier. He spotted the older man leaning against the parapet, his gaze fixed on the city below. Scott approached quietly, wondering what could be so important that Granier would insist on meeting in such a secretive location.

"Scott," Granier said without turning around, his voice low and serious. "Thanks for coming."

"Of course," Scott replied, moving to stand beside Granier. "What's this about? Why all the secrecy?"

Granier took a deep breath, as if gathering his thoughts. "Our mission, the one your father and I are planning... it's not going to be easy. We're going to be asking a lot of our team, and even more of the ARVN commanders we're trying to inspire."

Scott nodded, his brow furrowing. "I know. But we've got the best of the best on our side. We can do this."

"It's not just about the mission itself," Granier continued, turning to face Scott. "It's about what comes after. We need to make sure that our actions have the impact we're hoping for, that they can't be denied or covered up by the North Vietnamese."

"What are you getting at?" Scott asked, a sense of unease creeping into his voice.

Granier looked Scott straight in the eye, his expression grave. "We need a combat photographer, someone who can document our raids and provide irrefutable proof of what we've accomplished. And not just any photographer... we need the best."

Scott's eyes widened as he realized where Granier was heading. "You're talking about Karen, aren't you? My sister?"

Granier nodded. "She's the best there is, Scott. Her photos have already had a huge impact on public opinion back home. We both know that even if we succeed in our raids, the North Vietnamese will likely deny they ever happened. And the ARVN commanders might not believe us either, not without proof."

Scott nodded, understanding dawning in his eyes. "You're saying we need evidence, something tangible to show them."

"Exactly," Granier confirmed. "And not just any evidence. We need powerful, irrefutable images that will make them sit up and take notice. Photos that will give them the courage they lack."

Scott ran a hand through his hair, his mind racing. He knew that Karen was fearless, that she had put herself in harm's way countless times to get the perfect shot. But the idea of bringing her into this operation, of putting her life on the line alongside his own... it was almost too much to bear.

"I don't know, Granier," he said finally, his voice strained. "Karen's already been through so much. I don't know if I can ask her to take on this kind of risk."

"I understand your concern," Granier said, placing a hand on Scott's shoulder. "But think about what this could mean for her, too. Karen's always been driven to make a difference, to show the world the truth of what's happening here. This is her chance to do that on a whole new level, to be part of something that could change the course of the war."

Scott considered Granier's words, a faint smile tugging at the corners of his mouth. "Photograph a covert operation… She'd jump at the chance, wouldn't she? To be right in the thick of it, capturing those moments that no one else can."

Granier nodded, a glimmer of understanding passing between them. "It has to be her choice, of course. But I have a feeling she'll see the importance of what we're trying to do here."

"What about my father?" he asked finally, his voice barely above a whisper. "He'll never agree to this."

Granier's expression hardened, a flicker of something dark and determined crossing his features. "Your father doesn't need to know, Scott. Not yet. This is between you and me... and Karen, if she agrees to join us."

"When do you plan on telling him about Karen's involvement?"

Granier's jaw tightening almost imperceptibly. "I'll tell him right before we launch the first mission. He's not going to like it, but by then, it'll be too late for him to stop us."

Scott raised an eyebrow, a wry smile playing on his lips. "You're counting on Karen's stubborn streak to win him over, aren't you?"

Granier chuckled, a rare moment of levity in the midst of their somber discussion. "Your sister can be very persuasive when she wants to be. If anyone can make Coyle see the necessity of her role, it's her."

Scott knew that Granier was right, that they needed Karen's skills if they were going to have any chance of success. But the idea of going behind his father's back, of putting his sister in harm's way without his knowledge... it felt like a betrayal of everything he had ever been taught.

In the end, though, he knew what he had to do. The stakes were too high, the consequences of failure too great. If bringing Karen into the fold was what it took to turn the tide of this war, to give the people of South Vietnam a fighting chance... then that was what he would do.

"Alright," he said finally, his voice heavy with

resignation. "I'll talk to Karen. But if she says no, that's the end of it. I won't force her into this."

Granier nodded his agreement.

As the last rays of sunlight faded over the horizon, Scott and Granier fell into a contemplative silence, each lost in their own thoughts. They knew that bringing Karen into the fold was a risk, one that could have far-reaching consequences for all of them.

But they also knew that her talent, her passion, and her unwavering commitment to the truth could be the key to unlocking the hearts and minds of those they sought to inspire. With Karen by their side, documenting their every move, they would have a powerful weapon in their arsenal, one that could help them turn the tide of the war and give the commanders of South Vietnam the hope they so desperately needed.

Saigon, South Vietnam

The bustling Ben Thanh Market, a labyrinth of narrow alleys and vibrant stalls, provided an unlikely backdrop for the conversation between Scott and Karen Dickson. Amidst the cacophony of haggling vendors and the rich aromas of street food, the siblings found a small, secluded table in a corner cafe, far from the prying eyes and ears of the crowd.

Karen stirred her ca phe sua da, the iced coffee clinking against the glass as she studied her brother's face. "Alright, Scott, what's this all about? Why the sudden need for a secret meeting in the middle of the market?"

Scott leaned forward, his voice low and urgent. "I need your help, Karen. Granier and I are putting together a special team, one that could change the course of the war. But we need your skills, your eye for capturing the truth."

Karen raised an eyebrow, curiosity mingling with apprehension in her gaze. "You want me to document your missions, don't you? To provide proof of what you're doing out there."

Scott nodded, a flicker of pride in his eyes. "You're the best combat photographer in Vietnam, Karen. Your images have the power to move people, to make them see the reality of what's happening here. We need that now more than ever."

Karen sat back in her chair, a frown tugging at the corners of her mouth. "I don't know, Scott. I've always tried to maintain my objectivity, to show all sides of the conflict. If I join your team, it feels like I'm taking sides, becoming a part of the war instead of just documenting it."

"But don't you see, Karen?" Scott pressed, his voice filled with conviction. "This isn't about taking sides. It's about giving the people of South Vietnam a chance to survive, to build a future for themselves. The North Vietnamese and the Viet Cong, they're not going to stop until they've conquered the entire country. And when they do, the people here will suffer in ways we can't even imagine."

Karen's gaze drifted to the bustling market around them, taking in the faces of the vendors and shoppers, the families and friends going about their daily lives. "I've seen the aftermath of their attacks, Scott. The villages burned to the ground, the civilians caught in the crossfire. It's heartbreaking."

"Exactly," Scott said. "And that's why we need you. Your photos can show the world what's at stake here, the human cost of letting the communists win. You can give voice to the voiceless, Karen, and help us inspire the ARVN to keep fighting, to believe in themselves and their cause."

Karen met her brother's gaze, a flicker of determination kindling in her eyes. "You really believe that, don't you? That what you're doing can make a difference?"

Scott squeezed her hand, a smile tugging at the corners of his mouth. "I have to believe it, Karen. We all do. Because if we don't, then what are we even fighting for?"

For a long moment, Karen sat in silence, the weight of her brother's words settling over her like a mantle. She had always been driven by a desire to make a difference, to use her camera as a tool for change. And now, presented with the opportunity to do just that on a scale she had never imagined, she felt a surge of purpose, of clarity.

"Alright," she said finally, her voice steady and resolute. "I'm in. But I have one condition."

Scott raised an eyebrow, a hint of wariness in his gaze. "What's that?"

"I have complete editorial control over my photos. I'll document your missions, but I won't be a propaganda tool. The images I capture will be the truth, no matter how ugly or uncomfortable that truth might be."

Scott's smile widened, a glimmer of pride and respect in his eyes. "I wouldn't have it any other way, Karen. Your integrity is what makes you the best at what you do."

“Does Dad know about this?”

“Not until you tell him.”

“Coward.”

"I like to think I'm more of a survivor."

Karen laughed. As the siblings finished their coffee and melted back into the bustling crowd of the market, a new sense of purpose settled over them. They knew that they had the power to make a difference, to shape the course of history through their actions and their art.

Saigon, South Vietnam

Granier had waited years for this moment. Ever since that chaotic 1971 op across the border in Laos when he and Lucien Conein had parted ways with bullets rather than handshakes. Now Conein headed up DEA operations safely back in America while Granier continued his endless covert war here in Vietnam.

But new intel suggested Conein still kept a warehouse of weapons stockpiled in Saigon, selling arms through local gangster contacts. Granier became obsessed with locating the facility, seeing poetic justice in raiding one of Conein's operations to supply his teams with the weapons they needed.

It took several weeks, calling in favors from every shifty informant in Saigon before he got the lead that he wanted. A weaselly police detective, palms freshly greased, told Granier about unusual shipments being stored down by the wharf. "Big enough to equip a private army," the detective hinted. It had to be Conein's warehouse.

Under cover of night, Granier and six of his most trusted team members surrounded the guarded warehouse near the docks. He felt his heart pound with anticipation, gripped by thoughts of revenge.

With weapons ready, Granier crashed through the side entrance. Shocked shouts echoed inside as Granier and his men advanced through the warehouse.

Surveying the contents inside the building, Granier saw stacks of wooden crates stamped with US military stencils. Mortars, grenade launchers, rifles - it was a virtual armory. He also spotted two men huddled over an inventory list. One he pegged as a Chinese gang representative from the Snake Flowers triad. The nervous, sweat-soaked Vietnamese man next to him would be Conein's local sales agent and warehouse manager.

Granier signaled his team into flanking positions and stormed through the unlocked door, pistols and rifles at the ready. Both men inside threw up their hands in shocked surrender. Granier grabbed the agent by his shirt and slammed him into a crate stack. He forced the muzzle of his .45 into the panicking man's mouth as he sputtered in terror. Suddenly the agent's eyes went wide with recognition.

"Wait, Granier! It's you!" He mumbled around the pistol barrel jammed in his mouth. Granier eased up slightly and the agent coughed, hands still raised. "I heard you were back in country! Running some kind of covert missions near Laos right? Had a run in with your old friend Conein up in Long Tieng back in '71 if I remember. You two have quite the history!"

The agent rambled on anxiously while Granier debated how to proceed. This worm could identify him, complicate future clandestine operations. Perhaps permanently silence the loose end...

But the agent met his glare and spoke quickly. "Listen, Granier, take what you want! Guns, rockets, anything! Just leave me the rest to sell ok? And I'll square it with Conein back in D.C., tell him you and your team cleaned us out! It'll be easier for me that way, you understand?"

Granier searched the terrified man's face for any hint of deception. Seeing none, he finally nodded curtly and lowered the pistol. "Agreed. Have your triad contact stand aside." He turned to direct his men loading heavy crates of weapons into a US Army truck. The promise of vengeance against Conein made this inviting arrangement even sweeter...

Colombia, South America

The dense jungle canopy of the Sierra Nevada de Santa Marta mountains loomed before Lucien Conein as he stepped out of the UH-1 Huey helicopter. The oppressive heat and humidity hit him like a wall, but he remained focused on the task at hand. As the newly appointed head of DEA special operations, Conein was determined to make a name for himself in the Ford Administration, and this mission in Colombia was his chance to do just that.

Intelligence reports had indicated that a major cocaine shipment was set to move through this remote region, a key transit point for the notorious Medellín Cartel. Conein had assembled a team of his best agents, along with a contingent of Colombian special forces, to intercept the shipment and strike a blow against the cartel's operations.

The team moved through the dense undergrowth, following a narrow trail used by the smugglers.

Suddenly, the point man raised his fist, signaling the team to halt. Conein moved forward, his senses alert, his hand resting on the butt of his sidearm. As he reached the point man's position, he saw what had caused the stop: a small clearing ahead, with a ramshackle collection of huts and a makeshift airstrip.

Conein turned to his team, his voice low and urgent. "This is it. The shipment is likely being prepared for transport as we speak. We need to move fast and hit them hard. No one gets away, understood?"

The team nodded, their faces set in grim determination. Conein split them into three groups, one to flank the clearing from the left, the other from the right. He would lead the main assault down the center, using the element of surprise to their advantage.

As they moved into position, the jungle seemed to hold its breath, the only sound the distant chirping of birds and the occasional rustle of leaves. Conein's heart pounded in his chest, the adrenaline coursing through his veins. This was what he lived for, the thrill of the hunt, and if it benefited him personally all the better.

Suddenly, all hell broke loose. The sound of gunfire erupted from the clearing, followed by shouts and screams. Conein's team rushed forward, weapons at the ready, only to find themselves in the midst of a chaotic firefight. The cartel members, caught off guard by the surprise attack, fought back with a ferocity born of desperation.

Bullets whizzed past Conein's head as he dove for cover behind a stack of crates. He returned fire, his aim steady and true, dropping two cartel gunmen with well-placed shots. Around him, his team was engaged in close-quarters combat, the sound of gunfire and the acrid smell of smoke filling the air.

As the fighting raged on, Conein caught a glimpse of movement near the airstrip. A small plane, its engines already running, was preparing to take off. He knew that if the shipment made it onto that plane, they would lose their chance to strike a meaningful blow against the cartel.

Without hesitation, Conein sprinted towards the airstrip, his weapon drawn. He dodged bullets and leapt over fallen bodies, his focus solely on reaching the plane before it was too late. He fired several shots shattering the back window of the plane. As he neared the aircraft, he saw a figure emerge from the cockpit, weapon in hand.

Conein didn't hesitate. He raised his sidearm and fired, the bullet striking the figure in the chest. The man crumpled to the ground, his weapon falling from his grasp. Conein raced to the plane, pulling open the cargo door to reveal a staggering amount of cocaine, neatly packaged and ready for transport.

As the rest of his team secured the clearing and rounded up the remaining cartel members, Conein couldn't help but feel a sense of satisfaction. They had dealt a significant blow to the Medellín Cartel, disrupting their operations and seizing a massive shipment of cocaine. It was a big win for the DEA… and for Conein. He would make sure of it.

As they policed the area, Conein's assistant approached, his face drawn with grief.

"What's happened?" said Conein, never one to put off bad news.

"I just got a radio call. Your warehouse in Saigon was raided last night."

"By the government or the rebels?"

"Neither. A guy named "Granier."

Conein's face darkened on hearing the name. "Son of a bitch. What's the damage?"

"Everything."

"Everything? How is that possible?"

"I don't know. It just what your agent said."

"I'm sure Granier took the lion share, but I'm also sure my weasel of an agent took whatever remained and reported it as a total loss."

"What do you want to do?"

"I don't know yet. I've got to think about it. Planning revenge takes time."

First Strike

Bien Hoa Air Base, South Vietnam

The Spectre gunship hangar at Bien Hoa Air Base was a hive of activity as the team prepared for their inaugural mission. The elite group, handpicked by Granier and Coyle, worked with focused intensity, each member meticulously checking their equipment and rehearsing their roles.

Dao, the South Vietnamese sniper, calibrated his rifle with practiced precision. Harmon, the seasoned intelligence expert, pored over intelligence reports, seeking any detail that could give them an edge. The Spectre crew, led by the no-nonsense loadmaster, loaded ammunition and ran through pre-flight checklists with military efficiency.

As the final preparations were underway, Coyle and Granier called the team together for one last briefing. The men gathered around, their faces etched with a hint of anticipation.

Coyle cleared his throat, his voice filling the hangar. "I know each of you has faced your share of battles. You wouldn't be here if you hadn't. But what we're about to embark on is unlike anything we've done before. We're not just fighting for ourselves or even for South Vietnam. We're fighting for the future, for the chance to give the people of this country a shot at a better life."

Just as Coyle was about to continue, a figure entered the hangar, catching everyone's attention. Karen Dickson, Scott's sister and a renowned combat photographer, strode purposefully towards the group, her camera bag and rucksack slung over her shoulders. The team members exchanged glances, surprise and confusion evident on their faces.

Coyle's eyes narrowed as he realized the implications of Karen's presence. His jaw clenched, and without warning, he spun around and delivered a powerful punch to Granier's jaw, sending the man stumbling backward.

Chaos erupted as the team members rushed to separate the two men. Scott and Dao pulled Coyle back, while Harmon steadied Granier, who wiped a trickle of blood from the corner of his mouth.

"What the hell did you do, Granier?" Coyle demanded, his voice trembling with anger. "Karen, what are you doing here?"

Karen stepped forward, her gaze unwavering. "I'm here to join the team, Dad. As the combat photographer."

Coyle shook his head vehemently. "Absolutely not. It's too dangerous. I won't allow it."

"It's not your decision to make," Karen retorted, her voice calm but firm. "Granier and Scott approached me because they believe in the importance of documenting our missions, of showing the world what we're fighting for. And I agree with them."

Coyle's face reddened, a vein throbbing in his

temple. "This is unacceptable. I won't have my daughter putting her life on the line."

"Dad, I understand your concern, but I've been covering this war for years, and I know the risks. I also know that I can make a difference, that my photos can help change the course of this conflict. Please, trust me."

Coyle looked at his daughter, his expression a mix of pride and fear. Without another word, he turned and stomped out of the hangar, his shoulders rigid with tension. The team members exchanged nervous looks. They hadn't even started and the whole thing was falling apart.

Granier, rubbing his bruised jaw, glanced at the team. "Give us a moment," he said, before following Coyle out into the sunlight.

Outside, Granier found Coyle pacing, his hands clenched into fists. "Coyle," Granier began, his voice low and even. " I know you're angry, and you have every right to be, but Karen's right. We need her on this team. She's the best photographer still in the country."

Coyle whirled around, his eyes blazing. "Going behind my back to recruit my daughter? Have you lost your mind? You had no right to bring her into this, Granier. No right at all."

Granier met Coyle's gaze unflinchingly. "I didn't make this decision lightly. But Karen's skills and her commitment to the truth are invaluable to the success of our mission."

Coyle whirled around, his eyes blazing. "Success? You're putting my daughter's life on the line, and you're talking about success? I trusted you, Granier. I thought we were in this together."

"We are in this together, Coyle. But you have to see the bigger picture here. If we're going to have any chance of convincing the ARVN generals to leave the cities and fight the NVA and VC at the border, we need proof. We need to show them that victory is possible, that our missions are making a difference."

Coyle shook his head, his jaw clenched. "And you think Karen's photos are going to do that? You think a few snapshots are going to change the course of this war?"

Granier's gaze intensified. "Not just snapshots, Coyle. Karen's images have the power to show the truth, to capture the heart and soul of what we're fighting for. The generals, the politicians, the American public... they need to see what's really happening here. They need to understand the stakes."

Coyle turned away, his shoulders rigid with tension. "I can't believe you went to Scott first, that you two conspired to bring Karen into this mess."

"I went to Scott because I knew he would understand the importance of what we're trying to do. And Karen... she's a brave, capable woman who believes in this cause just as much as we do."

"Don't you dare try to tell me about my own daughter, Granier. I know her far better than you do."

"Then you know that she would never forgive you if you tried to stop her from doing what she believes is right."

Coyle was silent for a long moment, his gaze fixed on the distant horizon. Finally, he spoke, his voice low and resigned. "I don't like this, Granier. Not one bit. But you're right. We need every advantage we can get. And Karen is the best photographer in the country."

"I give you my word, Tom. I'll do everything in my

power to keep Karen safe, to make sure she comes back to you when this is all over."

"You'd better, Granier. Because if anything happens to her... I'll hold you personally responsible."

Granier held Coyle's gaze, unflinching. "I understand, Coyle. And I accept that responsibility."

The two men stood in silence for a moment longer, the weight of their commitment hanging heavy between them. Then, with a shared nod of resolve, they turned and walked back into the hangar, ready to lead their team into the heart of the conflict, to risk everything for the chance to save a nation and its people from the grasp of an unrelenting enemy.

Near Thanh Hoa, North Vietnam

The AC-130 Spectre gunship cut through the night sky like a ghostly predator, its engines humming a low, steady rhythm. Hugging the contours of the Vietnamese hills, the aircraft seemed to melt into the shadows, its black paint scheme rendering it nearly invisible against the starless backdrop.

As the gunship approached the drop zone, it popped up to eight hundred feet in a steep ascent, the lowest altitude possible for a jump. If any of the main parachutes failed, there would be no time to deploy a backup chute.

Inside the cargo hold, the team sat in focused silence, their faces illuminated by the dim red light of the jump indicators. Each member was a seasoned professional, handpicked for their skills and experience. They had trained relentlessly for this moment, honing their tactics and perfecting their coordination until they operated like a well-oiled machine.

Granier, his eyes hard and alert, stood near the jump door, his parachute already strapped tight to his body. He glanced at his watch, then addressed the team, his voice cutting through the drone of the engines. "Two minutes to drop. Remember, we're going in low and fast. Stick tight to your jump partner and watch your landing. The rice paddies are going to be soft and wet."

Beside him, Karen Dickson felt a potent mix of anticipation and adrenaline. She had made many jumps before, documenting the war from the front lines, but this felt different. The stakes were higher, the mission more critical than anything she had ever been a part of. It was a true last-ditch effort to save South Vietnam and its people.

She glanced at Granier, noting the coiled intensity of his posture, the unwavering focus in his gaze. He was a man on a mission, a warrior in every sense of the word. And yet, beneath the hardened exterior, she sensed a flicker of something else, a buried ember of humanity that drove him to fight for something greater than himself. She raised her camera and snapped a close up of Granier's face, then placed the camera in a waterproof satchel along with her film cannisters.

In the cockpit, Coyle and his co-pilot, a seasoned veteran, guided the Spectre through the treacherous terrain.

"Thirty seconds," Coyle called out, his voice crackling through the intercom. "Masks on. Opening jump door now."

The team members raised camouflaged masks to hide their faces from Karen's camera. Nobody would know who they were as they carried out their incredible acts of bravery. They would remain anonymous. With a hydraulic whine, the rear cargo door slowly lowered, revealing a yawning expanse of darkness punctuated by the scattered lights of distant villages. The rush of warm air filled the hold, whipping at the team's clothes and gear.

"Green light!" Granier shouted, his hand poised on the jump release. "Go, go, go!"

Two by two, the team members leapt into the void, their bodies swallowed by the night. Karen felt the familiar rush of freefall, the wind roaring in her ears as she plummeted towards the earth. Beside her, Granier's form was a study in controlled precision, his arms and legs positioned for maximum stability. Almost in sync, their chutes popped open.

As the ground rushed up to meet them, Karen braced herself for impact. She hit the soft, muddy surface of a rice paddy with a splash, her parachute collapsing around her in a tangle of fabric and cords. For a moment, she struggled to free herself, the thick, clinging mud threatening to drag her down.

Then, strong hands were pulling her up, hoisting her to her feet. It was Dao. He helped her untangle from the chute. Around them, the rest of the team was already moving, fanning out into a defensive perimeter as they scanned the surrounding darkness for any sign of the enemy.

Suddenly, a muffled grunt rang out from the edge of the paddy. Harmon had become mired in a particularly deep patch of mud, his legs sinking up to his knees. Instantly, the team swarmed around him, forming a protective circle as they worked to free him from the sucking morass.

Granier, his face grim, grabbed Harmon's arm and heaved, his muscles straining with the effort. Slowly, painfully, Harmon's legs came free, the mud releasing its grip with a sickening slurp. The team hustled him to firmer ground, their movements swift and silent, every sense attuned to the potential dangers lurking in the shadows.

As they gathered their gear and prepared to move out, Karen couldn't shake the feeling that this was just the beginning, that the real challenges still lay ahead.

The team was the last line of defense against the encroaching darkness. And as they melted into the night, moving silently towards their target, Karen felt a surge of pride and purpose. This was her mission, her calling.

Thanh Hoa Fuel Depot, North Vietnam

The team members moved through the dense jungle surrounding the Thanh Hoa fuel depot like wraiths, their footsteps nearly silent on the damp earth. The moonless night provided ample cover as they approached their target, the distant glow of floodlights and the low hum of generators guiding their path. There was no need to talk. Everything had been planned and everyone knew their job. Stealth and surprise were their key advantages.

At the edge of the treeline, Rene Granier raised a closed fist, signaling the team to halt. They crouched low, their weapons at the ready, as Granier surveyed the scene through a night vision scope. He spotted an NVA team patrolling the fence around the depot. He waited until the guards moved on before silently signaling Dao and his team, the vanguard, to move out.

Dao gestured to his fellow South Vietnamese operatives. They fanned out, melting into the shadows as they began their silent approach.

Karen Dickson, her camera at the ready, moved to follow Dao, but Granier's hand on her shoulder stopped her. He simply shook his head. Karen nodded, her grip tightening on her camera. She knew the importance of patience, of waiting for the right moment to capture the critical images.

As they waited, the minutes stretching out like hours, the distant sounds of the jungle filled the air. The chirp of crickets, the rustling of leaves in the gentle breeze, all seemed to amplify the tension that hung heavy over the team.

Suddenly, the sharp crack of a snapping twig shattered the stillness. Instantly, the team members dropped to a crouch, their weapons trained on the source of the sound. Karen felt her breath coming in short, shallow gasps.

But it was only Dao, emerging from the shadows. He gave a quick hand signal, indicating that the way was clear. Granier nodded, then motioned for the rest of the team to move forward.

They crept through the underbrush, the looming bulk of the fuel tanks growing larger with each step. As they reached a drainage culvert, Harmon took the lead, guiding them through the narrow, damp passage with a sure step.

Emerging on the other side, they found themselves in the heart of the compound, the towering tanks casting long shadows across the gravel-strewn ground. The air was thick with the pungent scent of petrol, the low hum of the generators a constant, droning presence.

Granier turned to his team and gave the hand signal for them to split up. He nodded to Karen, she should begin photographing the mission. He motioned that she should follow him and his team. She nodded that she understood.

As the team set to work, each member focused on their assigned task, Karen couldn't help but feel a surge of adrenaline. This was the moment she had been waiting for, the chance to capture the raw, unfiltered truth of a covert mission.

The Ghost Warriors moved swiftly and silently through the shadows of the fuel depot, each member focused on their assigned task. Harmon pointed out the location of each of the four massive storage tanks. The team split up.

Granier and his team approached the first massive storage tank, its rusted surface looming like a sleeping giant in the dim light. Karen followed. Before taking any photo she checked her surroundings to ensure that no NVA were within earshot of her camera's click.

Granier knelt beside the tank, his hands working deftly as he prepared the charges. He carefully molded a brick of C-4 plastic explosive, his fingers precise and sure as he inserted a detonator and a timed fuse. Beside him, Dao and his men kept a watchful eye on the surrounding area, their weapons at the ready.

Karen, her camera in hand, documented the process, the soft click of her shutter the only sound in the tense stillness. She marveled at the skill and precision of the team, the way they worked together like a well-oiled machine.

Suddenly, the distant sound of voices and footsteps sent a jolt of adrenaline through the team. Dao hissed a warning, his hand signals indicating that a patrol of NVA guards was approaching. The Ghost Warriors froze, their bodies tense and coiled like springs.

Karen crouched low behind a stack of oil drums, her camera clutched tightly to her chest. She watched as Granier and the others melted into the shadows, their dark clothing and camouflage paint rendering them nearly invisible.

The footsteps grew louder, the guttural voices of the NVA soldiers drifting on the night air. Karen held her breath, her eyes straining to pick out the shapes of her teammates in the darkness. She could see Dao, his body pressed flat against the side of a fuel tank, his finger resting lightly on the trigger of his suppressed submachine gun.

For a moment that seemed to stretch out into eternity, the NVA patrol passed by, their flashlight beams cutting through the gloom. Karen could hear the crunch of their boots on the gravel, the clipped cadence of their speech. She willed herself to remain perfectly still, hardly daring to breathe.

And then, just as suddenly as they had appeared, the patrol moved on, their voices and footsteps fading into the distance. The Ghost Warriors emerged from the shadows, their faces grim. They knew they had to work quickly now, before the patrol returned.

Granier and the others redoubled their efforts, their hands flying as they set the remaining charges. Karen moved with them, her camera capturing the urgency and intensity of the moment. She could feel the weight of history pressing down on them, the knowledge that what they were doing here could change the course of the war.

Harmon and another team member, a seasoned demolitions expert named Nguyen, began rigging their own charges on a different tank. They worked methodically, carefully placing the explosives at key structural points to ensure maximum damage.

As the last charge was set, Granier checked his watch, his jaw tight with tension. He signaled that they had three minutes before the charges detonated. It was time to leave.

The team began their withdrawal, moving swiftly and silently back towards the drainage culvert. Karen could feel the adrenaline surging through her veins, the knowledge that at any moment, the charges could detonate, turning the fuel depot into a raging inferno.

As they reached the culvert, Harmon paused, his head cocked to one side. His hand raised in warning.

The team froze, their weapons at the ready. Karen strained her ears, trying to pick out the source of the sound. And then she heard it - the distant rumble of engines, growing louder with each passing second.

Granier used his night vision to locate the source of the noise - a long convoy of supply trucks approaching the depot. NVA troops stood on each truck's runners. Even more road in troop trucks to protect the convoy and help load the fuel drums. The Ghost Warriors were now vastly outnumbered.

Granier motioned for everyone to move quickly as he and Dao took up sniper positions to protect their retreat. The team plunged into the culvert, the damp walls pressing in on them as they navigated the narrow passage. Karen could hear the ragged sound of her breathing in the close confines.

And then they were out, emerging into the hot night air of the jungle. Granier and Dao followed. Behind them, the rumble of the trucks grew louder, the glow of headlights visible through the trees. Granier checked his watch. They were out of time.

The team crouched low, their muscles coiled and

ready. Karen raised her camera, her finger poised over the shutter release. She knew that what came next would be a moment of truth, a test of all their training and preparation.

And then, with a deafening roar that seemed to shake the very earth beneath their feet, as the charges detonated. The night sky erupted in a blinding flash of orange and red, the hot shockwave slamming into the Ghost Warriors like a physical force, sucking the oxygen from the air.

Karen stumbled, her camera nearly slipping from her grasp. But she caught herself, her eyes fixed on the scene before her. She snapped photo after photo. The fuel depot was engulfed in flames, the massive tanks buckling and collapsing in on themselves like crumpled tin cans.

Secondary explosions ripped through the compound, sending geysers of burning fuel high into the air. The NVA trucks that were caught in the blast radius, flipped and cartwheeled like toys, their crews incinerated in the blink of an eye.

For a moment, the Ghost Warriors stood transfixed, the heat of the inferno washing over them in waves. Karen captured the apocalyptic scene in a series of rapid-fire shots. She knew that these images would be seared into her memory forever.

And then Granier was shouting, his voice cutting through the chaos like a knife. "Move, move, move!" he bellowed, his hand beckoning urgently. "The extraction point, now!"

The team broke into a run, their legs pumping as they raced through the jungle. Behind them, the fuel depot continued to burn, the flames casting a hellish glow over the landscape. Karen could hear the distant shouts of NVA soldiers, the crack of gunfire as they tried to mount a response.

But the Ghost Warriors were already gone, melting into the shadows like the phantoms they were named for. They had struck a blow against the enemy, a blow that would be felt across the length and breadth of Vietnam.

They ran, their hearts pounding and their lungs burning. They had done what they set out to do, against all odds. They had shown the world that the fight for freedom was far from over, that there were still those who were willing to risk everything to keep the flames of hope alive.

The Ghost Warriors raced through the dense jungle, their hearts pounding and their muscles burning with each stride. The harsh glow of the burning fuel depot faded behind them, replaced by the inky darkness of the night and the looming shadows of the trees.

Karen Dickson, her camera bouncing against her chest, pushed herself to keep pace with the others. She could hear the distant shouts of the NVA soldiers, the crack of gunfire echoing through the underbrush. They were being pursued, hunted like animals in the night.

At the rear of the group, Granier and Dao moved with a fluid, deadly grace. They took turns pausing to line up shots with their sniper rifles, the muffled cough of their suppressed weapons punctuating the stillness. Each shot found its mark, sending NVA soldiers tumbling to the ground in crumpled heaps. But the enemy continued its pursuit.

For every enemy they felled, it seemed two more took their place. The NVA was closing in, their numbers and determination overwhelming. Karen could feel the icy grip of fear tightening around her, the realization that they might not make it out of this jungle alive.

And then, just as despair threatened to engulf her, they burst into a clearing. The grass was flattened and trampled, the unmistakable signs of a landing zone. Karen felt a surge of hope, her eyes scanning the dark skies above.

Suddenly, the night erupted with the deafening roar of rotors. Two massive Chinook helicopters, their outlines barely visible against the starless sky, descended into the clearing like twin angels of mercy. Their door gunners opened fire, the chatter of their M60 machine guns ripping through the jungle and forcing the pursuing NVA soldiers to take cover.

Above them, a third helicopter, a Huey gunship, circled like a bird of prey. Its pilot, Scott Dickson, guided the aircraft with a sure hand, his eyes scanning the treeline for any sign of the enemy. Nothing yet, but he could see muzzle flashes deeper in the jungle. Not wanting to endanger the Ghost Warriors, he and his aircrew would wait until they had a clear shot at the enemy.

As the Chinooks touched down, their rotor wash whipping the grass into a frenzy, the Ghost Warriors made their move. They sprinted towards the waiting aircraft, their feet pounding against the damp earth. Karen could feel the heat of the jungle giving way to the cooler air of the helicopters, the promise of escape tantalizingly close.

Behind them, Granier and Dao continued to lay down covering fire, their rifles biting in short, controlled shots. They moved backwards towards the Chinooks, their eyes never leaving the treeline. Karen watched in awe as they worked in perfect unison, each one covering the other as they leapfrogged towards safety.

And then they were aboard, the Ghost Warriors piling into the cavernous holds of the Chinooks. The door gunners continued to fire, their bullets zipping past the heads of the approaching NVA soldiers. Karen could hear the ping of rounds ricocheting off the armored hulls of the helicopters.

In the Huey, now performing overwatch for the Chinooks, Scott gripped the cyclic, eyes scanning the clearing below. The Chinooks sat heavy, rotors whipping the grass as the team sprinted towards them. Muzzle flashes lit the jungle's edge - NVA closing in.

"Showtime, boys," Scott called to his crew. "Light 'em up!"

The door gunner leaned into his minigun, the barrels spinning with a whine. Tracers streaked down, stitching the treeline. Rocket pods thumped, explosive blooms walking back the NVA charge.

Scott circled tight, keeping the door gun on target. Figures crumpled and fell under the onslaught. Return fire whipped by, ineffective.

The team piled into the birds. Granier and Dao dove in last, rifles still firing.

Scott swung low, skids nearly brushing treetops. His gunner poured it on, the minigun burning through ammo.

"They're in!" the Chinook pilot crackled over the radio. Wheels lifted. As the Chinooks clawed for altitude, their powerful engines strained against the weight of the team and their gear, Karen felt a wave of relief wash over her. She looked out the open door, watching as the jungle receded beneath them, the burning fuel depot a distant, flickering glow on the horizon.

Beside her, Granier and Dao slumped against the bulkhead, their faces streaked with sweat and grime.

The Huey lingered, hosing the clearing. Better to be sure. The heavy bark of side-mounted .50 Cals joined the din, the copilot strafing the treeline as he took control of the gunship.

Smoking craters pocked the grass, bodies strewn. Enough. Retaking control of the aircraft, Scott nosed up, sliding into formation with the escaping Chinooks. The depot burned bright behind them - good work. He allowed a tight smile.

Plenty more to be done. But a good start. They had struck a blow against the enemy, a blow that would be felt across the length and breadth of Vietnam.

As the helicopters banked away from the burning depot, the rising sun painting the sky in shades of orange and gold.

And as Karen watched the jungle give way to the rolling hills and rice paddies of Vietnam, she knew that this was a moment she would never forget, a moment that would be seared into her memory for the rest of her days. They had struck a blow for freedom and justice in a land that had seen far too little of either.

Bien Hoa Air Base, South Vietnam

The roar of the Chinooks and Huey faded as they settled onto the tarmac, rotors whipping up clouds of dust. The hangar doors stood open, a welcome sight after the harrowing mission.

Granier and the team emerged from the helicopters, fatigue etched in their faces. They moved slowly, the adrenaline of combat giving way to the bone-deep weariness of a job well done.

Tom Coyle stood apart, his jaw set as he watched the team disembark. He caught sight of Scott approaching from the Huey and turned away, busying himself with post-flight checks on his Spectre gunship.

Scott hesitated, then squared his shoulders and walked over. "Dad, we need to talk."

Coyle didn't look up, his hands moving methodically over the aircraft's fuselage. "Not now, Scott. Debrief first, then rack time. You know the drill."

"No, this can't wait." Scott's voice was tight, controlled. "It's about Karen. About her joining the team."

Coyle's hands stilled. He turned slowly, his eyes hard. "There's nothing to discuss. You went behind my back, brought her into this mess. End of story."

"It's not that simple and you know it," Scott shot back. "We need her, Dad. Her skills, her camera - they can make a real difference out there."

"Don't give me that bullshit." Coyle's voice was low, dangerous. "You risked her life tonight, without even giving me the courtesy of a heads-up. What the hell were you thinking?"

"I was thinking about the mission, about what's at stake here." Scott met his father's glare unflinchingly. "Karen's a grown woman, Dad. She made her own choice."

"A choice you never should have given her!" Coyle's control slipped, his voice rising. Heads turned among the weary team members. "I am still your commanding officer, and more than that, I'm your father. You had no right—"

"What would you have had me do?" Scott cut in, his own temper flaring. "Keep her in the dark, just so you could feel better? She deserves to know the truth, to make her own decisions."

Coyle stepped closer, jabbing a finger at Scott's chest. "Her decision should have been made with all the information, including the fact that her own brother was planning to put her in the line of fire."

"She's not a child, Dad!" Scott's frustration boiled over. "When are you going to see that? When are you going to trust her - trust me - to do what's right?"

For a long moment, father and son stared each other down, the tension thick enough to cut with a knife. The hangar was utterly silent, the team frozen in place.

Finally, Coyle looked away, his shoulders slumping almost imperceptibly. "I do trust you, Scott. Both of you. But that doesn't make it any easier to watch you walk into danger, knowing I might not be able to protect you."

Scott softened, the anger draining away. "I know, Dad. But we're in this together, all of us. Karen included. We're stronger as a team, and you know it."

Coyle sighed heavily, rubbing a hand over his face. When he looked up, his eyes were tired but clear. "Alright. Alright. We'll figure it out, find a way to make this work. But, Scott - no more secrets, no more going behind my back. We do this as a family, or not at all."

Scott nodded, a weight lifting from his shoulders. "Agreed. And Dad - I'm sorry, for what it's worth. I never meant to hurt you."

Coyle clapped a hand on his son's shoulder, the gesture conveying more than words ever could. "I know, son. I know. Now come on - let's get this debrief over with so we can all get some chow and rack time. Something tells me we're going to need it."

As father and son walked towards the waiting team, the tension in the hangar eased, replaced by a weary but unshakeable sense of unity. They had come through the fire together, and emerged stronger for it - a team forged in the crucible of war.

Hanoi, North Vietnam

General Vo Nguyen Giap sat behind his desk, his weathered face illuminated by the soft glow of the lamp. The room was spartan, adorned only with a few maps and a portrait of Ho Chi Minh. Giap's eyes were fixed on the after-action report given to him by the young officer standing before him, his posture rigid with barely concealed unease. Finishing the report, he set it down on the desk and studied the officer's face. "Why is there not an exact count of casualties?" said Giap.

"Some of the men were fully incinerated by the fire when the depot was destroyed. We should have a full report on casualties once the coroner unit has sifted through ashes," said the officer.

"I see. The damage to the depot was complete? What does that mean?"

"In addition to the surrounding support structures, all four fuel tanks were destroyed along with a significant amount of fuel. We will have a more exact count shortly."

"And the supply trucks?"

"Seven were destroyed along with their drivers and passengers. We estimate twenty-one soldiers in all. The majority of our forces were able to evacuate before the fire spread."

"And the saboteurs?"

"Our troops gave chase, but the saboteurs were picked up by two Chinook helicopters before our men could reach them."

"So, they escaped… unharmed?"

"As far as we could tell, yes. An American gunship held our men at bay."

"What makes you think it was American?"

"There were no visible insignia on the helicopters and they were armed with miniguns. The South Vietnam helicopters lack these type of advanced weapons. We believe it was a covert operation… possibly CIA."

"The CIA?"

"Possibly. We will know better once we catch them."

"It's interesting that the CIA would carry out such an operation and not the ARVN."

"As far as our intelligence reports, no ARVN forces have left their bases around the cities."

"Good. It's better that the dogs slumber in their kennels."

Giap leaned back in his chair, his gaze never leaving the officer's face. "And what is the assessment of our local commanders? How significant a blow was this loss to our operations in the region?"

The officer shifted uncomfortably, glancing down at his notes. "They believe the impact will be minimal, Comrade General. The depot was one of many, and our supply lines are robust in this area. They see this as little more than a nuisance raid, a desperate attempt by the enemy to disrupt our inevitable victory."

For a long moment, Giap was silent, his expression unreadable. Then, slowly, he rose from his chair and walked to the map on the wall. His finger traced the lines of supply, from the North to the frontlines in the South.

"A nuisance, you say?" Giap's voice was soft, contemplative. "A minor inconvenience, easily brushed aside?"

"Yes, Comrade General. That is the consensus of the local command."

Giap turned, his eyes boring into the young officer. "They are fools."

The officer blinked, taken aback. "Sir?"

"This attack, however small, was no mere nuisance." Giap's voice was hard, unyielding. "It was precise, well-coordinated, and executed deep within our territory. That speaks to a level of intelligence and capability we have not seen from the enemy in some time."

He stalked back to his desk, his hands gripping the edge as he leaned forward. "I want a full investigation. Every detail of this attack must be scrutinized, every scrap of evidence analyzed. I want to know who was behind this, how they obtained their information, and what their next move might be."

"But sir," the officer stammered, "our resources are already stretched thin. Surely a minor raid like this doesn't warrant—"

"Enough!" Giap's fist slammed onto the desk, making the officer jump. "You think this enemy is weak, defeated? You think they will simply fade away, content with symbolic gestures? No. They are like the tiger, waiting in the tall grass. Ignore the rustle of leaves at your peril."

The officer swallowed hard, his face pale. "Yes, Comrade General. I will convey your orders immediately."

"See that you do." Giap's eyes were like flint, unyielding. "And let this be a reminder to all of our commanders - vigilance is the price demanded of victory. We must never underestimate our enemy, never assume their capabilities based on past performance. The moment we do, we invite disaster."

The officer bowed stiffly, then turned and hurried from the room. Giap watched him go, his mind already racing with possibilities.

He turned back to the map, his eyes tracing the lines of battle, the ebb and flow of the war. Somewhere out there, a new piece had entered the game, a wild card that could upset the delicate balance he had worked so hard to achieve.

But Vo Nguyen Giap had not come this far, had not led his people through decades of struggle and sacrifice, to be undone by a single opponent. He would find those responsible for this attack, and he would crush them without mercy.

In this war, there could be no half-measures, no room for doubt or hesitation. There could only be the relentless pursuit of the revolution, no matter the cost. And Giap would pay that price, as he always had - in blood, in sweat, and in the unshakeable will of the Vietnamese people.

Ambition Unchecked

Saigon, South Vietnam

President Nguyen Van Thieu stood at the window of his office, his hands clasped tightly behind his back. The ornate room, with its high ceilings and polished wood paneling, seemed to close in around him, the weight of his responsibilities pressing down like a physical force.

A knock at the door broke his reverie. "Enter," he called, his voice terse.

The door swung open, revealing the American Ambassador, Graham Martin, and the CIA Head of Station, Thomas Polgar. They strode into the room, their faces a mix of curiosity and concern.

"Mr. President," Ambassador Martin began, his tone diplomatically smooth, "we came as soon as we received your summons. How can we be of assistance?"

President Thieu turned from the window, his eyes hard. "Gentlemen, I have just received some disturbing news. Colonel Tran, if you would?"

An ARVN intelligence officer stepped forward, his

uniform crisp and his bearing ramrod straight. "Yes, Mr. President." He turned to the Americans, his English accented but precise. "Our sources in the North have reported a significant attack on a fuel depot near Thanh Hoa. The depot was completely destroyed, along with a number of supply trucks and a quantity of fuel."

Ambassador Martin frowned, glancing at Polgar. "I wasn't aware of any planned operations in that area. Were ARVN forces responsible for this attack?"

Colonel Tran shook his head. "No, sir. That's just it - we had no units operating in that region. This attack seems to have been carried out by unknown forces."

President Thieu leaned forward, his hands splayed on the desk. "Gentlemen, South Vietnam stands on the edge of a knife. One false move and the blade cuts deep. I must ask directly. Were American forces involved in this operation? CIA, perhaps?"

Polgar's eyebrows shot up, his surprise evident. "Absolutely not, Mr. President. We have no ongoing operations in that area, and certainly none that would involve an attack of this scale without coordination with ARVN command."

Ambassador Martin nodded in agreement, his face grave. "I can assure you, Mr. President, the United States had no involvement in this incident. Our policy has been one of support and advisement, not unilateral action."

Thieu's gaze bore into the two Americans, searching for any hint of deception. After a long moment, he sat back, his expression troubled. "Then we are left with a mystery. Who would have the capability and the motive to carry out such an attack, deep within North Vietnamese territory?"

Colonel Tran cleared his throat, drawing the room's attention. "Mr. President, there have been rumors... whispers of a new group operating in the shadows. Some say they're a coalition of our own special forces and American volunteers, working outside of official channels."

Polgar leaned forward, his interest piqued. "What do these rumors say about their goals, their methods?"

Tran shook his head, his frustration evident. "Very little, sir. Only that they seem to be targeting high-value North Vietnamese assets, and doing so with a level of skill and precision we've rarely seen."

President Thieu slammed his fist on the desk, making the room jump. "I will not tolerate rogue elements operating on Vietnamese soil. If these rumors are true, this group must be brought under control, and quickly."

Ambassador Martin raised a placating hand. "Mr. President, I understand your concern. But if this group is indeed working towards our shared goals, perhaps they could be an asset. An unconventional tool in an unconventional war."

Thieu's eyes flashed, his anger barely contained. "An asset? An uncontrolled variable, you mean. A wild card that could upset the delicate balance we are trying to maintain."

He stood abruptly, his gaze sweeping the room. "Gentlemen, I want answers. I want to know who these people are, what they want, and how they are able to operate with such impunity. And I want them brought to heel, one way or another."

The Americans exchanged a glance, the gravity of the situation sinking in. They were in uncharted waters now, facing an enigma that could unravel the fragile tapestry of the war effort.

But as they left the presidential palace, their minds raced with possibilities. Somewhere out there, a new element had entered the war. And whether ally or enemy, one thing was certain - they had just changed the rules, and nothing would be the same.

Bien Hoa Air Base, South Vietnam

The stifling heat of the Vietnamese summer clung to the air like a damp blanket as Coyle and Granier huddled over a map of North Vietnam in the dingy confines of their makeshift command center. The room, little more than a converted storage shed on the outskirts of the airbase, was lit by a single, flickering bulb that cast harsh shadows across the men's faces.

Coyle leaned back in his chair as he studied the map. "The fuel depot was a good start, but we need to keep the pressure on. Hit them where it hurts."

Granier nodded, his finger tracing a line along the coast. "I've been thinking about Haiphong Harbor. It's a major supply hub for the North, with ships coming in from China and the Soviet Union. If we could disrupt their operations there, even temporarily, it could put a serious dent in their ability to move men and materiel to the South."

Coyle's eyes narrowed, his interest piqued. "What did you have in mind?"

"A hijacking operation. We slip in, take control of one of their supply ships, and run it aground. It would block the harbor, create chaos, and send a message that nowhere is safe."

Coyle nodded slowly, his mind racing with possibilities. "It's bold, I'll give you that. But the risks...

infiltrating a heavily guarded harbor, taking on a crew, navigating an unfamiliar ship..."

Granier leaned forward, his eyes intense. "I know it's a gamble. But think of the payoff. We could cripple a key part of their supply chain for weeks, maybe longer. And the psychological impact... it would be a blow they wouldn't soon forget."

For a long moment, Coyle was silent, weighing the options. Then, with a heavy sigh, he pointed to another spot on the map. "What about this? A raid on their forward operating base near the DMZ. We could hit their command and control, disrupt their ability to coordinate attacks..."

Granier shook his head. "It's a valid target, but the security would be tight. We'd be going in against their best troops, on their home turf. The casualties..."

"...would be high," Coyle finished, his face grim. "I know. But we have to consider all the options."

Granier's finger moved again, settling on a cluster of symbols near Hanoi. "Then there's these - SAM sites and missile depots. Taking those out would give the South Vietnamese Air Force a fighting chance, make it easier to maintain air superiority."

Coyle frowned, his eyes tracing the distance from their current position. "It's a long way to go, deep in enemy territory. We'd be stretching our resources thin, and the risk of detection..."

"...is high, no matter what we do," Granier countered. "But that's the nature of the game we're playing. If we want to make a real difference, we have to be willing to take the big swings."

For a long moment, the two men stared at each other, the weight of their decisions hanging heavy in the air. Finally, Coyle sighed, his shoulders slumping.

"Alright. Haiphong Harbor it is. But we plan this one down to the last detail. We leave nothing to chance."

Granier nodded, a grim smile playing at the corners of his mouth. "Agreed. I'll start putting together the intel, work out the logistics. Now that we have their attention, we'll need to move fast, hit them before they have a chance to bolster their defenses."

"There's really not much for me to do on this one." Said Coyle.

"Unless something goes wrong," said Granier. "The Spectre is a powerful backup."

"True."

As the two men bent over the map, their voices low and urgent, the flickering light of the bulb cast their shadows long and dark against the walls. They were walking a tightrope now, balancing the need for bold action against the ever-present risk of failure.

But as they worked, a sense of purpose settled over them, a grim determination to see this through, no matter the cost. They were the tip of the spear, the ones who would strike the blows that others could not.

And in the heat and the sweat and the grime of that tiny room, they knew that they were exactly where they needed to be. There was no room for half-measures or hesitation. There was only the mission, and the unshakeable will to see it through.

Bien Hoa Air Base, South Vietnam

The hangar buzzed with a focused energy as the team of handpicked operatives gathered around the table. Granier, the architect of this unconventional unit, stood at the head, his presence commanding attention.

"Listen up," he began, his voice cutting through the low murmur of conversation. "Our target is Haiphong Harbor, the main supply artery for the North. But we're making a change to the plan."

He placed a hand on the map spread before them, his fingers tracing the outlines of the harbor. "Instead of seizing a ship, we're going to sink several. Limpet mines, placed strategically on the hulls of supply vessels waiting to unload. This tactic has the advantage of not requiring that we board any of the ships and we can hit multiple targets at the same time. With luck, we block the harbor and gum up their supply line as they clear the wreckage."

The men leaned in, their eyes sharp and attentive. They were no strangers to adaptability, to shifting gears on a moment's notice.

Granier's gaze swept the room, his expression serious. "A word of caution. We need to be selective in our targets. Under no circumstances are we to engage any Chinese or Soviet ships. The last thing we need is to give them an excuse to escalate their involvement."

Nods of understanding circled the table. These men knew the delicate balance of this war, the tightrope they walked with every operation.

"Sergeant Nguyen," Granier turned to the SCUBA team leader, "your men will be key. You'll need to place the mines discreetly, without drawing attention. Timing will be critical."

Nguyen met Granier's gaze. "We'll get it done, sir. My team is ready."

Granier's mouth twitched in a faint smile. He had no doubt about that. These were some of the best-trained men in the country.

"Lieutenant Donovan," he continued, "your role

will be support and overwatch. If anything goes sideways, it'll be on you to ensure a clean extraction."

Donovan nodded sharply, his eyes glinting with a steely resolve. "We've got their backs, sir. No man left behind."

Granier placed his hands on the table, leaning forward. "I don't need to remind you of the stakes here. Every ship we take out is a blow to the enemy's supply chain. But more than that, it's a message. A reminder that nowhere is safe, that we can and will strike at the heart of their operations."

The hangar was silent, the weight of Granier's words settling over the men like a mantle. They understood the risks, the potential consequences of failure. But they also knew the importance of their mission, the impact it could have on the course of the war.

"Alright," Granier said, his voice cutting through the stillness. "Let's go over the details. Approach routes, timelines, contingencies. We leave nothing to chance."

As the team huddled around the map, their focus narrowed to a laser point. They were professionals, each man a specialist in his field. And now, their skills, their dedication, would be put to the ultimate test.

As the briefing wound down and the men began to disperse, each to attend to their own preparations, Granier took a moment to survey the group. These were his men, his team. He was proud to fight beside them.

Refueling Pier, North Vietnam

The night was thick and heavy, the moon hidden

behind a veil of clouds as Granier and his team emerged from the dense jungle. They moved with a silent, practiced efficiency, their footsteps barely a whisper against the soft earth.

Ahead, the outline of a North Vietnamese patrol boat loomed, moored at a small refueling pier that jutted out into the inky black water. A single light flickered on the deck, casting eerie shadows across the weathered planks.

Granier held up a closed fist, signaling the team to halt. They melted into the shadows, their breathing slow and controlled, as they surveyed the scene before them.

Two sentries stood at the base of the pier, their rifles slung casually over their shoulders as they smoked cigarettes and spoke in low tones. On the deck of the boat, another figure could be seen moving about, a dim silhouette against the night sky.

Granier turned to his men, his voice a barely audible whisper. "Nguyen, Donovan, take out the sentries. Quick and quiet. The rest of you, with me. We secure the boat and neutralize any crew onboard."

Nods of acknowledgment passed through the group, each man readying himself for the task at hand. They had trained for this, honed their skills to a razor's edge. Now, it was time to put them to the test.

Nguyen and Donovan slipped away, blending into the shadows as they approached the sentries from either side. The rest of the team followed Granier, creeping towards the patrol boat with a silent, deadly intent, using the reeds along the shore as cover.

The takedown was swift and brutal. Nguyen and Donovan emerged from the darkness, their knives finding the sentries' throats with a vicious efficiency.

The men crumpled to the ground, their cigarettes still smoldering on the pier.

Climbing onto the boat, Granier and his men moved like a well-oiled machine. They swept the deck, dispatching the lone crewman with a muffled thud and a small splash as his body slipped into the water. Below decks, they found more sailors, sleeping in their bunks. Standing over each of the sleeping sailors, the team struck in unison with their knives. The enemy never had a chance to wake.

Granier crept into the boat officer's quarters. A lieutenant sat at a small desk writing a report to his commanding officer. Granier moved up behind him and plunged his knife into the back of his head. The wide-eyed officer gurgled for a moment before collapsing on his desk, dead.

With the boat secure, the team moved quickly, loading their supplies and gear with a practiced efficiency. Every second counted now. They knew that the longer they lingered, the greater the chance of discovery.

Granier took the helm, his eyes scanning the dark coastline. As the boat sliced through the water, leaving the refueling pier receding in its wake, Granier allowed himself a small, grim smile. They had passed the first hurdle, but the real challenge still lay ahead.

The stolen patrol boat cut through the inky darkness of the coastal waters, its engine thrumming a steady beat. Granier stood at the helm, his eyes fixed on the horizon, his mind focused on the mission ahead.

Suddenly, the silhouette of another patrol boat emerged from the gloom, its running lights casting an eerie glow across the water. Granier felt a surge of adrenaline, his grip tightening on the wheel.

"Stay calm," he murmured to himself as he flipped off the cabin light illuminating his face. "Act natural. We're just another patrol, out for a routine sweep."

The men on deck continued their duties with a practiced nonchalance. They knew the stakes, knew that any hint of suspicion could spell disaster. One of the team members calmly moved next to the forward deck gun, ready to take action if required.

As the two boats drew closer, Granier could make out the faces of the other crew, their features illuminated by the dim glow of their cockpit lights. They looked bored, disinterested, just another night on a thankless patrol.

The team members raised their hands in casual waves, gestures of camaraderie between fellow sailors. The other crew responded in kind, their hands lifting in halfhearted salutes.

The boats passed each other, the distance between them closing to mere meters. Granier could hear the thrum of the other boat's engine, could see the cigarette dangling from the lips of the helmsman.

For a moment, time seemed to stand still, the two boats suspended in a fragile bubble of silence and tension. Granier's breath caught in his throat.

Then, just as quickly as it had appeared, the other boat was gone, swallowed up by the night. Granier let out a slow, measured breath, his shoulders sagging with relief.

"Well done," he said to his team, his voice barely above a whisper. "We're clear."

The men nodded. They had passed the test, but they knew there would be more to come.

Haiphong Harbor, North Vietnam

As dawn approached, Haiphong Harbor loomed, a sprawling maze of docks and ships, of shadows and secrets. Somewhere in that labyrinth, their targets awaited.

They had to reach Haiphong Harbor before the alarm was raised, before the North Vietnamese realized that one of their own boats had been turned against them. Granier's eyes narrowed as he stared into the darkness. They were close now.

The stolen patrol boat cut a silent path through the night. The mission was all that mattered now, the mission and the men who would see it through.

The mines, nestled securely in their packs, were the key to the whole operation. Placed strategically on the hulls of the supply ships, they would cripple the enemy's ability to resupply their forces, sowing chaos and confusion in their wake.

But placement would be a delicate operation, requiring stealth, precision, and no small amount of luck. They would have to navigate the harbor undetected, slipping past patrols and watchful eyes to get close enough to their target ships.

The night stretched out before them, a vast, unknowable expanse of water and darkness. In the heart of enemy territory, a lone patrol boat cut through the waves.

Granier guided the stolen patrol boat through the maze of ships, his eyes scanning the docks for their targets. The North Vietnamese flags hung limply in the still night air, the only splashes of color in a world of gray steel and black water.

His eyes searched for the telltale signs of North

Vietnamese vessels. The flags, the markings, the small details that would betray their allegiance. Beside him, Nguyen waited. His team was ready, the mines primed and waiting. They needed only the word, the signal to begin their deadly work.

Granier spotted a small freighter, its hull rusted and pitted. The North Vietnamese flag hung limply from its stern, a splash of red against the black night. He pointed, a silent gesture that spoke volumes.

Nguyen nodded, his hand resting on the hilt of his knife. He knew what had to be done, knew the risks and the rewards.

They moved on, picking their way through the labyrinth of ships. The Chinese and Soviet vessels loomed large, their hulls dwarfing the smaller North Vietnamese boats. It would have been easy to target them, to strike a blow against the enemy's allies.

But Granier held back. This was not their fight, not their war. They would not drag others into the fray, would not risk escalation for the sake of a fleeting victory.

They stuck to their targets, the small, unassuming ships that flew the flag of their enemy. Each one a link in the chain, each one a step closer to their goal.

The minutes ticked by, the tension mounting with each passing moment. They knew that every second spent in the harbor was a second closer to discovery.

Finally, Granier held up a hand, a signal to halt. They had done all they could, had marked their targets and set the stage for the next phase. He turned to Nguyen, his voice low and steady. "Go," he said, the words heavy with meaning.

Nguyen nodded, his eyes gleaming in the darkness. He knew what had to be done.

As the stolen patrol boat slipped past each one of the targeted ships, the saboteurs slipped over the side of the boat, their movements silent and smooth. The water was cold, the darkness oppressive. But they pushed on, their minds fixed on the task at hand.

As they approached the last ship, a small, rusted freighter, Granier cut the engine, letting the boat drift silently towards the hull. Two shadowy figures emerged from the cabin, their movements fluid and purposeful. Nguyen and his partner, clad in dark wetsuits and scuba gear, slipped over the side of the boat, disappearing into the inky depths with barely a ripple.

Beneath the surface, the two men swam with powerful strokes, cutting through the water like torpedoes. They reached the hull of the freighter, their hands skimming along the barnacle-encrusted steel until they found the spots they had marked in their minds.

With practiced efficiency, they attached the limpet mines, one at each end of the ship, just below the waterline. The mines were compact, their magnetic clamps biting into the metal with a satisfying click. Each one was set to detonate on a timer, a failsafe to ensure that the team would be clear before the explosions ripped through the hulls.

Above, Granier watched the seconds tick by on his watch. He knew that every moment they lingered increased the chances of discovery. Dawn was quickly approaching and will it an increase in risk.

As the last mine was set, Nguyen and his partner resurfaced, their heads breaking the surface of the water like seals. They swam back to the patrol boat, their movements quick and silent, and hauled themselves aboard with a minimum of fuss.

Granier wasted no time, the engine roaring to life as he pointed the boat towards the opposite side of the freighter. They had to move quickly, had to pick up the other teams before the mines detonated and all hell broke loose.

They made their way around the ship, hugging the shadows, their eyes scanning the water for any sign of their comrades. One by one, the teams resurfaced, each one bearing the same look of grim satisfaction. They had done their job, had struck a blow against the enemy that would be felt for months to come.

As the last team clambered aboard, Granier gunned the engine, the boat leaping forward like a startled cat. They raced through the harbor, weaving between the ships, their hearts pounding in their chests.

Behind them, the mines ticked down, each second bringing them closer to their deadly purpose. And then, with a roar that seemed to shake the very foundations of the earth, they detonated.

The explosions were massive, the flames leaping high into the night sky. The ships shuddered and groaned, their hulls torn open like tin cans. Water poured into the gaping wounds, the vessels listing heavily to one side as they began to sink.

Chaos erupted on the docks, alarms blaring, voices shouting in confusion and fear. But the Ghost Warriors were already gone, the stolen patrol boat cutting through the waves like a knife through butter.

They had done it. And as the first light of dawn began to paint the sky, they knew that their mission was far from over. Sabotage was one thing, escape another.

The stolen patrol boat raced south, hugging the coastline, its engine roaring. Granier stood at the helm, his eyes fixed on the horizon. Behind them, three enemy boats gave chase, their deck guns barking into the night.

The shells fell short, the distance too great for accuracy. The pursuers were fast, but the stolen boat matched their speed. Granier pushed the engine to its limits, the hull vibrating beneath his feet.

The team braced themselves against the pounding waves. They knew that capture meant torture and certain death. But they were not afraid. They had faced worse odds and come out on top.

Donovan manned the rear gun, his eyes scanning the darkness for any sign of the enemy closing in. His finger rested on the trigger, ready to send a burst of lead into the night.

But the pursuit was futile. The enemy kept pace but was unable to close the gap. The stolen boat raced on, the wind whipping at their faces, the taste of salt on their lips. They were alive, victorious, the mission a success. But there was no time for celebration, no time for rest. For now, they had struck a blow, had shown the world that they were not to be underestimated.

Granier scanned the horizon, his eyes narrowing against the glare of the sun on the water. Two enemy boats appeared, their silhouettes growing larger as they closed in from the north. They were blocking the path to the border, cutting off the team's escape.

The situation was grim as the enemy patrol boats sandwiched the stolen patrol boat. Outnumbered and outgunned, Granier knew their chances of survival were slim. The team readied their weapons, preparing for a fight they could not win. They would go down fighting forcing the enemy to pay dearly for their lives.

As the enemy boats drew closer, the tension mounted. Granier's mind raced, searching for a way out, a glimmer of hope in a sea of despair. There was none.

Suddenly, one of the enemy boats exploded, a fireball erupting from its hull. The Spectre gunship appeared, flying low over the waves, its Vulcan cannons spitting fire. Coyle and his crew had arrived just in time, raining destruction upon the enemy. The Ghost Warriors cheered.

The second boat tried to fight back, its deck gun firing into the sky as the Spectre passed by. But it was no match for the gunship's firepower. It too erupted in flames, its crew leaping into the water as the vessel sank beneath the waves.

The three commanders of the pursuing boats, seeing the destruction wrought by the Spectre, broke off their chase and turned back. They had no desire to face the same fate as their comrades.

But the team's troubles were not over yet. As they approached the border, Granier knew they could not risk contacting the South Vietnamese Navy. Their stolen North Vietnamese boat would raise too many questions and expose their covert operation.

Instead, Granier pointed the boat towards the shore, pushing the engine to its limits. "Brace," he shouted to the team.

The hull slammed into a grove of mangroves snapping roots. The patrol boat wedged itself between two massive tree trunks. Recovered quickly from the crash, the team grabbed their weapons and leapt from deck disappearing into the trees.

Granier stayed behind, pulling incendiary grenades

from his pack. He tossed them into the boat, the flames consuming the evidence of their mission and destroying the craft. No trace could be left behind, no clue to their true identities.

With the boat destroyed, Granier joined his team, moving quickly through the jungle towards the rendezvous point. They had to keep moving, had to stay ahead of any pursuit.

As they broke from the grove, the sound of rotors filled the air, a welcome sight in the chaos of their escape. Scott's Huey appeared, flanked by the Chinooks, ready to extract the team and bring them to safety. In the doorway of the Huey, Karen snapped photos of the team below as they ran toward the landing Chinooks.

The Ghost Warriors had made it, against all odds. The mission was a success, the enemy dealt a blow they would not soon forget.

As the team boarded the helicopters, their faces lined with exhaustion and relief, Granier allowed himself a small smile. They had done the impossible, had struck at the heart of the enemy and lived to tell the tale.

The Ghost Warriors rose into the sky, leaving the smoking ruins of the enemy boats behind. They had proven their mettle, had shown the world what a small, dedicated team could accomplish.

The Blame Game

Hanoi, North Vietnam

The politburo was a grand, imposing building in the heart of Hanoi. The structure, a relic of the French colonial era, loomed over the surrounding streets, its façade a mix of European grandeur and Vietnamese austerity. The walls were a faded, mottled gray, the windows tall and narrow, like the eyes of a watchful sentry.

Inside, the corridors were wide and echoing, the floors polished to a high sheen. The air was cool and still, heavy with the weight of history and the gravity of the decisions made within these walls. The politburo chamber itself was a large, rectangular room, its walls lined with dark wood paneling and its ceiling adorned with an elaborate, crystal chandelier.

At the head of the room sat Le Duan, the General Secretary of the Communist Party. He was a man of medium height, with a thin, wiry build, and a face that seemed carved from granite. His eyes were dark and piercing, his gaze unwavering as he surveyed the room. He radiated an aura of power and authority, a man who was used to being obeyed without question.

To his right sat Truong Chinh, the Chairman of the National Assembly. He had a sharp, angular face and a perpetual frown. His eyes darted around the room, as if searching for any sign of dissent or disloyalty. He was known for his hardline stance, his unwavering commitment to the party line.

Next to him was Pham Van Dong, the Prime Minister. He was a tall, slender man with a gray goatee and an air of quiet dignity. He spoke softly, but his words carried weight, his opinions respected by all who heard them. He was seen as a moderating influence, a voice of reason in a sea of ideological fervor.

Across the table sat Le Duc Tho, the chief negotiator with the Americans. He was a small, wiry man with a quick, nervous energy. His eyes were constantly in motion, his hands fidgeting with the papers in front of him. He was known for his cunning and his ability to outmaneuver his opponents, both at the negotiating table and in the halls of power.

And then there was General Giap, the hero of Dien Bien Phu and the head of the military of North Vietnam. He sat at the far end of the table, his uniform crisp and his medals gleaming in the light of the chandelier. His face was lined and weathered from the years of struggle and sacrifice he had endured. But his eyes were clear and sharp, his mind as quick and agile as ever.

These were the men who held the fate of Vietnam in their hands, the leaders who would guide the nation through the trials and tribulations of the war. They were a diverse group, with different backgrounds and different agendas. But they were united in their commitment to the revolution, their determination to see their country free and independent.

And as they sat in that grand, imposing room, the weight of history bearing down upon them, they knew that the decisions they made would echo through the ages. For better or for worse, they were the architects of Vietnam's future, the guardians of its destiny. And they would not fail, would not falter in their duty until the final victory was won.

The room was thick with tension, the air heavy with the weight of unspoken accusations. "Comrade General," Le Duan began, his voice deceptively calm. "We have called you here to answer for the recent attacks on our coastal installations. The sabotage at Haiphong Harbor, the raids on our supply lines. What do you know of these incidents?"

Giap met Le Duan's gaze, his own eyes unwavering. "I have received reports, Comrade Secretary. My men are investigating as we speak, working to uncover the truth behind these attacks."

"The truth?" Le Duan leaned forward, his hands clasped on the table before him. "The truth is that our allies are concerned. The Soviets and the Chinese have both expressed their worries that their ships may have been targeted. They threaten to cut off aid by sea if we cannot secure our own waters."

Giap bristled at the accusation, his voice low and steady. "I assure you, Comrade Secretary, that no Soviet or Chinese vessels were targeted. The enemy's focus seems to be on our own supply lines, our own infrastructure."

"And how can you be so certain?" Another member of the politburo spoke up, his tone skeptical. "These attacks were carried out with a precision and skill we have not seen before. This is not the work of the South Vietnamese alone."

Giap turned to face the speaker, his expression grave. "I agree, Comrade. The nature of these attacks suggests a new enemy, a force we have not yet encountered. But I assure you, my men will find those responsible and bring them to justice."

Le Duan slammed his hand on the table, the sudden noise making the room jump. "Justice is not enough, Comrade General. We must have security, must have the confidence of our allies. If we cannot protect their interests, they will abandon us, leave us to fight this war with one hand tied behind our backs."

Giap drew himself up to his full height, his voice ringing with conviction. "I understand the gravity of the situation, Comrade Secretary. But I urge you not to let fear cloud your judgment. We have faced worse odds and emerged victorious. We will find a way to overcome this challenge, just as we have all the others."

For a long moment, the room was silent, the weight of Giap's words hanging in the air. Finally, Le Duan sat back in his chair, his expression unreadable.

"See that you do, Comrade General. The fate of our revolution hangs in the balance. We cannot afford to let these attacks go unanswered."

Giap bowed his head, a gesture of respect and acknowledgement. "I will not fail you, Comrade Secretary. Nor will I fail our people. We will find those responsible and we will make them pay for their crimes against our nation."

As the meeting adjourned, Giap strode from the room, his mind already racing with plans and possibilities. He knew the stakes, knew the price of failure.

The Ghost Warriors had struck a blow, had shown that they were a force to be reckoned with. But they had also awakened a sleeping giant, had provoked the wrath of a nation that would stop at nothing to defend its sovereignty. One thing was certain - the people of Vietnam would never surrender, never bow to the will of their enemies. They would fight on, until the last breath, until the last drop of blood. This was their land, their home. And they would defend it to the end, no matter the cost, no matter the sacrifice.

Saigon, South Vietnam

The U.S. Embassy hummed with activity as Coyle walked through the bustling corridors, his footsteps echoing on the polished marble floor. He had been summoned to the office of Thomas Polgar, the CIA's top man in Saigon, and he knew it could only mean trouble.

Coyle knocked on the heavy wooden door. He heard Polgar's muffled voice from within, inviting him to enter. He wiped the sweat from his brow before opening the door.

The room was spacious and well-appointed, with large windows that overlooked the city. Polgar sat behind a massive desk with an American flag behind him and the CIA crest on the wall. He motioned for Coyle to take a seat in one of the leather chairs facing him.

"Tom," Polgar began, his voice even and measured. "Thank you for coming on such short notice."

Coyle nodded, his mouth suddenly dry. "Of course, sir. What can I do for you?"

Polgar leaned back in his chair, his fingers steepled in front of him. "Tom, you're known for being a straight shooter. I like that about you. It builds trust."

"Thank you, sir. I try."

"That's why I was concerned when I've received a report from one of our Navy destroyers off the coast. They claim to have witnessed a Spectre gunship engaging North Vietnamese patrol boats near the border."

"Really? Maybe it was the South Vietnamese."

"I thought so too. But the head of their Air Force assures me that none of the gunships we have given them have been used along the coast in quite some time. It's seems they're saving them for when the NVA mount their next offensive."

Coyle felt his stomach drop, but he kept his expression neutral. "Is that so, sir?"

"Yes, it is." Polgar's gaze bore into him, searching for any hint of deception. "Now, as far as I'm aware, we have no sanctioned operations in that area. So, I'm curious, Tom. What do you know about this?"

Coyle took a deep breath, his mind racing. He knew he had to tread carefully, had to protect his men and their mission at all costs.

"I'm not sure what to tell you, sir," he said, his voice steady. "I haven't heard anything about a Spectre operating in that region. Could it have been a case of mistaken identity?"

Polgar's eyes narrowed, his expression hardening. "The destroyer's crew is quite confident in what they saw, Tom. They're not in the habit of making such mistakes."

Coyle shrugged. "All I can say, sir, is that if there was a Spectre out there, it wasn't ours. We've been focusing our efforts on interdiction missions along the Ho Chi Minh Trail. We haven't been near the coast."

For a long moment, Polgar was silent, his gaze never leaving Coyle's face. Finally, he sighed, leaning forward and placing his hands on the desk.

"Tom, I know you and your men have been doing good work out there. But I need to know that you're playing by the rules, that you're not going off the reservation on some unsanctioned mission."

Coyle met Polgar's gaze unflinchingly, his voice firm. "I assure you, sir, that my men and I are doing everything by the book. We're here to support the South Vietnamese, to help them win this war. Nothing more, nothing less."

Polgar held his gaze for a moment longer, then nodded, sitting back in his chair. "Alright, Tom. I'll take you at your word. But I want you to know that I'll be keeping a close eye on your operations from here on out. We can't afford any rogue elements. We're almost out of this thing. The president doesn't want us stirring the pot if you know what I mean."

Coyle stood. "I understand, sir. You can count on us to do our duty, to the best of our ability."

As he left Polgar's office, Coyle felt a weight lift from his shoulders. He had navigated a dangerous situation, had kept his men and their mission safe.

But he knew that the road ahead would only get harder, that the risks would only grow greater. They were playing a dangerous game, walking a tightrope between duty and necessity. And one misstep, one moment of carelessness, could bring it all crashing down around them. They had to be careful, had to be smart.

Saigon, South Vietnam

The AP office was a ghost town, the once-thriving hub of journalism now reduced to a handful of diehards clinging to the remnants of a dying war. Granier navigated the maze of empty desks and abandoned offices, the silence broken only by the soft hum of the air conditioner.

He found Karen in the darkroom, hunched over a tray of developer, her face bathed in the eerie red glow of the safelights. She looked up as he entered, a wry smile playing on her lips.

"Granier," she said, her voice tinged with exhaustion. "I thought you'd be out celebrating with the rest of the team."

Granier shrugged, leaning against the doorframe. "Celebrations can wait. I wanted to see the photos first."

Karen nodded, turning back to the tray. She fished out a print, holding it up to the light. It was a shot of Nguyen, his eyes filled with fierce concentration as he prepared to place the limpet mines. The water swirled around him, a vortex of chaos and danger, but his eyes were steady, his hands sure.

"Look at this one," she said, handing the print to Granier. "The determination in his eyes, the coiled energy in his muscles. It's like he's ready to take on the whole damned North Vietnamese Army himself."

Granier studied the image, his brow furrowed. "It's a powerful shot, Karen. They all are. But are you sure this is the best place to be developing them? I mean, the AP office... it's not exactly secure."

Karen let out a snort of laughter. "Secure? Granier, have you looked around lately? There's nobody here who gives a damn anymore. Anybody with half a brain and a shred of ambition left Saigon a long time ago, chasing the next big story."

She shook her head, a wistful smile playing on her lips. "The war's over, Granier. At least, the war that the rest of the world cared about. The only ones left are the diehards, the true believers. And believe me, they've got bigger things to worry about than a few photos of some unnamed commandos."

Granier was silent for a moment, his gaze distant. "But you stayed, Karen. Why? Why keep fighting when everyone else has given up?"

Karen's smile faded, her eyes taking on a faraway look. "I guess... I guess I just couldn't let go. This war, these people... they got under my skin. They became a part of me."

She looked down at the tray of photos, the images of bravery and sacrifice, of hope and despair. "I made a promise to myself, a long time ago. To see this thing through, to the bitter end. To bear witness to the truth, no matter how ugly or uncomfortable it might be."

Granier nodded, a glimmer of understanding in his eyes. "I know what you mean. It's the same for me, for all of us. We're here because we believe in something, because we know that what we're doing matters. And your photos, Karen... they're a big part of that. They're the proof that we were here, that we fought, that we made a difference."

She turned back to the tray, pulling out another print. It was a wide shot of the harbor at Haiphong, the smoking ruins of the enemy ships still smoldering in the dawn light. In the foreground, a group of commandos huddled together, their faces etched with the hard lines of exhaustion and triumph.

"Look at their faces," she said, her voice soft with reverence. "The pride, the relief, the sheer fucking joy of knowing that they made it out alive."

Granier studied the image, his brow furrowed. "It's a powerful shot. Full of emotion, full of raw energy. But do you think it will be enough? To convince the ARVN commanders, I mean."

Karen sighed, hanging the print up to dry. "I don't know. These photos, they tell a story. They show the bravery and the sacrifice of our men, the lengths they're willing to go to for the cause. But will it be enough to change minds, to inspire action? I can't say for sure."

Granier was silent for a moment, his gaze distant. "I know what you mean. We're asking a lot of these men, of these commanders. To put aside their doubts, their fears, and to take a stand against an enemy that seems unbeatable."

Karen turned to face him, her eyes searching his face. "But that's why we're doing this, isn't it? To give them hope, to show them that victory is possible, even against the odds."

And as he looked around the darkroom, at the images of bravery and sacrifice that lined the walls, he knew that he would never forget this moment, this place, these people. They were the Ghost Warriors, the ones who fought on when all others had given up.

Saigon, South Vietnam

The tension in the room was palpable as General Cao Van Vien, the Chief of the Joint General Staff, and President Nguyen Van Thieu, the leader of South Vietnam, sat across from each other. The fate of their nation hung in the balance, and both men knew that the decisions made in this room would have far-reaching consequences.

"Mr. President," General Vien began, his voice firm and insistent, "I must speak frankly. While I understand the importance of protecting our cities and the Mekong Delta, I believe that our current strategy of not engaging the enemy at the borders is a grave mistake."

President Thieu's eyes narrowing. "General, we have discussed this before. Our resources are limited, and we cannot afford to overextend ourselves. The cities are our strongholds, our last line of defense. When the North Vietnamese launch their offensive, they will be decimated by our prepared defenses and overwhelming forces around the cities."

Vien leaned forward, his gaze intense. "Sir, with all due respect, if we allow the North Vietnamese to gain a foothold in the border regions, it will only be a matter of time before they stockpile enough weapons and men to overrun our cities even with our prepared defenses. We must take the fight to them, disrupt their supply lines and troop movements. We must reduce their strength while there is still time. If history has taught us anything it is that stationary defenses, no matter how strong they seem, cannot withstand a modern army with modern weaponry. By staying within our defenses, we lose the power of maneuver. It is the enemy that determines where they attack next, not us. As sure as the monsoons, they will find our weak points and use them to their advantage. Stationary defenses are a bad idea in modern warfare."

"Then how do you explain the Siege of Khe Sanh, General? The American Marines withstood NVA forces for months and in the end, it was the NVA that withdrew after suffering tremendous losses."

"It is true, the American did defeat the NVA at Khe Sanh, but only after expending a huge amount of resources and air support for its defense. The US Marines are well-known for their tenacious nature and their training. While we do have some limited forces that are similar, we don't have nearly enough to sustain multiple assaults on the cities and areas we are protecting. Once those forces had been reduced, there will be nothing to stop the NVA if they are allowed to stockpile weapons and supplies so close to the battlefields."

"Let's assume for a moment that you are correct and that allowing the NVA to stockpile weapons and supplies within our borders is a strategic mistake. How do you propose to attack the NVA while protecting our cities and our major food growing provinces. Our forces are already stretched thin, and we cannot risk leaving these areas vulnerable."

Vien's mind raced, the gears of his strategic intellect turning. "Mr. President, I suggest a series of targeted strikes, quick and decisive. We use our air power to hit their supply depots, their staging areas. We drop our special forces behind enemy lines to sabotage their infrastructure, sow chaos in their ranks."

He paused, his voice dropping to a low, intense tone. "We don't need to engage them in pitched battles, sir. We need to be smart, surgical. Hit them where it hurts, then fade back into the jungle before they can respond. We do the same thing they have been doing to us since the war began. We fight like guerillas. Never engage the enemy unless we know we can win. That strategy will allow us to use our forces for maximum effect while still protecting them so they can be used for city defenses when the time comes."

Thieu was silent for a long moment, his expression unreadable. Finally, he spoke, his words measured and deliberate.

"General Vien, your proposals are bold, and not without merit. But I fear that even these targeted strikes you speak of would require a significant commitment of resources. The recent fifty percent reduction in American support has put us in a precarious position. We must be even more strategic in how we allocate our funds and resources. Expensive training exercises and large-scale offensives are simply not feasible at this time."

“Mr. President, I don’t see how we cannot go on the offensive and survive the coming enemy offensive.”

Thieu sighed, the weight of his office bearing down on him. "The North Vietnamese are like a flood, General. We cannot hope to stop them at the source. Our only hope is to build our dams high and strong, to weather the deluge until they have spent their fury."

Vien's frustration was evident, but he knew that he had to choose his words carefully. "Mr. President, I hear your concerns, and I understand the difficult position we are in. But I fear that if we do not act now, if we do not seize the initiative, the dams will eventually break and the flood will consume us all.”

“I will admit, that is a possibility. But our options are few and our financial resources are even less.”

“Sir, if I may, one way we could stretch our available funds is by curbing corruption among our generals and ARVN officers. It could ensure that all resources are being used efficiently and it would greatly improve our ability to defend against the enemy."

"General, while I agree that corruption is a significant issue, we must tread carefully. Launching an internal campaign against corruption at this critical juncture could seriously undermine the loyalty of our generals to the government. The last thing we need right now is a coup that destabilizes our leadership and gives the North Vietnamese an opening to accelerate their offensive. The risks are simply too high."

"I agree that a coup would be disastrous at this point and the north would certainly take advantage of any instability. But we must do something to boost our ranks if we are to stand on equal footing with the NVA."

"Remember, General, that the Vietnamization program was designed to replace American soldiers with well-trained Vietnamese forces. However, with the reduction in U.S. aid, the extensive training required to make this transition is no longer financially viable."

"I understand, Mr. President. But if we cannot rely on the Americans, perhaps we could seek aid from other countries to help us in our fight against the communists."

"I'm afraid that is unlikely, General. No other nation has shown a willingness to step in and fill the void left by the Americans. We are, for all intents and purposes, on our own in this struggle. We must make do with what we have and find a way to persevere."

Resigned, Vien took a deep breath, his voice steady and resolute. "I will obey your orders as I always do, sir. I will do everything in my power to fortify our cities, to protect our people. But I implore you, do not let us become a fortress under siege. Let us strike back, let us show the enemy that we are not afraid, that we will not go quietly into the night."

Thieu's eyes met Vien's, a flicker of understanding passing between them. "Your words are passionate, General, and your dedication to our cause is beyond question. I will consider your proposals, and I will do what I believe is best for our nation. But for now, we hold the line. We stand firm, and we do not waver."

Just as Thieu was about to dismiss the General, Vien spoke up, his voice hesitant but determined. "Mr. President, there is one more matter I wish to discuss, if I may."

Thieu's curiosity piqued. "Go on, General."

Vien leaned forward. "Sir, I'm sure you are aware of the recent covert assaults across the border, the raids that have struck deep into enemy territory."

Thieu's eyes narrowed, his expression growing guarded. "I am aware, yes. What of them?"

"I was wondering, sir, if you had discovered any more information about who might be behind these attacks. They are bold, daring, and they seem to be having an impact on the enemy's operations."

Thieu was silent for a long moment, his gaze distant. When he finally spoke, his voice was low and conspiratorial. "General, I have my suspicions, but no hard evidence. Not yet. But if I were to hazard a guess, I would say that our American friends, particularly those in the CIA, are involved."

Confusion was evident on Vien's face. "But sir, I thought that Mr. Polgar, the CIA chief of station, had denied any involvement in these actions."

Thieu's laugh was short and bitter. "General, you are a brilliant military strategist, but you still have much to learn about the world of espionage and diplomacy."

He fixed Vien with a piercing stare, his words

measured and deliberate. "Mr. Polgar is a professional liar, General. It is his job to deceive, to misdirect, to keep his true motives hidden from all but a select few and we are not on that list."

Vien shifted uncomfortably in his seat, the implications of Thieu's words sinking in. "So, you believe that the CIA is acting without our consent, conducting operations that could have a major impact on the course of the war?"

"It would not be the first time, General. The Americans have their own agenda, their own interests. They will pursue them, regardless of the consequences for our nation. But we cannot afford to confront them directly, not now. We need their support, their resources, if we are to have any hope of holding back the tide of communist aggression."

Vien's jaw clenched, frustration evident in his tone. "So, we are to simply sit back and let them operate with impunity, to let them shape the course of this war without our input or consent?"

"For now, yes. We play the game, we dance to their tune. But we keep our eyes open, we gather what information we can. And when the time is right, when we have the leverage we need, we will make our move. We will take control of our own destiny, and we will do what needs to be done to secure the future of South Vietnam."

Vien sat back in his chair, his mind reeling with the implications of Thieu's words. He had always known that the relationship between South Vietnam and the United States was a complex one, fraught with hidden agendas and competing interests. But to hear it laid out so starkly, to realize the depth of the deception and the manipulation that was taking place behind the scenes...

it was a bitter pill to swallow. And yet, as he looked into the steely gaze of his president, Vien knew that he had no choice but to trust in Thieu's judgment, to follow his lead as they navigated the treacherous waters of this war.

For better or for worse, they were in this together, the fate of their nation resting on their shoulders. And they would do whatever it took, whatever sacrifices needed to be made, to see South Vietnam through to a brighter future.

Vien rose to his feet, his hand clasping Thieu's in a firm grip. "Of course, Mr. President. I am a soldier, and I will follow your orders. But I will also continue to provide my best advice, to use every ounce of my strategic knowledge to help guide us through these dark times."

As he left the room, Vien's heart was heavy, but his resolve was unshakable. He knew that the fate of South Vietnam hung by a thread.

Armor Versus Air

Bien Hoa Air Base, South Vietnam

The air in the makeshift command center was thick with tension as Coyle and Granier stood on opposite sides of the map-strewn table, their voices rising with each passing minute.

Coyle slammed his hand down on the table, his frustration evident. "Dammit, Granier, we can't just keep nibbling at their heels! We need to hit them where it hurts, and those SAM sites along the border are the perfect target. Without SAMs, our air assaults will make short order of the NVA troops and supply transports. We'll cut them off at the knees."

Granier shook his head, "Yeah, but for how long? We take out a handful of SAM sites, and they'll just replace the SAMS and reinforce the ground defenses. We don't have the resources to keep up that kind of campaign."

Granier jabbed a finger at the map. "But this armored vehicle staging area in the foothills near Lang

Vei, that's a different story. If we hit them there, we force them to pull back some of their front-line troops to defend their staging areas. It could put a serious dent in their offensive capabilities."

Coyle snorted, his arms crossed over his chest. "And how do you propose we get close enough to hit that staging area? It's heavily guarded by crack NVA guard units. It's not like we can just waltz in there and start shooting."

Granier leaned forward, his voice low and intense. "We do the opposite of what we've been doing. We don't use the ground team to take out the vehicles. We use them to take out the anti-aircraft units, then let the Spectre do the heavy lifting and take out the armor. If you had a clear path, how many vehicles do you think you could take out?"

"It's hard to say. Depends on the vehicle and the thickness of the armor on top of the turret. It varies from vehicle to vehicle and who makes it. Russian armor is thicker than Chinese armor."

"So, what's your best guess?"

Coyle cracked a smile, "A lot. We could cut back on the minigun ammo and replace the weight with armor piercing rounds for the 20mm Vulcans. And if the Vulcan doesn't get the job done, we can hit them with the 40mm Bofors autocannon."

"That's the attitude."

"I haven't agreed yet. That close to the border, we still need to worry about their MiGs. The Spectre is not designed for air-to-air combat, especially against jets."

"Any idea where they will be coming from?"

"If I have to venture a guess, I would say Hoa Loc Air Base along the coast. Why?"

"What if we split the ground team in two? We sent

one team along the coast to Hoa Loc and sabotage their MiGs. Meanwhile, a second team goes to the forward staging around Lang Vei to take out the anti-aircraft units."

"Do we have enough men to split the team?"

"We'd be stretching things pretty thin, but we could recruit some more team members to make it work. We just need to define the main targets and not go after any targets of opportunity."

"What if your team went after the runway instead of the MiGs? We only need to stall them for an hour until the air assault is over and we can retreat back behind our own air defenses."

"Well, that would be easier than going after the MiGs. That's for sure."

"Plus, it's certain that you ground all the aircraft."

"Right. Nothing gets off the ground if we take out their runway. Still, cratering a runway would need a lot of explosives."

"Yeah, and they need to be shaped charges fired in unison. Tricky, but doable. So, what do you think?"

Coyle considered for a moment, then… "I say, if you can split the team and take out the airfield and the anti-aircraft units, then it's a go from my side."

"Good. I agree. It shouldn't take long to recruit the soldiers we need. Dao's got a list of potential volunteers. Getting that many shaped charges is a bit tricky, but it's doable."

They leaned over to examine the map, Coyle's finger tracing a path from their current position to the staging area. "But we need to do this fast and hard. The longer we wait, the more time they have to reinforce their positions and push further into South Vietnam."

Granier nodded. "Agreed. We'll need to coordinate

closely, make sure our timing is perfect. Both ground teams will have to move quickly to take out those air defenses, and then the Spectre needs to be ready to swoop in and finish the job."

"My guys will be ready."

"If we succeed, it's going to give the NVA one hell of a bloody nose. They'll think twice about how fast they should advance into the south."

"I like the sound of that."

Coyle and Granier worked late into the night, hammering out the details of the multiple raids.

And as the first light of dawn began to creep over the horizon, Coyle and Granier were ready to lead their men into the heart of the storm. The Ghosts were coming, and Heaven help anyone who stood in their way.

Bien Hoa, South Vietnam

The bar was a dingy, smoke-filled den, the kind of place where soldiers came to forget the war for a few precious hours. The walls stained a nicotine yellow that spoke of countless nights of debauchery.

In a corner booth, far from the prying eyes of the other patrons, Granier and Dao sat across from a group of potential recruits, their faces illuminated by the flickering glow of a single bare light bulb overhead. The men were a motley crew, a mix of ARVN Rangers and Marines, each of them battle-hardened and hungry for a chance to strike back at the enemy.

Granier leaned forward. "Gentlemen, I'll get right to the point. We're putting together a team for a mission that could change the course of this war. It's dangerous, it's dirty, and there's a good chance some of us won't make it back."

He paused, letting his words sink in. "But if we succeed, we'll be striking a blow against the NVA that they won't soon forget. We'll be showing them that they don't own this country, that the people of South Vietnam are still in this fight."

One of the men, a wiry Ranger with a heavily tattooed arm, spoke up. "What kind of mission are we talking about?"

Dao answered, his voice a low growl. "We're going to hit them where it hurts. An armored staging area, deep in their territory. We take out their anti-aircraft guns, and then our friends in the sky come in and rain hell down on their tanks and APCs."

Another man, a thick-necked Marine with a scar running down his cheek, grunted in approval. "About damned time we took the fight to them. I'm sick of sitting around waiting for the NVA to make the first move."

Granier nodded. "That's the spirit. We're not going to win this war by playing defense. We need to be proactive, to hit them hard and fast before they can launch their offensive."

A third man, a young ARVN soldier with a nervous energy about him, leaned in, his eyes wide. "But how are we going to get close enough to take out those anti-aircraft guns? They'll have that whole area locked down tight."

Dao chuckled. "We'll hit them like a typhoon, fast and hard before they know what's happening."

The tattooed Ranger shook his head, a smile spreading across his face. "I like it. It's bold, it's risky, but it's the kind of thing that should have been doing all along."

Granier leaned back, his eyes scanning the faces of the men around him. "It won't be easy. We'll be outnumbered, outgunned, and deep in enemy territory. But I look around this table, and I see some of the finest soldiers I've ever had the privilege to serve with. If anyone can pull this off, it's you."

The Marine with the scar nodded. "We're with you, sir. Just point us in the direction of the enemy and let us loose."

As the recruiting session stretched late into the night, the smoke and the alcohol and the sweat mingling in the air, Granier knew that he had found his team. These were the men who would fight and bleed and die for the chance to make a difference in this war.

The mission was taking shape. It was a daunting prospect that could easily end in disaster. They were the tip of the spear in a war that had dragged on for far too long. The NVA may have had the numbers and the momentum, but they didn't have the sheer stubborn will to fight that he saw in the eyes of his men. And in the end, that would make all the difference.

Spectre Hangar

Inside the hangar with Spectre in the background, the team gathered around a large table covered with reconnaissance photos and maps of the target area. The air was thick with the smell of coffee and cigarette smoke as they pored over the details, each focused on their specific role in the upcoming mission.

Harmon, the intelligence specialist, studied the grainy black and white images intently. "Alright, based on these photos, it looks like they have four ZPU-4 anti-aircraft guns set up around the perimeter of the staging area." He tapped a series of circled locations on the map. "Two here, one here, and another over on this ridge. Those will be our primary targets for the ground team."

Coyle leaned in, squinting at the photos. "What about the armor? Can you make out what types of vehicles they have?"

Harmon nodded, sliding a magnifying glass over a particularly clear image. "Looks like a mix of PT-76 light tanks and BTR-60 armored personnel carriers. The PT-76s have pretty thin top armor, only about 10-15mm. The Spectre's 20mm Vulcan cannons should be able to punch right through that."

Coyle grunted in approval. "Good. And the BTRs?"

"Thicker, around 20mm on the top. But the 40mm Bofors autocannons should still be effective, especially with armor-piercing rounds."

Across the room, Dao was hunched over a typewriter, carefully forging requisition forms for the specialized ammunition they would need. "I'm putting in requests for 5,000 rounds of 20mm PGU-28A/B armor-piercing incendiary and 2,000 rounds of 40mm L/70 AP. That should give us plenty of firepower to take out those vehicles."

Granier glanced up from a roster of potential recruits, his eyes narrowed. "What about the airfield? We'll need to put that runway out of commission."

Dao nodded, pulling out another form. "Already on it. I'm requisitioning 500 pounds of C-4, plus enough det cord and synchronized detonators to rig the entire width of the runway. We'll plant the charges in a double, staggered pattern to ensure maximum damage."

Coyle and his aircrew were clustered around

another table, examining the approach routes to the staging area. "If we come in low from the south, using this ridgeline as cover, we should be able to avoid their radar until we're right on top of them," Coyle said, tracing a line on the map with his finger.

The loadmaster, a grizzled veteran named Johnson, tapped a spot near the center of the staging area. "This looks like the best spot to start our run. It's got the highest concentration of vehicles."

Coyle nodded. "Alright, that's our plan then. We'll come in low and fast, hit them hard, and then get the hell out before they can respond."

Meanwhile, Granier was deep in discussion with a group of new recruits, outlining the details of the mission. "We'll be inserting two teams, one to take out the anti-aircraft guns at the staging area, and another to rig the airfield with explosives."

He pointed to a spot on the coast, just north of the target. "Team one will infiltrate by sea, using a dredge ship as cover. The bay is filled with silt so the dredge shouldn't raise any suspicions. We've got a local pilot who can get us close to the airfield. We will go in at night using an inflatable boat."

Turning to another map, he indicated a winding route through the hills. "Team two will approach overland, using this old smuggling trail to avoid the main roads. It's a tough hike, but it should keep us away from their patrols."

One of the recruits, a wiry man with a heavily scarred face, raised his hand. "What kind of resistance are we expecting?"

Granier's expression tightened. "Heavy. They'll have patrols around the perimeter, and once we engage, they'll throw everything they have at us. But if we move fast and hit hard, we should be able to achieve our objectives before they can organize a coherent defense. Then we pull back and the Spectre do it worst."

He looked around the room, making eye contact with each of the men. "Some of us may not make it back from this mission. It's a tough one with a great deal of risk. But what we're doing here could change the course of this war. It could give our people a fighting chance. And I figure that's worth putting our lives on the line."

As the team continued their preparations, a sense of determination settled over the room. They all knew the stakes, knew the risks they were taking. But they also knew that they were the only ones who could pull off a mission like this.

And so they planned and plotted and prepared, each of them focused on their own piece of the puzzle. Harmon with his intel, Dao with his requisitions, Coyle with his flight plans, and Granier with his ground strategy.

Separately, they were just cogs in a machine. But together, they formed a lethal weapon, a precision instrument of war that would strike deep into the heart of the enemy and bring them to their knees.

Bien Hoa Air Base, South Vietnam

The armory was a squat, unassuming building tucked away in a corner of the base, its weathered, brick walls and rusting roof giving no indication of the deadly arsenal contained within. Dao and his teammate, a wiry Ranger named Hien, approached the entrance with a casual air, their forged requisition papers tucked neatly into a folder under Dao's arm.

The guard at the door, a bored-looking ARVN corporal, barely glanced up as they approached. "Papers?" he grunted, his hand outstretched.

Dao handed over the folder with a confident smile. "All in order, Corporal. We're here to pick up some specialized equipment for a training exercise."

The guard gave the papers a cursorily glance, then handed the folder back, and waved them through.

As they entered the armory, they approached a sergeant sitting at a desk. “Papers?” he said.

Dao handed him the folder. He flipped through the papers, his eyes scanning the dense blocks of text and official-looking stamps.

For a moment, it seemed like he would simply give them what they requested. But then he looked up at Dao with a suspicious glint in his eye.

"20mm and 40mm armor-piercing rounds? C-4 explosives? This is some heavy gear for a training exercise."

Dao's smile never wavered, but Hien could see the tension in his jaw. "You know how it is, Sergeant. The brass wants us to simulate real combat conditions. Can't do that with blanks and firecrackers."

The sergeant hesitated, clearly torn between his natural suspicion and the authoritative tone of Dao's voice. "I don't know. I should probably call this in, just to be sure."

Dao leaned in, his voice low and conspiratorial. "Look, Sergeant, I get it. You're just doing your job. But let me level with you. This exercise, it's not exactly on the books, if you know what I mean."

The sergeant's eyes widened slightly, a spark of understanding dawning on his face. "Off the record, huh?"

Dao nodded, his expression serious. "That's right. The less people who know about it, the better. I'm sure you understand the need for discretion in these matters."

For a long moment, the sergeant was silent, his gaze flicking back and forth between Dao and the papers in his hand. “I want ten percent when you sell it,” said the sergeant in a whisper.

“Five percent and nothing more,” said Dao.

The sergeant considered for a long moment, then, “You already have a buyer?”

“Of course.”

“Alright… five percent. Do you need anything else?”

“Do you have any of those new sniper rifles from the Americans?”

“We have two.”

“I'll take them both.”

“But I get ten percent on those. Specialty items.”

“Alright… ten percent on the sniper rifles.”

“And I don't want to come looking for my money. You understand?”

“We're professionals. We understand perfectly.”

The guard handed Dao back his folder and said, “Good. I'll get your gear. Where's your truck?”

“Out front.”

“Back it up to the door. My boys will help you load it.”

After a few minutes, the items on the list were loaded on the truck. Dao checked off each item. The 20mm and 40mm rounds, the C-4, the det cord and detonators - all of it carefully packed and loaded onto the back of the truck.

As they drove away from the armory, the supplies safely stowed in the back, Hien glanced over at Dao, a look of admiration on his face. "That was some smooth talking back there, sir. I thought for sure that guard was going to call in the MPs on us."

Dao shrugged, a slight smile playing at the corners of his mouth. "It's all about confidence, Hien. You act like you belong and most people won't question it."

As they drove back to the hangar, Dao knew the mission was a long shot, a gamble of the highest order. But then again, that was what the team was all about. Taking the risks that no one else would, fighting the battles that others feared to even contemplate.

South China Sea, off the coast of North Vietnam

The sun was just beginning to dip below the horizon as Dao and his team boarded the rusty, weathered dredging ship. The vessel, a relic of the French colonial era, had seen better days, its paint peeling and its engines sputtering as it chugged out of the harbor and into the open sea.

But for Dao and his men, it was the perfect cover. Who would suspect a group of elite soldiers to be hiding aboard such a decrepit ship? They blended in with the crew, donning grease-stained overalls and battered hard hats, their weapons and gear carefully concealed in waterproof duffels.

As the ship made its way up the coast, hugging the shoreline to avoid the prying eyes of North Vietnamese patrols, Dao gathered his team in a secluded corner of the hold. The space was cramped and dimly lit, the air thick with the stench of diesel fuel and stale sweat.

"Alright, listen up," he said. "We'll be approaching

the drop point in a few hours. From there, we'll be on our own. We need to make our way to the airfield, neutralize any enemy patrols, and set the charges on that runway before midnight."

He paused, his gaze sweeping over the faces of his men. "We're deep in enemy territory, and they'll be on high alert. But I have faith in each and every one of you. We've trained for this, and we're ready."

The men nodded. They were a seasoned bunch, veterans of countless covert operations behind enemy lines. They knew the risks, knew the price of failure. But they also knew the importance of their mission, the impact it could have on the war.

As the hours ticked by and the sun began to set, painting the sky in shades of orange and red, Dao and his team made their final preparations. They checked and double-checked their weapons, ensuring that each one was in perfect working order. They went over the plan again and again, committing every detail to memory.

And then, as the last sliver of sunlight disappeared below the horizon and the sky faded to an inky black, they made their move. Silently, they slipped over the side of the ship, lowering themselves into an inflatable raft that bobbed gently in the dark waters.

The journey to shore was tense, the only sound the gentle lapping of waves against the raft's rubber sides. They paddled with muffled strokes, their eyes straining to pierce the gloom, alert for any sign of the enemy.

As they neared the beach, Dao signaled for the team to hold position. He scanned the shoreline with his night vision goggles, looking for any indication of patrols or sentries. But the coast was clear, the only movement the gentle swaying of the palm fronds in the warm, humid breeze.

With a silent nod, he gave the order to move in. The team paddled the final few meters to shore, beaching the raft on the sandy expanse. They moved quickly, efficiently, dragging the raft up past the high-tide line and concealing it beneath a camouflage tarp and covering it with fallen palm fronds.

And then they were off, moving inland with a swift, silent purpose. They kept to the shadows, darting from tree to tree, their footsteps muffled by the soft, loamy soil of the jungle floor.

Dao took point, his senses heightened, his body coiled like a spring. He knew that the enemy could be anywhere, that a single misstep could spell disaster for him and his men.

As Dao and his team crept through the dense jungle, the sound of distant voices suddenly brought them to a halt. Dao held up a closed fist, then signaled for his men to take cover. They melted into the foliage, their bodies still as statues.

Through the gaps between the leaves, Dao could see the shapes of six North Vietnamese soldiers as they made their way along a narrow trail. They were chatting casually, their rifles slung carelessly over their shoulders, clearly not expecting any trouble this deep in their own territory.

Dao listened as the patrol drew closer, their boots crunching on the dry leaves and twigs that littered the forest floor. He could see the glowing tips of cigarettes, the smoke curling lazily in the humid air.

One of the soldiers, a young man with a wiry build and a cocky grin, took a final drag from his cigarette before flicking it carelessly into the underbrush. The smoldering butt landed on the brim of a camouflaged hat mere inches from the face of Tuan, one of Dao's Rangers, who lay hidden behind a rotting log.

Tuan's eyes widened as the cigarette singed the edge of his hat, the acrid smell of burning fabric filling his nostrils. But he remained utterly still, his body rigid with tension, not daring to move a muscle.

Dao watched as the patrol passed by, oblivious to the hidden soldiers that lay just feet from their path. He could see the whites of their eyes, could hear the low murmur of their conversations, and yet they remained undetected, invisible to the enemy. To remain so still, so utterly invisible in the face of the enemy, was no small feat.

As the last of the soldiers passed out of sight, their voices fading into the distance, Dao allowed himself a small sigh of relief. He signaled for his team to move out, to continue their silent trek towards the airfield, but not before catching Tuan's eye and giving him a nod of approval.

The Ranger grinned back, plucking the smoldering cigarette butt from his hat and crushing it beneath his boot.

As they pressed on, the jungle seeming to close in around them, Dao couldn't shake the feeling of unease that had settled in the pit of his stomach. The encounter with the patrol, though uneventful, was a stark reminder of the razor's edge upon which their mission balanced. He pushed those thoughts aside, focusing instead on the task at hand.

The airfield loomed ahead, a sprawling complex of runways and hangars, bristling with the hardware of war. Hidden on the edge of the jungle, Dao signaled for the team to halt, dropping to a crouch as he surveyed the terrain ahead.

The airfield was heavily guarded, the perimeter bristling with watchtowers and patrolling sentries. But Dao had expected this, had planned for it. With a series of hand signals, he directed his men to fan out, to take up positions around the airfield's perimeter. Having reached their target, they would wait until the agreed upon time before sabotaging the runway and trapping the MiGs on the ground. And when that moment came, they would move with the speed and precision of a well-oiled machine.

Dao looked out over the enemy airfield and knew that there was nowhere else he would rather be. This was his fight, his war.

Near Lang Vei, South Vietnam

Beneath the cover of darkness, the two Chinook helicopters emerged from the night sky like silent behemoths, their rotors a muted whisper against the backdrop of the star-studded heavens. The Huey gunship hovered protectively overhead, its watchful presence a reassuring sight for the men aboard the transports.

Inside the lead Chinook, Granier and his team sat in focused silence, their faces illuminated by the dim red glow of the cabin lights. They were a hardened bunch, each man a veteran of countless operations behind enemy lines. Tonight, they were tasked with a mission that could alter the course of the war - a raid on the North Vietnamese armor vehicle staging area.

Scott's steady hand guided the helicopter toward the designated drop point, a small clearing just a few klicks from the target. As they neared the LZ, he spoke into the intercom, his voice cool and controlled. "Two minutes to drop. Masks on."

The men donned their camouflaged masks, their identities concealed beneath layers of greasepaint and cloth. Karen was there, capturing the moment with her camera.

As the Chinooks flared for landing, Granier gave the signal. The men rose as one, their movements fluid and rehearsed. The rear ramp lowered, and they filed out into the inky darkness, their boots sinking into the soft earth of the jungle floor.

Scott watched as the ground team melted into the shadows, their forms swallowed by the dense foliage. He knew the challenges they faced, the dangers that lurked in the enemy-held territory. But he also knew the caliber of the men under Granier's command. If anyone could pull off this mission, it was them.

With the ground team deployed, Scott lifted the Chinook back into the night sky, the Huey falling into formation beside them. They would orbit at a safe distance, ready to provide support or extract the team if needed.

The dense jungle canopy provided cover as they moved towards the armor staging area, their objective clear in their minds - neutralize the anti-aircraft units to pave the way for Coyle and the Spectre's attack.

Granier took point, his senses heightened, scanning the surroundings for any signs of enemy activity. The distant rumble of engines and the clatter of metal from the staging area grew louder as they approached. Each man knew the success of the entire operation hinged on their ability to eliminate the air defenses.

Bien Hoa Air Base, South Vietnam

Inside the Spectre's hangar, Coyle and his crew made their final preparations for the assault on the armored vehicle staging area. The ground crew hustled to load the last pallets of ammunition, their faces glistening with sweat in the dim light. The 20mm Vulcan rounds and 40mm Bofors shells were carefully stacked and secured, each one a promise of destruction to be unleashed upon the enemy.

Coyle had no idea if Dao and Granier's teams would be successful until he was just a few minutes away from the enemy staging area. If Granier failed, then the Spectre and his aircrew would be chewed up by the enemy's extensive anti-aircraft emplacements. And if Dao failed, the Spectre would most likely be shot down by enemy MiG jets for which his aircraft had no defense and was too slow to evade. Both teams had to succeed in their objectives for Coyle and his crew to survive.

As the last pallet was loaded, he gathered the crew around him, his voice cutting through the hum of activity.

"Alright, men. I'll save the pep talk for another mission. We all know what's at stake here. Granier and Dao's teams will clear the way. It'll soon be our turn to deliver the knockout blow. We're flying into the heart of enemy territory, and they're going to throw everything they have at us. Focus on your job, trust your instincts, and watch out for each other up there. We're a team, and we'll succeed or fail together. Let's go win the war."

With a final nod, Coyle dismissed his men to their stations. The engines roared to life, the propellers churning the air as the ground crew disconnected the last of the umbilical cords. Coyle climbed into the cockpit, settling into his seat with a familiar sense of purpose.

As he ran through the pre-flight checklist, his mind was already racing ahead to the mission at hand. The Armored Vehicle Staging Area was a high-value target, and taking it out would deal a harsh blow to the enemy's offensive capabilities.

With a final thumbs up from the ground crew, Coyle eased the throttle forward and guided the Spectre out of the hangar. The aircraft lumbered onto the taxiway, its massive frame dwarfing the other planes scattered about the tarmac.

As they approached the runway, the tower cleared them for takeoff, and Coyle pushed the throttle to full. The Spectre surged forward, its engines roaring as it hurtled down the runway. The wheels lifted off the ground, and suddenly they were airborne, climbing into the night sky like a giant, predatory bird.

Coyle banked the aircraft towards the target area, the dark landscape of Vietnam stretching out below them.

In the darkness of that cockpit, illuminated only by the glow of instruments, Coyle felt a sense of clarity wash over him. This was his mission and his purpose.

As the Spectre roared through the night sky, a lone beacon of American might in a war-torn land, Coyle knew that he and his crew were ready to bear that weight, ready to do whatever it took to secure victory.

Near Lang Vei, South Vietnam

Halting the team at the edge of the treeline, Granier surveyed the armored vehicle staging area through his binoculars. The anti-aircraft units were strategically positioned around the perimeter, their guns pointed skyward, ready to engage any aerial threat. The plan of attack on the anti-aircraft emplacements had already been formulated. They would attack the emplacements in unison so as not to tip off the enemy that an assault was underway until it was too late. The only thing left was execution.

With a series of hand signals, Granier directed his men to split into their four groups, each assigned one of the four enemy guns. Surprise and speed were their allies, and they intended to make full use of both.

As the team moved out, Karen captured the moment with her camera, the soft click of the shutter barely audible above the ambient sounds of the jungle.

Granier led his group forward, their footsteps muffled by the dense undergrowth. As they neared the first anti-aircraft position, he signaled for the team to hold. Two sentries stood guard, their AK-47s held loosely at their sides, cigarettes dangling from their lips. The anti-aircraft emplacement gunner and loaders slept nearby in hammocks tied to trees. Knowing that the ARVN were ensconced within the cities, the NVA troops did not expect any assault from their enemy.

Granier's team would kill both the guards and gun's operators in one swift strike eliminating any warning to the others. Acting as conductor, Granier signaled which team member would kill which enemy soldier. He watched as his men drew their knives and moved into position beside their assigned targets. He studied his watch to ensure that his unit attacked at the same moment as the other units in the team.

Once he was sure that everyone was ready and the timing was right, he wasted no time. He gave the signal and the knives struck in unison, the edge of their blades flashing in the dim light, their enemy's lives snuffed out before they could even register the danger. There were soft thuds as the enemy hit the ground in the muted throes of death. It was over in seconds. Silence reined once again. The enemy was none the wiser.

The team's sapper moved up and placed explosives with timers on the anti-aircraft gun and the ammunition boxes. Again, the destruction of the weapon and ammunition would be timed with the other assault units. Nothing was left to chance. No warning would be given to the enemy. Granier's team withdrew, swiftly, silently.

As the teams regrouped at the predetermined rallying point at the edge of the jungle, Granier checked his watch. They were right on schedule. As the second hand swept to the designated time, the night erupted in a series of coordinated explosions lighting up the sky.

The anti-aircraft positions vanished in balls of flame, the concussive force of the blasts rippling through the staging area. Alarm klaxons blared as the enemy scrambled to respond, but it was too late. The air defenses were out of commission, leaving the armor vulnerable to the impending aerial assault.

Granier and his team melted back into the jungle, their mission accomplished. Now it was up to Coyle and the Spectre to deliver the decisive blow. As they made their way back to the extraction point, the men allowed themselves a moment of satisfaction. They had paved the way for a larger victory.

But even as they savored their success, each man knew that the enemy would regroup, adapt, and strike back with renewed fury. But for now, under the canopy of the jungle, they had given their brothers-in-arms a fighting chance. And that, in itself, was a victory.

Hoa Loc Air Base, North Vietnam

Dao and his team crouched at the edge of the Hoa Loc Air Base, their faces painted and covered with masks. They were hundreds of miles from the armored vehicle staging area where Granier and his men were carrying out their part of the mission, but their role was no less crucial.

The lead sapper, Minh, carefully checked each shaped charge, ensuring they were primed and ready. The explosives were the key to neutralizing the airfield's runway, preventing the MiGs from taking off and engaging the Spectre during its attack on the distant armor staging area.

Dao surveyed the airfield, his mind racing through the plan they had rehearsed countless times. With a series of hand signals, Dao directed his team to take up positions. They moved silently, cutting through the perimeter fence and slipping onto the airfield quickly and quietly. A weapons team set up their light machine gun, prepared to provide covering fire when the inevitable response from the NVA came.

The sappers moved swiftly, placing the shaped charges along the runway in a staggered pattern designed for maximum damage. Minh followed closely, connecting each charge to individual terminals on the detonator, his hands steady, working their magic.

Suddenly, shouts erupted from across the airfield as the NVA soldiers spotted the intruders. Gunfire shattered the night, tracers streaking through the darkness like angry fireflies. Dao and his men returned fire, their weapons thundering in defiance. "Keep placing those charges!" Dao yelled over the cacophony of battle.

The sappers worked frantically, racing against time as bullets whizzed past, kicking up chunks of concrete. The weapons team laid down a withering barrage, keeping the enemy at bay, but Dao knew they couldn't hold out forever.

Just as the last charge was set, an enemy grenade landed mere yards from their position. "Grenade!" Dao shouted, diving for cover. The blast shook the earth, showering them with debris.

Ears ringing, Dao rallied his men. "Charges set! Fall back to the extraction point!"

The team began bounding back towards the breach in the fence, leapfrogging each other and providing covering fire as they went. The NVA pressed hard, their numbers growing with each passing moment, advancing down the runway.

As they reached the perimeter, Minh showed Dao the detonator, primed and ready. "On your command, sir."

Dao took one last look at the runway, the charges they had placed now hidden in the darkness. The NVA were closing in, their shouts and gunfire growing ever louder.

"Blow it," he ordered.

The night erupted in a series of thunderous explosions as Minh pressed the detonator. The shaped charges tore into the runway, ripping apart the concrete with ruthless efficiency. The shock wave nearly knocked them off their feet.

As the smoke cleared, Dao allowed himself a moment of satisfaction. Miles away, the Spectre would now have a clear run at the armored staging area, free from the threat of MiGs scrambling to engage them.

Dao and the team were retreating from the airfield when Minh, the lead sapper, suddenly froze. His eyes widened as he stared at the runway behind them, a look of horror etched on his face.

"One of the charges didn't detonate!" he shouted over the sound of gunfire. "There's a gap in the damage!"

Dao followed Minh's gaze and saw the unbroken stretch of concrete, a glaring flaw in their carefully laid plan. If even one MiG managed to take off, it could spell disaster for the Spectre and the entire mission.

Suddenly, the roar of a jet engine shattered the night. A MiG was taxiing onto the runway, preparing for takeoff. The pilot had seen the opportunity and was seizing it.

Without hesitation, Minh sprinted back towards the runway, his satchel of tools bouncing against his hip. He had to repair the damaged wire and finish the job, no matter the cost.

Dao screamed for him to stop, but his words were lost in the chaos. He watched in horror as Minh raced across the open ground, bullets kicking up dirt at his feet. The young sapper dove for the damaged section of the runway, his hands working furiously to splice the wire.

But it was too late. A burst of enemy fire caught Minh in the chest, and he crumpled to the ground, his life ebbing away on the cold concrete.

The MiG's engines roared to life, and the jet began hurtling down the runway, rapidly gaining speed. In a matter of seconds, it would be airborne, and all their efforts would be for naught.

Dao knew he had only one chance. He unslung his sniper rifle and dropped to one knee, bringing the weapon to his shoulder in a single, fluid motion. The world seemed to slow down as he lined up the shot, his crosshairs settling on the cockpit of the speeding jet, then giving his target a lead that only a master sniper could correctly measure.

He fired once, twice, three times, the recoil slamming into his shoulder with each shot. At this distance and with a moving target, it was an almost impossible shot. But Dao was beyond caring. He would not let Minh's sacrifice be in vain. He would not allow the mission to fail.

For a heart-stopping moment, nothing happened. The MiG continued its relentless charge down the runway, the gap in the damage looming ahead.

Then, as if in slow motion, the jet began to veer off course. It had hit the damaged section of the runway, and the uneven surface wrenched at the landing gear. With a sickening crunch, the gear tore free, and the MiG lurched sideways, careening out of control.

The jet slammed headlong into the runway, a massive fireball erupting from the wreckage. The twisted metal carcass came to rest in the middle of the airstrip, effectively blocking any further takeoffs.

Dao didn't have time to celebrate. The NVA were closing in, their shouts and gunfire growing ever louder. He rallied his team and plunged into the jungle, the darkness swallowing them whole.

As they ran, jumping over giant roots, the adrenaline pumping through their veins, Dao couldn't shake the image of Minh's lifeless body on the runway.

Another ghost to haunt him, another sacrifice in this endless war.

But even in the midst of his grief, Dao knew that Minh's bravery had not been in vain. The runway was destroyed, the MiGs grounded. Miles away, the Spectre would have a clear run at the armored staging area, free from aerial interference.

They had done their part, but the cost had been high. As the sounds of pursuit faded into the night and the distant glow of the burning airfield lit the horizon, Dao knew that this was just one more battle in a war that seemed to have no end.

Near Lang Vei, South Vietnam

The night sky stretched out before Coyle as he guided the Spectre towards the armored vehicle staging area. The cockpit was alive with the glow of instruments and the hum of the engines, a symphony of power and purpose.

Beside him, his co-pilot scanned the horizon, his eyes searching for any sign of enemy activity. The crew were at their stations, each man focused on his task, ready to unleash the Spectre's weapons on the unsuspecting NVA below.

Suddenly, a flicker of light caught Coyle's eye. As they drew closer, the light resolved into a series of flickering flames, the wreckage of the anti-aircraft guns burning like beacons in the darkness.

"Granier's team did it," Coyle said, a slight smile tugging at his lips. "The air defenses are down."

But even as the words left his mouth, the night erupted with the chatter of machine gun fire. Tracers streaked up from the ground, the NVA using the armored vehicles' mounted weapons in a desperate attempt to fend off the approaching gunship.

"Looks like they know we're coming," the co-pilot said.

Coyle's grip tightened on the controls, his eyes narrowing as he lined up the first target in his sights. "Then let's give them a proper welcome. Guns up!"

The crew sprang into action, the weapons systems humming to life. The 40mm Bofors and 20mm Vulcan cannons swiveled into position, their barrels glinting in the dim light of the cockpit.

As the Spectre approached the target area, Coyle's grip tightened on the controls. He knew that the key to their success and survival was to stay out of range of the enemy's machine guns while still being able to rain down devastating fire on the armored vehicles below.

"Initiating pylon turn," Coyle announced over the intercom, his voice steady and focused.

With a deft touch on the controls, he brought the Spectre into a tight, circular pattern, maintaining an altitude of 2,000 feet. This maneuver, known as a pylon turn, would allow the gunship to keep the target area with the gunship's sight while presenting a challenging profile for enemy gunners on the ground.

As the Spectre approached the target area, Coyle's eyes were fixed on the reticle on the side cockpit window. This was his instrument of precision, the tool that would allow him to bring the gunship's fearsome array of weapons to bear on the enemy armor below.

In the back of the aircraft, the gunners and loaders were poised and ready. They knew their roles, knew the importance of keeping the guns fed and operational.

"Targets acquired," the sensor operator called out,

his voice tense with concentration. "Armor concentration confirmed, bearing zero-nine-zero."

"Copy that," Coyle acknowledged. His hand hovered over the weapon selection panel, ready to unleash the Spectre's deadly payload.

As the reticle settled over the first target- a Soviet-made T-54 tank, Coyle depressed the trigger on the steering yoke. The Bofors cannon roared to life, its heavy rounds tearing into the enemy tank with a devastating impact. Explosions blossomed across the vehicle's hull, the armor unable to withstand the punishing onslaught.

Coyle swiftly transitioned to the next target, the reticle dancing across the formation of armored personnel carriers. With a flick of the weapon selector, he brought the Vulcan cannons online, their high-speed buzz saw sound filling the air as they spat out a hail of 20mm rounds.

In the back, the loaders worked feverishly to keep pace with the guns' voracious appetite, their hands a blur as they fed belt after belt into the weapons. The gunners monitored the systems, their eyes scanning for any sign of malfunction, ready to spring into action at a moment's notice.

The Spectre tore through the enemy armor like a scythe through wheat. The night lit up with the glow of burning wreckage, the NVA soldiers scattering in panic as their vehicles were reduced to smoldering husks.

Through it all, Coyle remained focused on the reticle, on the delicate dance of keeping the guns on target while the Spectre roared over the armored vehicle staging area, its guns leaving a trail of destruction in its wake. Tanks and APCs erupted into fireballs as the Bofors and Vulcan cannons found their marks.

As Coyle brought the gunship around for another run, a sudden burst of tracer fire erupted from the jungle below. A well-hidden anti-aircraft gun had found its mark, its heavy rounds slamming into the Spectre's fuselage with a sickening crunch.

Alarms blared in the cockpit as warning lights flashed across the instrument panel. Coyle felt the gunship shudder beneath him, the controls growing sluggish and unresponsive.

"We're hit big time!" the co-pilot shouted, his hands flying across the switches and dials as he tried to assess the damage.

In the back, one of the gunners slumped over his station, blood pooling beneath him. The round had found its way through the armored plating, a one-in-a-million shot that had claimed a life.

Coyle fought to keep the Spectre in the air. The gunship was wounded, but it wasn't dead yet. And he'd be damned if he let that anti-aircraft gun finish the job.

With a herculean effort, Coyle wrenched the Spectre into a tight turn, the airframe groaning under the strain. The co-pilot worked frantically to reroute power and bypass damaged systems.

As they came around, Coyle spotted the telltale muzzle flashes of the anti-aircraft gun, nestled beneath the jungle's double canopy amidst the foliage. He lined up the reticle, his finger hovering over the trigger.

"Guns, standby to engage!" he called out, his voice steady despite the chaos.

The anti-aircraft gun opened up again, its rounds stitching a line of holes across the Spectre's wings. In the back, the loaders and gunners redoubled their efforts, pouring ammunition into the weapons even as the aircraft shuddered and lurched around them.

Coyle squeezed the trigger, and the Bofors cannon roared to life. The heavy rounds slammed into the anti-aircraft gun's position, exploding in a geyser of dirt and shattered trees, killing several in its crew.

But the gun wasn't finished. It returned fire, its rounds ripping into the Spectre's already damaged hull. Warning lights flashed red, and the smell of smoke filled the cockpit.

Coyle didn't let up. He hammered the gun position, walking the Bofors fire across the jungle until the muzzle flashes fell silent and the leaves grew still.

"Cease fire!" he called out. "Damage report!"

The crew's voices crackled over the intercom, a litany of damage and malfunctions. But the Spectre was still flying, still in the fight.

"Ammo check!" Coyle demanded, his mind already racing ahead to the next target.

"Bofors at twenty percent, Vulcans at fifteen percent," came the reply, the loaders' voices strained with exhaustion.

Coyle paused for a moment, weighing his options. They had taken a heavy blow, had lost a man. The smart thing would be to break off, to head for home, lick their wounds, and fight another day.

But the mission wasn't finished. The enemy armor still lay below, shattered but not destroyed. Coyle and the crew still had ammunition and a desire for revenge.

"We finish this," Coyle declared, his voice hard with determination.

The Spectre came around once more, its guns blazing, its crew united in a final, defiant stand. They poured fire into the staging area, the Bofors and Vulcans chewing through their remaining ammunition like ravenous beasts.

As the last shell casing clattered to the deck and the guns fell silent, Coyle looked down upon a field of burning wreckage. The staging area was no more, the enemy's armor reduced to twisted, smoldering ruins.

With a final, sweeping pass over the battlefield, Coyle steered the wounded Spectre around towards home. They had paid a heavy price, but they had done their duty.

As they limped back through the night sky, the rising sun painting the horizon in shades of orange and gold, Coyle allowed himself a moment of grief for their fallen comrade. But even in his sorrow, he felt a fierce pride burning in his chest.

For their brothers, for their country, for the cause of freedom, they would fly and fight and bleed. Until the last round was fired and the last enemy vanquished, the Spectre would haunt the skies of Vietnam, a avenging angel in a war without end.

Bien Hoa Air Base, South Vietnam

The Spectre limped back to base, its battle-scarred fuselage evidence of an operation gone wrong. As the wheels touched down on the runway, Coyle could feel the weight of the mission settling on his shoulders like a physical burden.

The ground crew swarmed around the aircraft, their faces etched with concern as they took in the damage. Bullet holes peppered the wings and fuselage, and the acrid smell of smoke still lingered in the air. The Spectre's aircrew gently lifted the body of their dead gunner, placed it in a body bag, then carried it into the hangar.

Coyle climbed down from the cockpit, his jaw set in a hard line. He strode across the tarmac, his eyes searching for Granier.

He found him in the hangar, huddled over a map with Harmon. Coyle's anger flared at the sight of them, the men whose mistakes had cost him a member of his crew.

"Granier!" Coyle barked, his voice cutting through the din of the hangar like a knife.

Granier looked up. "Coyle? What happened out there?"

Coyle closed the distance between them in a few quick strides, his fists clenched at his sides. "What happened? I'll tell you what happened. We flew into an ambush, that's what happened. A hidden anti-aircraft gun, one that your team missed."

Granier's eyes widened, a flash of realization crossing his face. "Coyle, I... we destroyed everything we could see in the recon photos. Every gun emplacement, every fortified position. If there was another gun out there, we had no way of knowing."

Coyle's anger boiled over, his voice rising to a shout. "No way of knowing? It's your job to know, Granier! It's your job to make sure we have all the information we need, that we're not flying blind into a damned trap!"

Harmon stepped forward, his hands raised in a placating gesture. "Coyle, please. Granier and his team did everything they could with the intel they had. If there was a mistake, if they missed something, that's on me. I take full responsibility."

Coyle rounded on Harmon, his eyes blazing.

"You're damned right it's on you, Harmon. Your intel, your mistake. And now I've got a dead gunner and a shot-up plane to show for it."

The hangar fell silent, the weight of Coyle's words hanging in the air like a palpable thing. Granier and Harmon exchanged a glance, their faces filled with guilt and regret.

Finally, Granier spoke, his voice low and steady. "Coyle, I'm sorry. We let you down out there. But we can't change what happened. All we can do is learn from it, adapt our tactics, and make sure it never happens again."

Coyle stared at Granier for a long moment, his anger still simmering beneath the surface. But he knew, deep down, that Granier was right. They couldn't undo what had been done, couldn't bring back the man they'd lost.

With a final, frustrated sigh, Coyle turned away. "Just make sure it doesn't happen again, Granier. We can't afford any more mistakes, not with what's at stake."

As he stalked out of the hangar, Coyle could feel the weight of the operation pressing down on him once more. They had struck a blow against the enemy, had achieved their objective. But the cost had been high, and the road ahead was uncertain.

In the end, they were all in this together, all fighting for the same cause. They would have to learn from their mistakes, adapt and overcome, if they hoped to see this war through to its bitter end.

A Change of Plan

Hanoi, North Vietnam

In the heart of Hanoi, the imposing stone edifice of the North Vietnamese government headquarters loomed against the gray sky. Inside, in a dimly lit conference room, General Vo Nguyen Giap and Le Duan, the General Secretary of the Communist Party, sat across from each other, their faces showing their frustration.

On the table between them lay scattered reports and photographs, evidence of the latest attacks on their armored vehicle staging area and the Hoa Loc airfield.

Giap leaned forward, "These attacks are becoming more than just a nuisance. The destruction of our armor spearhead and the damage to the airfield will undoubtedly slow our offensive plans."

Le Duan nodded. "Indeed, General. It seems we have underestimated the ARVN's willingness to leave the safety of their cities and strike at our supply lines."

"Not just the ARVN," Giap corrected, tapping a photograph of the burnt-out remains of an anti-aircraft gun. "These are not the tactics of a conventional army. The precision, the audacity... this has the hallmarks of American involvement, likely their CIA operatives."

Le Duan showed a flicker of anger passing across his face. "The Americans... even in retreat, they seek to undermine our cause."

Giap sighed, leaning back in his chair. "Regardless of who is behind these attacks, it is clear that we must adapt our strategy. We have been moving too quickly, too boldly, assuming the ARVN would not dare to challenge us beyond their city walls."

"What do you propose, General?"

"We must reinforce our existing depots and forward bases, harden their defenses against infiltration and sabotage. We cannot allow these phantom warriors to disrupt our plans any further."

Le Duan nodded, his mind already racing with the logistics of such an undertaking. "It will delay our offensive, but it is a necessary step. We cannot hope to crush the South if our own supply lines are in disarray."

Giap was silent for a moment, his gaze distant. Then, slowly, an idea began to take shape in his mind. "Comrade, I believe we may be approaching this problem from the wrong angle."

Le Duan raised an eyebrow, curious. "How so, General?"

"We have been chasing these saboteurs across the country, reacting to their attacks, always one step behind. But what if we could turn the tables, make them come to us?"

Le Duan's eyes glinting with intrigue. "Go on, General."

Giap leaned forward. "We must be patient if we are to defeat the entire group of saboteurs and not just a select few."

"Wise."

"As I see it, the plan would have three phases. The first is to identify one or more of the saboteurs. We do this by creating a trap, a target too tempting for them to resist. A key command center, perhaps, or a vital supply hub. We let it be known that this target is essential to our war effort, that its loss would be a crippling blow. It is also essential that they must not be able to study the target from the air and are forced to perform their recon on the ground. This way we can have our own recon forces take photos of the saboteurs and maybe even follow them to their nest. I suggest we use a dedicated recon unit. The best we have to deal with a worthy opponent."

"A cunning strategy, General."

"Phase two will require us capturing one of the saboteurs and interrogating him. If possible, we will turn him and make him an informant. The key will be finding a weakness and exploiting it mercilessly. Once we have him on our side, we can feed him information to lure their leaders wherever we wish."

"And where might that be?"

"Somewhere we can surround all of them and ensure nobody escapes. Once trapped, we will crush them like the insects that they are."

"And that will end their schemes once and for all."

"Yes. Then we will be free to move our offensive forward without fear of our supply lines and depots being sabotaged."

"We will also send a powerful message to our enemies – the North is not to be trifled with."

"Exactly."

Le Duan stood then offer his hand to Giap who took it. "Then let us begin, General. Let us set the stage for a confrontation that will be remembered for generations. "

As the two men shook hands, a sense of purpose filled the room. The war had entered a new phase, a battle not just of arms but of wits and will.

Bien Hoa Air Base, South Vietnam

In the dimly lit command room, Harmon spread out a series of reconnaissance photos and intelligence reports across the table. Coyle and Granier leaned in, their eyes scanning the documents with practiced intensity.

"I've got a list of potential targets for our next mission," Harmon began. "Supply depots, troop concentrations, forward command posts. But there's one that stands out, one that could really turn the tide in our favor."

Coyle looked up, his interest piqued. "What is it?"

Harmon tapped a grainy aerial photo, his finger resting on a shadowed cave entrance near the border. "SAM missiles. A whole stockpile of them, hidden away in this cave system. If we could take them out, it would be a game-changer for our air support."

Coyle's eyes revealed a glint of excitement in his gaze. "SAMs have been a thorn in our side since day one. Taking out a stockpile that size would free up the South Vietnamese Air Force to really hammer the NVA as they cross the border."

Granier leaned forward, his expression cautious. "How solid is this intel, Harmon? We can't afford to commit resources to a wild goose chase."

Harmon nodded, his face serious. "The source is reliable, someone who's come through for us before. But you're right, we need to confirm the target before we make any moves."

Coyle stood, his hands planted on the table. "Then let's confirm it. We send a recon team, get eyes on the ground. If the SAMs are there, we take them out. Simple as that."

Granier held up a hand, his tone measured. "Not so fast, Coyle. We need to think this through. A cave system like that, it's not going to be an easy target. We need to know what we're walking into before we commit the team."

Harmon cleared his throat, his voice hesitant. "I could go. I've got experience with this kind of terrain, and I know what to look for. My team can be in and out before they even know we're there."

Coyle and Granier exchanged a glance, a silent conversation passing between them. Finally, Granier spoke, his words careful and considered.

"Alright, Harmon. You'll lead the recon. But we do this smart. Minimal exposure, maximum discretion. We get the confirmation we need, and then we plan our next move."

Coyle nodded. "And if the SAMs are there, we hit them hard. We'll show the NVA what happens when they try to ground our birds."

The three men bent over the table, as they planned the details of the recon mission. It was a good opportunity if it panned out.

Borderlands, South Vietnam

The jungle was a green wall, the air heavy with the scent

of rotting vegetation and the chirping of insects. Harmon crouched low, his M16 held at the ready, as he led his small team of recon specialists through the dense undergrowth.

Behind him, Scott's Huey gunship receded into the distance, the thump of its rotors fading into the ambient noise of the jungle. They were on their own now, deep in enemy territory.

The jungle was a living, breathing entity, a tangle of foliage and shadow that seemed to close in around Harmon and his recon team with every step. They moved silently through the undergrowth with a cautious, practiced ease, their senses attuned to the dangers that lurked in the green depths.

Harmon took point, his eyes scanning the jungle ahead for any sign of enemy activity. Behind him, his team followed in a staggered column, their weapons sweeping the flanks, their footsteps barely a whisper on the damp earth.

They had been moving for hours, navigating the treacherous terrain with the aid of a map and compass, avoiding the well-worn trails and clearings that were sure to be watched by enemy patrols. It was slow going, a painstaking process of advance and pause, of reading the subtle signs of the jungle and adapting their route accordingly.

Harmon held up a closed fist, bringing the team to a silent halt. He had spotted something up ahead, a glint of metal in the diffused light filtering through the canopy. He signaled for his team to take cover, then crept forward, his every sense on high alert.

As he drew closer, the shape resolved into a tripwire, a thin strand of metal stretched taut across the narrow game trail they had been following. Harmon's heart raced, his mind immediately jumping to the deadly possibilities: a claymore mine, a grenade bouquet, a punji pit lined with sharpened stakes.

With infinite care, he followed the tripwire to its source, a small, innocuous-looking bundle nestled in the undergrowth. He recognized it immediately as a Soviet-made MON-50 directional mine, a nasty piece of work that would spray the area with hundreds of steel pellets if triggered.

Harmon signaled for his demolitions expert, a wiry sergeant named Nguyen, to come forward. With deft, practiced movements, Nguyen disarmed the mine, carefully removing the detonator and rendering the device harmless.

They were lucky, Harmon knew, to have spotted the trap before it was too late. The NVA were masters at boobytrapping the jungle, of turning the very land itself into a weapon. They would need to be even more vigilant going forward, lest they fall victim to the enemy's deadly ingenuity.

With the mine disarmed, they pressed on, the jungle seeming to grow thicker and more oppressive with every passing meter. The heat was stifling, the humidity a physical weight that seemed to sap the strength from their limbs and fog their minds.

After what seemed an eternity of green hell, they saw it. The cave entrance, a yawning void in a rockface, shadowed and foreboding.

Harmon signaled for the team to halt, his eyes scanning the surrounding jungle for any sign of the enemy. The area seemed clear, but he knew better than to take anything at face value. The NVA were masters of concealment, of blending into the jungle like wild animals.

Where are the guards? he thought. *Strange. I don't like strange.*

With a series of hand signals, he directed his team to take up positions around the cave entrance, their weapons trained on the inky darkness within. He would take the lead, probing the depths with cautious, measured steps, ready for anything.

Harmon stepped into the cool, damp air of the cave, his senses on high alert. The darkness seemed to swallow him whole, the only light coming from the narrow beam of his flashlight. He swept the beam across the rocky walls, searching for any sign of the promised SAM missiles.

But the cave was empty, a yawning void of shadow and silence. No crates, no ammunition boxes, no indication that anything of value had ever been stored here. Harmon's unease grew with each passing moment, a prickling sense of wrongness that he couldn't quite shake.

As he ventured deeper into the cavern, a flicker of movement caught his eye. He jerked his flashlight towards the source, his free hand tightening on the grip of his M16. There, scuttling across the rough stone wall, was a Vietnamese giant centipede, its segmented body glistening in the pale light.

Harmon's breath caught in his throat. He had heard stories of the centipede's venomous bite, of grown men reduced to whimpering agony by the creature's toxic sting. Carefully, he edged around the centipede, giving it a wide berth as he continued his search.

But there was nothing to find, no hidden stockpile of enemy armaments, no secret cache of weapons. Just the empty, echoing darkness and the skittering of insectoid feet on stone.

With a growing sense of frustration, Harmon made his way back to the cave entrance. As he stepped out into the humid air of the jungle, he blinked in the sudden brightness, his eyes struggling to adjust after the gloom of the cavern.

He scanned the surrounding foliage, his senses on high alert. Something wasn't right, some subtle wrongness that he couldn't quite put his finger on. The intel had been too perfect, too convenient. And now, with the cave proving to be a dead end, his suspicions only grew.

Harmon's skin prickled with the sensation of being watched, of unseen eyes observing his every move. He signaled for his team to regroup, his mind racing with the implications of what he had found, or rather, what he hadn't found.

They had been played, led on a wild goose chase into the heart of enemy territory. But to what end? And by whom? Harmon didn't have the answers, but he knew one thing for certain. They had to get out of here, had to report back and regroup.

As the team disappeared into the jungle, a North Vietnamese recon soldier hidden in the foliage snapped a final photo of Harmon looking back at the mouth of the cave. The question of his face clear – Why?

Hanoi, North Vietnam

In a dimly lit room deep within the heart of Hanoi, Colonel Tran stood before General Giap, a folder clutched tightly in his hands.

"Comrade General," Tran began, his voice steady and sure, "our reconnaissance team has made a significant discovery."

Giap leaned forward in his chair, his eyes sharp and probing. "Go on, Colonel."

Tran opened the folder, placing a series of photographs on the table before the General. "The man in these images, the one who entered the cave, has been identified as an American intelligence officer. Alex Harmon, CIA, currently operating out of Saigon."

Giap studied the photographs intently. "Harmon," he mused, the name rolling off his tongue like a curse. "One of their intelligence leaders, no doubt. CIA or rogue? I suppose it doesn't matter."

Tran nodded, a glimmer of excitement in his eyes. "There's more, Comrade General. Our intel has uncovered a critical piece of information. Harmon has a Vietnamese son, a radio operator serving with the ARVN. He's stationed at an outpost in the Mekong Delta."

At this, Giap's eyes flickered with a predatory gleam. "A son," he murmured, his mind racing with the possibilities. "This could be the leverage we need, the key to unraveling the enemy saboteurs from within."

Tran leaned in. "If we can capture the son, we can use him to force Harmon's hand. A father's love is a powerful thing, a weakness that can be exploited."

Giap sat back in his chair, his gaze distant and calculating. "A turned agent would be quite a feat," he mused, the gears of his strategic mind turning. "We could anticipate their every move, strike at them where they are most vulnerable."

A knock at the door interrupted the moment, and Le Duan entered, his face a mask of curiosity and concern. "General Giap, Colonel Tran," he greeted, his eyes scanning the photographs on the table. "I trust you have news of import?"

Giap gestured for Le Duan to take a seat, a smile playing at the corners of his mouth. "Indeed, Comrade Le Duan. Colonel Tran has brought us a gift, a weakness in the armor of our most troublesome foes."

Quickly, Giap outlined the discovery of Harmon's identity and the existence of his son, the pieces falling into place like a child's puzzle.

Le Duan listened intently. "This is the opportunity we have been waiting for," he declared, his voice ringing with conviction. "These saboteurs have been a thorn in our side for too long."

Giap nodded. "I agree. We must move quickly and strike while the iron is hot."

Mekong Delta, South Vietnam

The jungle was a living, breathing entity, a tangle of foliage and shadow that seemed to pulse with a heartbeat of its own. Through this green hell, a column of North Vietnamese Army soldiers moved with a silent, deadly purpose. The mangrove roots sprawling in every direction, threatening to brake ankles made the trek even more dangerous.

At the head of the column, Captain Nguyen Huu An led his men forward, his eyes scanning the dense undergrowth for any sign of the enemy. He was a veteran of countless battles, a true believer in the cause of his people.

Behind him, his soldiers moved in a disciplined line, their AK-47s and RPGs held at the ready, their faces smeared with camouflage paint. They were the best of the best, handpicked for this mission by the high command in Hanoi.

Their objective was simple: to capture the ARVN

outpost at Trung Nghia and secure a foothold in the Mekong Delta. From there, they could launch further attacks, bleeding the South Vietnamese and their American allies dry.

As they moved through the jungle, Captain An's mind drifted to the briefing he had received before the mission. His superiors had stressed the importance of taking the outpost quickly and efficiently, with minimal losses.

But An knew that in war, nothing was ever that simple. The ARVN soldiers at Trung Nghia would fight like cornered rats, defending their position to the last man. And the South Vietnamese Air Force, with its superior firepower, was always a wild card.

Still, An had confidence in his men and in the rightness of their cause. They were fighting for the freedom of their country, for the right to determine their own destiny. No force on earth could stand against the will of the Vietnamese people.

As the sun began to set, casting long shadows across the jungle floor, An called a halt. They were close now, the outpost just a few kilometers ahead. It was time to prepare for the final assault.

The men fanned out, taking up positions around the perimeter of the outpost. An watched as they set up their machine guns and mortars, preparing to rain down a hail of fire on the unsuspecting ARVN soldiers.

He could feel the tension in the air, the anticipation of the battle to come. His men were ready, their weapons primed, their hearts filled with the fire of revolutionary zeal.

An himself carried a special burden, a secret mission entrusted to him by the high command. Somewhere in the outpost was a young ARVN radio operator, a half-

American soldier with valuable intelligence on the enemy's communications network.

An's orders were clear: the radio operator was to be taken alive, at any cost. He was the key to unlocking the secrets of the ARVN's defenses, to striking a blow against the imperialist aggressors and their puppet regime in the South.

As night fell over the Mekong Delta, Private Bui sat outside the communication bunker of the Trung Nghia outpost. With his rifle leaning against the sandbags beside him, he listened for any incoming radio calls as his eyes scanned the darkness beyond the perimeter. The humid air clung to his skin, the stillness broken only by the occasional chirp of insects and the soft murmur of his fellow soldiers.

Bui's thoughts were far from the battlefield, dwelling instead on the letter he had received from his mother that morning. She had written of his father, the American serviceman Alex Harmon, and the love they had shared amidst the chaos of war.

Growing up, Bui had always felt torn between two worlds, his Vietnamese heritage and the American blood that flowed through his veins. His mother had raised him with stories of his father's bravery and loyalty, instilling in him a deep sense of pride and duty.

Now, as he stood watch, Bui felt a renewed sense of purpose. He was there not just as a soldier of the ARVN, but as a son carrying on his father's legacy of service and sacrifice.

Bui's commander had often remarked on his intelligence and resourcefulness, traits that set him apart from his fellow soldiers. He had a quick mind and a natural aptitude for technology, skills that had earned him a position as the outpost's radio operator.

But Bui was more than just a skilled technician. He was a leader, a man who inspired loyalty and respect in those around him. His fellow soldiers looked to him for guidance and reassurance, knowing that he would always put their well-being first.

As he scanned the treeline, Bui's thoughts turned to the future. He dreamed of a day when the war would be over, when he could use his skills and knowledge to help rebuild his country. He imagined himself working alongside his father, bridging the gap between their two cultures and forging a new path forward.

Little did Bui know that his fate was already sealed, that forces beyond his control were conspiring to tear him away from everything he held dear. Across the jungle, Captain Nguyen Huu An and his NVA soldiers were closing in, their sights set on the young radio operator and the secrets he held.

But in that moment, as he stood tall and proud, Private Bui was a soldier like any other, a man doing his duty with honor and courage. He was a son of Vietnam and a son of America, a living embodiment of the complex tapestry that was the Vietnam War.

As the last light of day faded from the sky, An gave the signal to advance. The jungle erupted with the sound of gunfire and explosions as the NVA soldiers stormed forward, their battle cries piercing the night.

As the first shots rang out across the outpost, Private Bui sprang into action. All around him, the night erupted with the chaos of battle. The sharp crack of AK-47s and the deeper thud of machine guns filled the air, punctuated by the shouts and screams of the soldiers on both sides. Without orders from his commanding officer, Bui dove back into the communications bunker, his focus on one thing – get word to headquarters that the Trung Nghia outpost was under attack.

Bursting into the small, cluttered room, Bui grabbed the radio handset and began to transmit. "This is Trung Nghia outpost! We are under heavy attack by NVA forces, requesting immediate support! I repeat, we are under heavy attack!"

As he spoke, Bui could hear the telltale whistle of incoming mortar rounds. The NVA were targeting the outpost's defenses, trying to soften them up before the main assault.

Suddenly, a deafening explosion of a heavy mortar round rocked the radio bunker, sending Bui sprawling to the floor.

Bui hauled himself to his feet and staggered back to the radio. But as he reached for the handset, his heart sank. The antenna had been destroyed, the delicate wires and metal rods shattered by the force of the mortar blast. The radio was useless, the outpost cut off from the the outside world. Bui felt a momentary surge of despair, the weight of their isolation pressing down on him like a physical force.

But he was a soldier, trained to fight and defend. And right now, his comrades needed him more than ever.

Grabbing his M16, Bui raced out of the radio shack and into the maelstrom of battle. All around him, the outpost erupted into chaos. Men leapt from their bunks, grabbing weapons and racing to their positions. The chatter of automatic weapons fire filled the air, tracers streaking through the darkness like deadly fireflies.

Bui could see the enemy soldiers swarming over the outpost's defenses, their faces twisted in fierce battle cries. They were well-armed and well-trained, fighting with a discipline and ferocity that matched anything the ARVN could muster.

But Bui and his comrades would not give in, would not surrender. They fought with the strength of men who knew that everything they held dear was on the line.

Bui charged into the fray, his rifle bucking and roaring in his hands. He could feel the heat of the muzzle flash, the acrid smell of cordite filling his nostrils.

He jumped into his fighting hole and crawled to the edge, aiming his M16's barrel toward the advancing enemy. Beside him, his fellow soldiers fought with equal bravery. They knew the odds were against them, that they were outnumbered and outgunned.

For Bui, the battle was a test of everything he had ever learned, every skill he had ever honed. He fought with the instincts of a born soldier, the courage of a man who knew that his very identity was on the line.

Even as the NVA pressed in, even as the ARVN lines began to crumble, Private Bui fought on. He would not yield, would not surrender, would not let the enemy take him alive.

An himself led the charge, his AK-47 spitting fire, his heart pounding with the thrill of combat. He could see the ARVN soldiers scrambling to respond, their positions crumbling under the ferocity of the assault.

And then, through the smoke and the chaos, he saw

him. The radio operator, a young man with the features of a foreigner, fighting with the desperate courage of a cornered animal.

An felt a surge of exultation. His mission was almost complete, his objective within reach. With a roar of triumph, he led his men forward, determined to capture the radio operator and secure the victory that would bring his country one step closer to liberation.

In that moment, as the battle raged around him and the ARVN soldiers fell before the might of the NVA, Captain Nguyen Huu An knew that he was a part of something greater than himself. He was a soldier of the revolution.

With that knowledge burning in his heart, An pressed forward into the maelstrom of fire and blood, ready to meet his destiny on the battlefield of Trung Nghia.

All around Bui, the battle raged with a terrible intensity. The Viet Cong swarmed over the outpost's defenses, their faces twisted in fierce battle cries. They wore the simple black clothing of the local farmers, indistinguishable from the civilians until their weapons were in hand.

Bui could see the muzzle flashes of the enemy's AKs, could hear the zip and whine of bullets passing perilously close.

Beside him, his comrades fought with a desperate fury, pouring fire into the advancing enemy. But the Viet Cong seemed to absorb the bullets like sponges, shrugging off the hits and pressing forward with a relentless determination.

Bui's rifle bucked and kicked against his shoulder, the hot brass casings spitting from the ejection port.

He fired until his magazine ran dry, then scrambled to reload, his hands shaking with the rush of adrenaline.

A sharp pain lanced through his upper arm, and Bui gasped, nearly dropping his rifle. A Viet Cong round had found its mark, the bullet tearing through flesh and muscle. Hot blood ran down his arm, soaking into his uniform.

Impervious to the pain, Bui switched his weapon to his other hand and kept firing. He would not give in, would not let his comrades down. His father had taught him to be strong, to fight for what he believed in, and Bui would honor that legacy.

The battle raged on, the minutes stretching into an eternity of smoke and fire and blood. The Viet Cong pressed their attack, surging over the outpost's defenses like a tidal wave. Bui saw his friends falling, cut down by the merciless storm of lead.

And then, through the chaos and the carnage, he saw the sappers. Three men, low crawling through the mud and the blood, satchel charges strapped to their backs. They were making their way towards the outpost's command bunker, intent on the head of the serpent.

Bui knew he was the only one who could stop them. His comrades were pinned down, fighting for their lives against the main VC assault. If the sappers reached the command bunker, it would be all over. Leaderless, he had little doubt the ARVN defense would buckle.

With a roar of defiance, Bui leapt from his fighting hole and charged towards the sappers. Pain shot through his wounded arm, but he pushed it aside, his focus narrowing to a single, burning point.

He pulled the trigger on his rifle as he ran, but the gun didn't respond. He was out of ammunition. He reached the first sapper just as the man was rising to his knees, his hand reaching for the detonator on his satchel charge. Bui lashed out with the butt of his rifle, catching the sapper across the temple with a sickening crunch. The man crumpled, his charge falling harmlessly to the ground.

But the other sappers were on him in an instant, their knives flashing in the firelight. Bui felt the hot sting of a blade across his ribs, felt the warm rush of blood soaking his uniform.

He fought like a man possessed, his rifle swinging in deadly arcs, his bayonet stabbing and slashing. He could feel the heat of the flames on his face, could taste the coppery tang of his own blood on his lips.

One of the sappers lunged at him, his knife seeking Bui's heart. Bui twisted aside, but the blade caught him across the chest, drawing a line of fire. He staggered back, his vision blurring, his strength failing.

And then, a blow to the back of his head sent him sprawling to the ground. Bui's rifle flew from his grasp, clattering away into the darkness. He tried to rise, but his body betrayed him, his limbs heavy and unresponsive.

Through the haze of pain and confusion, he saw a figure looming over him - an NVA soldier with an AK-47 leveled at Bui's chest, the barrel smoking. Beside the soldier, an NVA captain – An.

Bui closed his eyes, his thoughts turning to his mother and father. He had tried to make them proud, had fought with everything he had. But in the end, it hadn't been enough.

He waited for the final shot, for the searing heat of

the bullet that would end his life. But it never came. Instead, rough hands seized him, dragging him up and away from the burning outpost.

Bui struggled weakly, but his body was broken, his strength gone. He could feel himself slipping into unconsciousness, the world around him fading to a dull, distant roar.

As the darkness claimed him, Bui saw the faces of his captors, hard and unyielding in the flickering light of the flames. They were the faces of the enemy, the men who had taken everything from him.

But even in that moment of despair, Bui felt a flicker of defiance. He was a soldier of the ARVN, a son of two worlds. And no matter what torments he might face, he would never stop fighting.

For the moment, Trung Nghia and its ARVN outpost were overrun by the enemy. The NVA had a new launching point against Saigon and the ARVN.

In the darkness of the Mekong night, as the smoke of battle drifted on the wind and the cries of the wounded echoed across the rice paddies, a new chapter in the war had begun. The Ghost Warriors, so long the hunters, had become the hunted. And the fate of one young soldier, caught in the crosshairs of a conflict he barely understood, hung in the balance.

Bien Hoa Air Base, South Vietnam

Granier and Coyle sat in the cramped, dimly lit room, the tension palpable in the air between them. On the table before them lay a stack of photographs, the visual record of their covert missions deep behind enemy lines.

Coyle picked up one of the photos, studying it

intently. It showed the smoldering ruins of a North Vietnamese supply depot, the twisted metal and blackened earth demonstrating the destructive power of their raids.

"These are powerful images," he said. "Karen's really captured the essence of what we've been doing out there."

Granier nodded, his eyes fixed on another photograph, this one depicting an enemy jet, its cockpit shattered, and its fuselage riddled with bullet holes. "She's got a gift, that's for sure. These photos tell the story better than any mission report ever could."

There was a long moment of silence, both men lost in their own thoughts. Finally, Coyle spoke, his tone somber. "We're losing men, Granier. Good men. Each mission, it seems like the price gets higher."

Granier sighed, leaning forward. "I know. And it's not just our losses. The NVA, they're getting smarter, adapting to our tactics. Their security is tighter than ever, making our job that much harder."

Coyle's frustration evident in his voice. "We can't keep this up forever. Sooner or later, our luck's going to run out."

Granier was silent for a long moment, the weight of Coyle's words hanging heavy in the air. When he finally spoke, his voice was tinged with determination. "It's time to show our hand."

"…to the ARVN commanders?" said Coyle.

"Yes. We give them the proof they need to see that the tide can be turned, that victory is within their grasp."

Coyle leaned back in his chair. "It's a big risk," he said. "If we reveal our operations, we're putting everything on the line. Our careers, our freedom, maybe even our lives."

"Then we'll have sacrificed everything for nothing," Granier finished. "But it's a risk we have to take. We can't keep fighting in the shadows, not when the enemy is growing stronger every day."

Coyle was silent for a long moment, his eyes distant. Finally, he spoke, his voice filled with a quiet conviction. "You're right. If we don't act, if we don't give the South Vietnamese a reason to fight, then what's the point of any of this? We might as well just pack up and go home. Let's bring in the expert. Let's get Karen in here, have her walk us through what she's captured. If anyone can gauge the power of these images, it's her."

Granier hesitated, then nodded his assent. "Alright. But we do this carefully. We're walking a fine line here, and one misstep could bring it all crashing down around us."

A few minutes later, Karen entered the room, her camera bag slung over her shoulder. She could sense the tension in the air, the weight of the decision that hung over them all.

"You wanted to see me?" she asked.

Coyle gestured to the photographs scattered across the table. "We need your opinion, Karen. Granier and I think it's time to show your photos to the ARVN commanders. We need your professional assessment on which images will have the biggest impact."

Karen stepped closer, her gaze sweeping over the array of photographs. She picked one up, studying it intently. It was a shot of Granier and his team, their faces smeared with camouflage paint, their eyes hard and determined as they prepared for a mission.

"This one's powerful," she said. "They show the

bravery, the sacrifice, the sheer guts it takes to do what you've been doing out there."

She picked up another photo, this one of a burning NVA tank, its crew stumbling away from the wreckage, their faces contorted in pain and fear. "And this one shows the consequences of the enemy's aggression, the price they're paying for their campaign of terror."

Granier leaned forward, his eyes locked on Karen's face. "But will they be enough? Enough to convince the ARVN to leave their fortresses, to take the fight to the enemy?"

Karen was silent for a long moment, her gaze distant. Finally, she spoke, her voice filled with a quiet conviction. "I can't guarantee anything. No one can. But I believe in the power of the truth, in the ability of images to change hearts and minds."

She looked up, her eyes meeting Granier's with an unwavering intensity. "These photographs are the truth of what you've done, of what our soldiers are capable of. If anything can give the South Vietnamese the courage to stand and fight, it's this."

Granier nodded. "Then it's decided. We pick out the best and take them to the commanders, show them what we've been doing, and how they can still take on the north."

Coyle stood, his posture rigid. "And we pray that they have the wisdom to see the opportunity we're giving them, to seize the chance to turn the tide of this war."

As the three of them stood there, surrounded by the evidence of their covert war, they knew that they were taking a step into the unknown. They were risking everything on the power of the truth, on the strength of their convictions.

But they also knew that they had no choice. They had to take this final, desperate gamble.

Saigon, South Vietnam

The room was deathly silent as Coyle and Granier stood before the assembled group of South Vietnamese commanding generals. The air was thick with tension, the only sound the soft rustle of starched uniforms and the occasional clink of medals.

At the head of the table, General Ngo Quang Truong, commander of I Corps, a grizzled veteran of countless battles, leaned forward, his eyes narrowing. "Officer Coyle," he said, his voice low and dangerous, "I was under the impression that this meeting was called by your superior, Mr. Polgar. And yet, he is nowhere to be seen."

Coyle took a deep breath. "You're right, General. Mr. Polgar is not aware of this meeting. We called it ourselves, under false, but necessary pretenses."

The room erupted in a chorus of angry mutters and shocked exclamations. Several of the generals pushed back their chairs, ready to storm out in indignation.

Admiral Tran Van Chon, commander of the Navy, a hawk-faced man with a reputation for ruthlessness, slammed his fist on the table. "This is an outrage!" he snarled, his eyes flashing with fury. "You dare to deceive us, to go behind the backs of your own superiors? Give me one good reason why we shouldn't have you arrested for treason right now!"

Granier stepped forward, his expression calm and unruffled in the face of the commanders' anger. "Because, gentlemen," he said, his voice cutting through the clamor like a knife, "we have something you need to see."

Granier tossed a stack of photographs onto the table. They fanned out across the polished wood, a visual record of the Ghost Warriors' covert missions behind enemy lines.

For a moment, the generals simply stared at the photos, their expressions a mix of curiosity and wariness. Then, slowly, almost hesitantly, General Le Nguyen Khang, commander of the Marine Corps, reached out and picked one up.

It was a shot of a burning NVA supply depot, the flames casting an eerie glow over the twisted metal and shattered concrete. Khang's eyes widened, his breath catching in his throat.

"What is this?" he demanded, his gaze snapping up to meet Granier's. "What have you done?"

Granier's voice was filled with a quiet intensity. "We've been fighting, General. Fighting the enemy on their own turf, hitting them where they're most vulnerable."

He gestured to the photos. "These are the results of our missions. Supply depots and armored vehicle staging areas destroyed, enemy supply ships sabotaged and sunk, key targets eliminated. We've been waging a secret war, a war that the North Vietnamese never saw coming and were ill prepared to stop."

The generals were silent, their gazes locked on the photographs. More picked up photos to study them closer. Some shook their heads in disbelief, others muttered under their breath in a mix of awe and apprehension.

General Truong picked up another photo, this one showing the fuel storage tanks ruptured and burning out of control.

"These images are the result of months of covert operations, carried out by a team of Americans, Vietnamese, and indigenous warriors," said Coyle. "We've been striking at the heart of the enemy, hitting their supply lines, their command centers, their key infrastructure."

General Tran Van Minh, commander of the RNVAF, picked up one of the photos, studying it intently. "And you did all this with, what, a handful of men? A few scraps of intelligence?"

Coyle nodded. "We had to be smart, General. We couldn't match the NVA in numbers or firepower. So, we used what we had - speed, surprise, and audacity. We hit them where they least expected it, and we hit them hard."

"And what do you expect us to do with this information?" he asked, his voice tight with barely contained anger. "Why bring this to us, instead of your own chain of command?"

Granier stepped forward. "Because, General, everyday you give the enemy a pass, they get stronger, they build up their supplies, weapons, and troops. South Vietnamese military needs to take the fight to the enemy, to leave the safety of the cities and strike at the NVA as they cross the border. "

He gestured to the photos, his voice rising with conviction. "These images prove that it can be done, that the enemy is vulnerable."

General Minh leaned back in his chair, his expression unreadable. "And what makes you think we'll agree to this? To risk our forces on the word of a pair of rogue Americans, operating outside the bounds of their own command?"

"Because you have no choice, General. The North Vietnamese grip on this country is tightening like a noose. If you don't act now, if you don't seize this chance to turn the tide, then all will be lost."

He swept his gaze across the room, taking in the faces of the assembled generals. "We're showing you a way to strike back with little risk, to show the world that South Vietnam is still a force to be reckoned with. But you have to be willing to take that chance, to step out of the shadows and into the fight."

For a long, tense moment, the room was silent. The generals exchanged glances, some uncertain, others calculating.

Admiral Chon scoffed. "You speak of turning the tide, American, but what do you know of the pressures we face? President Thieu has made it clear that we are to conserve our resources, to husband our strength for the defense of the cities. We cannot risk everything on a gamble in the wilderness."

Granier's voice took on a hard edge. "And what good will your cities be, Admiral, when the enemy is at the gates? The North Vietnamese will not stop at the borders, they will not be content with the scraps you throw them. They want it all, and they will take it, unless you find the courage to stand and fight."

General Khang shook his head. "You speak of courage, Officer Granier, but what of the courage it takes to follow orders? To put the needs of the nation above our own desires for glory and adventure? We are soldiers, sworn to obey, not to question."

"Then change your president's mind. If you all go to him he will have to listen," said Coyle.

"I am afraid that is not possible. President Thieu

has made his will known and it is up to us to obey," said Khang.

Granier's fist slammed down on the table, the sudden violence of the gesture making the generals flinch. "Damn your orders, and damn your blind obedience! Is this what we have fought for, what we have bled for? To watch you squander our sacrifices, to see you cower behind your walls while the enemy runs rampant? The people of South Vietnam are crying out for leadership, for a sign that their government, their military, has not abandoned them. And yet here you sit, counting your gold and polishing your medals, while the country burns."

General Nguyen Ngọc Loan, commander of the National Police, surged to his feet, his face flushed with anger. "How dare you, American! How dare you lecture us on leadership, on sacrifice! We have given everything for this country, and we will not be dictated to by a pair of foreign interlopers with delusions of grandeur!"

Granier's voice cut through the clamor like a knife. "Delusions? Look around you, General. Look at the fear in your eyes, the desperation in your hearts. You know, deep down, that we are right. That the only path to victory lies in taking the fight to the enemy, in showing them that the will of the South Vietnamese people is unbreakable."

He gestured to the photographs. "We have given you the key, gentlemen. The key to unlocking the true potential of your forces, of your nation. But it is up to you to use it, to find the courage to break free of the chains of fear and inertia that bind you."

For a long, tense moment, the room was silent, the generals exchanging glances filled with uncertainty and doubt. Then, slowly, General Truong spoke, his voice heavy with the weight of his office. "While I appreciate the passion and conviction you have brought to this meeting, I am afraid that our decision must stand. We cannot, in good conscience, divert our forces from the defense of our cities and our heartland. The risks are too great, the stakes too high."

Coyle's expression was one of utter disbelief. "General, I implore you, reconsider. The fate of your nation hangs in the balance. If you do not act now, if you do not seize this chance, then all that your people have fought for, all that they have sacrificed, will be for nothing."

But Truong's gaze was resolute with finality. "I am sorry, but our course is set. We will not be swayed by the words of outsiders, no matter how well-intentioned they may be."

As the generals rose to leave, Granier and Coyle were left alone, the weight of their failure crushing down upon them like a physical force.

Granier's shoulders slumped, his voice filled with a bitter resignation. "Cowards, all of them."

"We tried," said Coyle. "We gave it everything we had. But in the end, it wasn't enough. Their fear, their shortsightedness, it was too much to overcome."

Coyle was silent for a long moment, his gaze distant and haunted. "I just keep thinking about all the lives that will be lost, all the suffering that could have been prevented.

"We had a chance, Coyle. A chance to make a real difference, to change the course of this goddamned war. And we blew it."

"We didn't blow it, Granier. We did everything we could, everything in our power. It's not our fault that they couldn't see the truth, that they were too blind, too stubborn, to seize the opportunity we gave them."

"I just don't know where we go from here."

"We go home. It's over. We played our last card and we lost."

"I don't know if I can do that… go home."

"Yeah. Me neither. It's been so long. This is all I know."

As they left the room, the photographs of their triumphs scattered across the table like the ashes of a dying dream, Coyle and Granier knew that they were facing their darkest hour, a moment of truth from which there could be no turning back.

The Bamboo Pentagon

Bien Hoa Air Base, South Vietnam

The sun hung low in the sky, casting long shadows across the tarmac as Coyle and Granier made their way back to the Spectre hangar. The weight of their failure pressed down upon them like a physical burden, the memory of the generals' dismissal still fresh in their minds.

As they entered the hangar, the sound of power tools and the acrid scent of welding fumes assaulted their senses. The maintenance crews were hard at work, trying to patch up the damage the Spectre had sustained in their last mission.

Karen looked up from her camera, her eyes searching their faces for any sign of hope, of progress. The slump of their shoulders, told her all she needed to know.

"What happened?" she asked, her voice barely audible over the din of the hangar.

Coyle shook his head, his expression bleak. "They wouldn't listen. They're too afraid, too set in their ways. They'd rather hide behind their walls and watch the country burn than take the fight to the enemy."

Granier leaned heavily against the fuselage of the Spectre, his gaze distant. "We gave them everything, Karen. Every scrap of evidence, every ounce of passion we had. But in the end, it wasn't enough. They couldn't see past their own fear, their own shortsightedness."

Around them, the rest of the team had gathered, their faces etched with the same mix of exhaustion and despair. They had put their faith in Coyle and Granier, had believed that their leaders could sway the generals, could bring the full might of the ARVN to bear against the enemy.

But now, seeing the defeat in their eyes, the hopelessness in their posture, they knew that their faith had been misplaced. The Ghost Warriors, once the tip of the spear, now found themselves adrift, their purpose and direction lost in the fog of war.

Coyle surveyed his team, his heart heavy with the weight of their trust, their loyalty. "I'm sorry," he said, his voice thick with emotion. "I wish I had better news, a clearer path forward. But the truth is, I don't know what comes next. We've given everything we have, and it still wasn't enough."

Just then, Harmon burst into the hangar, his face flushed with excitement. "Coyle, Granier, I need to talk to you. Now."

The two men exchanged a glance, then followed Harmon to a quiet corner of the hangar. "What is it, Harmon?" Coyle asked with concern.

Harmon leaned in, his voice low and urgent. "What is the one place that has eluded us the entire war? The biggest prize constantly out of our grasp?"

Coyle and Granier looked at each other, realization dawning in their eyes. "COSVN," they said in unison, their voices hushed.

Harmon nodded, a grin spreading across his face. "That's right. And my team of intelligence operatives, they've done it. They've uncovered the location of the Central Office for South Vietnam, the nerve center of their entire operation in the South."

For a moment, Coyle and Granier were speechless, their minds reeling with the implications of Harmon's words. COSVN had been the holy grail of the war effort, the key to unraveling the enemy's command and control structure.

And now, after years of fruitless searching, after countless lives lost and sacrifices made, it was within their grasp. By destroying COSVN they would destroy heart and mind of the Viet Cong and the NVA in the South. There was little doubt that Hanoi would need to rethink their entire final offensive, delaying it months, maybe even years as they rebuilt their command center in the South.

Granier's eyes gleamed with a newfound intensity. "This is it, Coyle. The opportunity we've been waiting for. If we can take out COSVN, if we can cut the head off the snake, then maybe, just maybe, we can give the ARVN the breathing room it needs to regroup and fight back."

Coyle nodded, his mind already racing with the possibilities, the logistics of mounting such a daring operation. "It won't be easy," he said, his voice filled with a grim determination. "They'll have that place locked down tighter than a drum, and we'll be going in blind, without any support from the brass."

But even as he spoke the words, Coyle could feel the fire reigniting in his belly, the sense of purpose that had driven him through the long years of the war. This was their chance, their moment to make a difference, to strike a blow that would echo through the annals of history.

As the three men huddled around a planning table, A flicker of doubt crossed Granier's face. He turned to Harmon. "Harmon, I know you've always been our go-to man for intelligence, but we can't ignore the fact that the last two missions we've run on your intel have gone sideways. How can we be sure that this location for COSVN is the real deal?"

Harmon met Granier's gaze unflinchingly, his expression one of quiet confidence. "I understand your concerns. The last thing I want is to lead us into another dead end or worse, a trap. But I can assure you, this intel is rock-solid. We've vetted it six ways from Sunday, and I even sent a recon team to scout out the defenses and confirm the location."

Coyle's head snapped up, his eyes widening with a hint of anger. "You sent a recon team? Without consulting us? Dammit, Harmon, we're supposed to be in this together, making these decisions as a unit."

Harmon raised his hands in a placating gesture, his voice calm and even. "I know, Coyle, and I apologize for not bringing you both in on that decision. But you have to understand, after the last two missions, I couldn't afford to take any chances. COSVN is too important, too critical to our success, to leave anything to chance."

He leaned forward, his gaze intense and unwavering. "I take full responsibility for the failures of our previous operations. That's on me, and I own that. But I also know that we can't let those setbacks define us, can't let them shake our resolve or our commitment to the mission at hand."

Granier's expression softened, a glimmer of understanding in his eyes. "You're right, Harmon. We can't afford to second-guess ourselves, not now, not when we're this close to striking a blow that could change everything."

Coyle nodded slowly, the tension in his shoulders easing slightly. "Alright, I get it. You did what you thought was necessary, what you believed was in the best interest of the team and the mission. I can respect that, even if I don't necessarily agree with the way you went about it."

"I know, Coyle, and I appreciate your understanding. From here on out, we make these decisions together, as a team, as brothers-in-arms."

Granier's voice filled with a quiet intensity. "Agreed. We're in this together, until the end. And with this intel, with the location of COSVN finally within our grasp, I believe that end may be closer than we ever could have imagined."

As the initial rush of adrenaline began to fade, Coyle felt a nagging sense of doubt creeping into his mind. He cleared his throat, drawing the attention of Granier and Harmon.

"Listen," he began, his voice hesitant, "I know we're all eager to jump on this and I am too. But we need to think this through, to consider all of our options."

"What are you suggesting, Coyle?" said Granier.

Coyle took a deep breath, steeling himself for the reaction he knew was coming. "COSVN is going to be well protected, and our resources are severely limited. We're only going to get one shot at this thing and we need to make sure we complete the mission successfully. Taking down COSVN, it's a tall order for our small team, even with our skills and experience."

"Okay. I don't disagree."

"I think we should consider bringing this to the South Vietnamese commanders, or at least talk to Polgar at the embassy to get more support and resources. "

Harmon shook his head vehemently, his expression one of disbelief. "No way, Coyle. We can't risk this getting out, can't take the chance that the brass will shut us down or, worse, take credit for our work."

Granier nodded in agreement. "Harmon is right. We've come too far, sacrificed too much, to let this slip through our fingers. If we bring in the commanders, or even Polgar, we lose control of the situation, lose the element of surprise that is our greatest asset."

Coyle's mind raced with the potential consequences of their decision. "But what if we fail? What if we go in there and get ourselves killed, or captured? We've got no backup, no support. It's just us against the entire Viet Cong and NVA command structure."

"That's always been the case, Coyle. From the very beginning, it's been the Ghost Warriors against the world, doing what needs to be done, no matter the odds. And if we fall, if we don't make it back, then at least we'll know that we gave it everything we had, that we didn't shy away from the fight when it mattered most."

Harmon's voice filled with a quiet conviction. "Granier's right, Tom. This is our mission, our moment. We can't let fear or doubt hold us back, not when we're this close to striking a blow that could change everything."

For a long moment, Coyle was silent, the weight of his friends' words sinking into his very bones. They were right, he knew. To bring in outsiders, even allies, was to risk everything they had worked for, everything they had bled for.

Finally, he nodded, his resolve hardening like tempered steel. "Alright," he said, his voice steady and sure. "We do this ourselves, and we don't stop, we don't hesitate, until COSVN is nothing but a smoking ruin and the enemy is running around like a chicken with its head cutoff."

Granier and Harmon grinned. "That's the spirit," Harmon said.

"But what about our own team? Surely, they need to know what we're planning, what we're risking," said Coyle.

Harmon leaned forward, his gaze intense. "Not necessarily. The more people who know, the greater the risk of exposure. We can brief the team on a need-to-know basis, give them just enough information to carry out their roles effectively."

"Harmon's right. We're walking a tightrope here, balancing the need for secrecy with the need for operational efficiency. The three of us, we'll carry the burden of this knowledge, make the hard decisions that need to be made," said Granier. "Now let's get to work, figure out how we're going to make this happen."

Saigon, South Vietnam

The U.S. Embassy in Saigon was a sprawling complex located in the heart of the city. The main embassy building was a modernist structure, its clean lines and stark white facade standing in sharp contrast to the bustling streets and colonial architecture that surround it. The building was designed to project an image of strength and modernity, a physical manifestation of America's commitment to South Vietnam and its determination to fight the spread of Communism in Southeast Asia.

Inside, the embassy was a hive of activity, with diplomats, military personnel, and intelligence operatives working around the clock to provide support to the South Vietnamese government. The halls were lined with offices and conference rooms, each one humming with the constant chatter of typewriters, telephones, and urgent conversations.

At the heart of the embassy was the Ambassador's office, a spacious and well-appointed room that served as the nerve center of American diplomacy in Vietnam. The walls were lined with bookshelves and adorned with portraits of American presidents and Vietnamese leaders, a visual reminder of the long and complex history of the two nations.

Beyond the main building, the embassy compound was a vast and sprawling affair, encompassing several city blocks and ringed by high walls and razor wire. Within its confines were a variety of other structures, including residential quarters for embassy staff, a medical clinic, a commissary, and even a swimming pool and tennis courts for off-duty recreation.

As the war entered its final stages, the embassy took on an even greater significance, becoming a focal point for the desperate efforts to evacuate American personnel and their South Vietnamese allies before the fall of Saigon.

Deep inside the embassy, Thomas Polgar, the CIA

Chief of Station in Saigon, sat behind his desk as he pored over the latest intelligence reports. The situation in Vietnam was growing more precarious by the day, and he could feel the weight of his responsibilities bearing down on him.

A sharp knock at the door jolted him from his thoughts. "Come in," he called out.

The door swung open, revealing the imposing figure of General Tran Van Minh, commander of the RNVAF. The general's face barely contained his anger, his eyes flashing with a mix of frustration and accusation.

"Mr. Polgar," he said, his tone clipped and formal, "we need to talk. It seems that you have a problem with some of your officers."

Polgar's eyebrows shot up, a flicker of surprise crossing his features. "I'm not sure I understand, General. What problem are you referring to?"

Minh strode forward, his hands clenched into fists at his sides. "I'm talking about your men, Coyle and Granier. They had the audacity to call a meeting in your name with myself and the other commanders, trying to convince us to abandon our posts in the cities and take the fight to the North Vietnamese at the border."

Polgar had always known that Coyle and Granier were unconventional, that they often skirted the edges of official protocol. But to go behind his back, to try and influence South Vietnamese military strategy without authorization - that was a line he never thought they would cross.

"General, I can assure you, I had no knowledge of this meeting, or of any attempts by my officers to convince you to change your tactical approach. If what you're saying is true, then they acted entirely without my consent or approval."

"Mr. Polgar, my collogues and I have tolerated a great deal from your agency over the years. We have allowed you to operate with a degree of autonomy, trusting that you had our best interests at heart. But this - this is an unacceptable breach of that trust, a direct challenge to our authority and our ability to prosecute this war as we see fit."

Polgar held up his hands in a placating gesture, his mind racing as he tried to find a way to defuse the situation. "General, I understand your anger, and I share your concerns. I give you my word that I will get to the bottom of this, that I will find out exactly what Coyle and Granier were thinking, and that I will take appropriate action to ensure that nothing like this ever happens again."

"See that you do, Mr. Polgar. Because if you cannot control your own agents, if you cannot keep them in line and prevent them from undermining our efforts, then perhaps it is time for us to reevaluate the nature of our relationship with your agency."

With that, Minh turned on his heel and strode out of the office, leaving Polgar alone with his thoughts and the growing sense of unease that threatened to consume him.

He leaned back in his chair, his mind racing as he tried to make sense of what he had just heard. Coyle and Granier, two of his most trusted agents, going rogue and trying to dictate military strategy to the South Vietnamese commanders. It was a nightmare scenario, one that could have devastating consequences for the CIA's position in the country, and for the war effort as a whole.

Polgar knew that he had to act quickly, had to find

a way to rein in his wayward officers and reassure the South Vietnamese that the CIA was still a reliable and trustworthy partner in the fight against the communist insurgency.

But even as he picked up the phone to begin making calls, to set in motion the wheels of an internal investigation, he could not shake the feeling that this was just the beginning, that the actions of Coyle and Granier were a symptom of a much deeper problem, a sign that the war in Vietnam was slipping further and further out of control.

Bien Hoa Air Base, South Vietnam

Coyle and Granier sat in the hangar waiting for Harmon to arrive to continue planning the new mission to destroy COSVN. The weight of their actions over the past few months and the failure to convince the South Vietnamese generals hung heavy in the air between them. They had always known that their unsanctioned missions could come with a heavy price - but now, with the specter of treason charges looming over them, that price felt more real than ever.

It wasn’t fear of what would happen to them that concerned them. It was the fate of the other team members that troubled them. They had been loyal to Coyle and Granier as the team leaders and done whatever had been asked. It seemed unfair that prison might be their only reward for their fidelity.

Coyle leaned forward. "Polgar's not going to let this slide," he said, his voice low and heavy with resignation. "He can't afford to, not with the South Vietnamese breathing down his neck. He'll come after us with everything he's got."

Granier nodded. "I can't really blame him. He has to maintain discipline of those under his command or he'll lose all credibility. We always knew this was a possibility, that our actions could be seen as a betrayal of our country, of our oath."

"But we also knew that we couldn't sit back and watch as this country tears itself apart, as the people we'd sworn to protect were left to fend for themselves," said Coyle. "And what about the others? The team, my kids?"

"They knew the risks just as we did," said Granier. "They knew these were treasonable offensives."

"I doubt the Montagnard even know what treason is. It was our little crusade. We brought them into this. We need to get them out of it, even if it means we have to throw ourselves on the altar."

"I'm not afraid of the altar. I'd gladly sacrifice my life to save the people of Vietnam. But that's not our decision. It's Polgar's."

"If he catches us."

"What do you mean?"

"To try us, he has to catch us. The others too."

"Do you wanna go to guerrilla and hide in the mountains?"

"No. That's your style, not mine. But I don't want to make it easy for him either. Take the team and go to ground, find a way to finish what we started without getting caught in Polgar's net. We load up everything we can and move."

"To where? We need an airfield."

"The ARVN have abandoned plenty of airfields in the last few months. We find one and occupy it."

"The NVA and VC are sure to attack once they find out we're there. Hell, the ARVN might even attack it.

Those commanders looked pretty pissed off."

"It's a risk we'll have to take. It's better than getting thrown in the slammer."

"What kind of shape is Spectre in? Can it make a journey like that?"

"It'll be rough, but with a few more critical repairs and yeah… it can make it."

"Polgar will never stop hunting us, never give up until he'd brought us to heel."

"Look… our main objective is the assault on COSVN. If we succeed, there is no telling what will happen. It could be good."

"…or bad."

"Always a possibility. But we're only defeated if we stop fighting."

"Well, you know how I feel about fighting."

"Me too. We were born to this. At least we'll know that we did what we believed was right, that we fought for something bigger than ourselves."

"Amen."

"We need to send a recon team to possible airfields right away while we finish up the critical repairs. Scott and his aircrews can start shuttling equipment and ammunition as soon as we find a new home."

"I'll put a recon team together and I'll get Harmon working the aerial photos of the potential airfields."

"Shall we tell the team what we plan on doing and why?"

"Yeah. COSVN is one thing. That's operational security. But I don't like keeping things from the team if we can help it."

"Me neither. Do you think they'll come onboard?"

"It's hard to say until we ask them."

As Coyle and Granier called the team, the roar of

jeep engines interrupted their ad hoc meeting. A squad of CIA officers, heavily armed and clad in dark fatigues, rolled into the Spectre's hangar.

The Ghost Warriors, already on edge and preparing for their next mission, instinctively reached for their weapons.

At the head of the CIA unit was a familiar face - Jack Keller, a seasoned officer who had worked with Coyle and Granier in the past. His eyes scanned the rogue team until they settle on the two leaders. His expression was grim, his eyes filled with a mix of regret and determination as he approached the two men.

"Coyle, Granier..." he said, his voice heavy with the weight of his duty, "I'm sorry, but I have orders from Polgar. You're to come with us, both of you. You're under arrest for treason."

Coyle and Granier exchanged a glance, a silent acknowledgment of the moment they had both known was coming.

"Polgar moves quick," said Granier.

"Yeah. I should have known," said Coyle.

"I'm not getting into a gunfight with our own guys."

"Me neither. They're not the enemy."

"Well?" said Keller.

"Relax, Jack. We're coming," said Granier.

As they stepped forward, their hands raised in surrender, the Ghost Warriors surged to life around them. These were men who had fought and bled alongside Coyle and Granier, who had followed them into the jaws of hell and back again. They were not about to stand by and watch as their leaders were dragged away in handcuffs.

"Hold it right there," growled Scott Dickson. He leveled his M16 at Keller, his finger hovering over the trigger. "You're not taking them anywhere."

Keller's men fanned out, their own weapons at the ready. "Stand down, Officer Dickson," Keller barked, his hand resting on the butt of his sidearm. "This doesn't concern you. We have our orders."

But Scott was not alone. All around him, the Ghost Warriors were taking up positions, their faces etched with grim determination. Karen raised her camera, ready to document whatever was about to happen, especially who fired first.

"Orders be damned," Scott spat. "Coyle and Granier are with us. They're family. And we don't abandon family."

Keller's gaze swept the hangar, taking in the hardened faces and unwavering stances of the Ghost Warriors. He had seen their kind before - men and women who had been forged in the crucible of war, who had learned to trust and rely on each other above all else. He didn't relish the idea of a fire fight with these veterans.

And then, with a whirring sound that sent a chill down his spine, he saw it - the minigun mounted inside of the Spectre, its barrels spinning up to speed as a gunner operating it manually swung it around to point directly at him and his men.

Keller knew the devastating power of that weapon, had seen the carnage it could unleash in the blink of an eye. He also surmised that the Ghost Warriors would not hesitate to use it, not if it meant protecting their own.

For a long, tense moment, the two sides stared each other down with the tension of a standoff that could erupt into violence at any second. Coyle and Granier stood in the middle, their hearts swelling with a fierce pride even as they prepared themselves for the worst.

But then, slowly, almost reluctantly, Keller raised his hand, signaling his men to lower their weapons. "Stand down," he said, his voice tight with frustration and undisguised anger. "We're pulling out."

As the CIA unit began to back away, their eyes never leaving the bristling guns of the Ghost Warriors, Keller turned to Coyle and Granier, his expression a mix of disappointment and grudging respect. "Polgar won't let this slide. He'll come for you, with everything he's got and then some. And when he does, even your loyal band of misfits won't be able to save you."

Granier stepped forward, his chin lifted in defiance. "So be it," he said, his words ringing with the conviction of a man who had already accepted his fate. "We'll be waiting."

Keller shook his head, a sad smile playing at the corners of his mouth. "I hope you guys know what you're doing. For all our sakes."

And with that, he turned and led his men out of the hangar, the sound of their jeep engines fading into the distance as the Ghost Warriors watched them go.

"Well, that was exciting," said Karen.

In the sudden stillness that followed, Coyle turned to his team. "I don't know what to say," he began, his voice thick with emotion. "What you just did..."

But Scott cut him off, his hand coming to rest on his father's shoulder. "You don't have to say anything, Dad. We know what's at stake. And we know where we stand - with you, and with Granier, until the end."

"Keller is right. They'll be back. And next time, I doubt they'll back down," said Granier.

"Load everything you can into the Spectre and the Chinooks," said Coyle. "It's time to go."

"We need forty to fifty minutes to button up the Spectre," said the lead maintenance officer.

"You got until the aircraft is loaded and not a minute more."

The officer nodded and went back to work. The team began loading the aircraft.

"Any idea where we're going?" said Scott.

"For the moment… Da Nang," said Coyle. "From now on, we've gotta keep moving, one step ahead of Polgar."

"Roger that," said Scott and moved off to help the others.

Da Nang Airbase, South Vietnam

The Spectre lumbered through the sky, its engines straining as it approached the sprawling expanse of Da Nang Air Base. The bullet holes and scorch marks that marred its fuselage were evidence of the fierce battles it had endured, a reminder of the sacrifices made by the men who called it their home.

Beside the gunship, a pair of Chinook helicopters flanked its sides, their rotors beating a steady rhythm against the wind. These were the birds of the Ghost Warriors, the faithful steeds that had carried them into the heart of the enemy's territory time and time again.

As the small fleet began its descent, Coyle felt a knot of unease tightening in his gut. He glanced over at Granier, seeing the same flicker of doubt in his eyes. They had defied orders, had stood against the very organization they had sworn to serve. And now, as they prepared to touch down on South Vietnamese soil, they couldn't help but wonder if their actions had already been reported, if they were walking into a trap of their own making.

Granier scanned the airfield below, searching for any sign of trouble. "We need to be careful," he said over the intercom. "If the commander here has gotten word from Saigon, we could be in for a rough reception."

Coyle nodded, his mind racing as he tried to formulate a plan. "We'll play it cool," he said, his tone a forced calm. "We're just here for repairs, to get the Spectre patched up before we head back to base. That type of thing happens all the time. No need to raise any suspicions."

As the gunship and its escort touched down on the tarmac, the Ghost Warriors inside tensed, their hands instinctively reaching for their weapons. They had become a unit forged in the fires of war who trusted each other with their lives. But now, in the face of an uncertain future, that trust was about to be put to the ultimate test.

The South Vietnamese soldiers milled around the airstrip, watching with guarded eyes as the American aircraft rolled to a stop. Coyle could sense their unease, the flicker of doubt and suspicion that played across their faces.

He turned to Karen. "Stick close," he said. "Keep your head down and your camera at the ready. We may need a record of what happens here."

Karen nodded, her hand tightening on the strap of her camera bag. She had seen the horrors of war through her lens, had captured the moments of triumph and tragedy that defined this conflict. And now, as she stepped out onto the tarmac alongside her father and her brother.

Coyle and Granier led the way as they approached

the South Vietnamese commanding officer. The man was a hardened veteran, his eyes sharp and calculating as he watched the Americans draw near.

"Colonel," Coyle said. "I apologize for the unannounced arrival. We had a bit of a rough mission up North, and the Spectre here is in need of some repairs before we can head back to Saigon."

The colonel's gaze flickered over the bullet-riddled fuselage, taking in the scorch marks and shattered windows. For a moment, Coyle thought he saw a flash of suspicion in the man's eyes, a hint of the knowledge that had surely already reached him from the capital.

But then, with a curt nod, the colonel waved them forward. "See to your repairs quickly," he said, his voice tight with barely concealed tension. "We do not have the luxury of time here. There is a major offensive brewing, and we must be ready to meet it."

Coyle nodded, then motioned his copilot in the Spectre's cockpit towards the waiting maintenance hangars. They had bought themselves a reprieve, however temporary, but their time was running out.

Somewhere out there, in the halls of power in Saigon and Washington, the wheels of retribution were already turning. Polgar and his allies would stop at nothing to bring them to heel, to make an example of the rogue operatives who had dared to defy the chain of command.

And so, with, they set to work on the Spectre, their hands moving with a fierce urgency as they raced against the clock and the forces that sought to bring them down.

"We need Harmon and his aerial photographs to identify a new base of operation," said Coyle.

"I'll try to get word to him, but it's not going to be

easy without tipping our hand to Polgar," said Granier.

"What the base's intelligence unit? Could we get the aerial photos from them?"

"Maybe. I'll give it shot."

"Make it good shot. We need a new home and fast."

"Yeah. I get it," said Granier as he moved off.

A few hours later…

Granier strode into the hangar as he clutched a folder filled with aerial photographs and hastily scribbled notes. The rest of the team was gathered around the Spectre, making what repairs they could with the limited resources at their disposal.

Coyle looked up from the engine he was working on, his eyes narrowing as he caught sight of the folder in Granier's hand. "What've you got there?" he asked, wiping his grease-stained hands on a rag.

"Our ticket out of here," he said with a small smile. "I just came from the intelligence unit. Managed to sweet-talk the captain in charge into giving me a list of abandoned airfields in the region, along with some recon photos of the most promising candidates."

Coyle's eyebrows shot up, a flicker of hope kindling in his eyes. "Let's see 'em."

Granier nodded, spreading the photos out on a nearby workbench.

The rest of the team gathered around, their faces etched with a mix of curiosity and concern. Karen leaned in, her gaze sharp and appraising as she studied the grainy images.

"These are pretty remote," she said, her finger tracing the outline of a runway overgrown with jungle vegetation. "Some of them look like they haven't been used in years."

"That's the point," said Granier. "We need a place where we can disappear, where we can operate without interference."

He turned to Coyle, "Sooner or later, word will get back to Saigon about what happened with Keller and his men. And when it does, the colonel here will have no choice but to either lock us up or hand us over to Polgar."

Coyle nodded, his expression grim. "Yep. We need to move, and fast. But we need to cover our tracks, so Polgar doesn't find us."

"Yeah, and we also need to recon the airfields to make sure we're not falling into a trap. I'll handle the recon with Scott and his aircrew. You need to wrap up repairs to the Spectre."

"I'm gonna need another day for that."

"I need a night and day for recon."

"So, we hope our luck holds out and we plan to leave at sunset tomorrow."

"Alright. Everyone keep their weapons close. This could get hairy."

Granier rounded up a four-man recon team while Scott refueled his Huey gunship. Within the hour they took off and disappeared over the nearby hills.

Abandoned Airfield – South Vietnam

The Huey skimmed low over the dense jungle canopy, its rotors kicking up a swirling maelstrom of leaves and debris as it searched for a suitable landing site. In the chopper's belly, Granier and his four-man recon team sat in tense silence, their faces smeared with camouflage paint and their weapons held at the ready.

It was a daylight drop and that was always more risky for everyone.

At the controls, Scott Dickson guided the aircraft with a sure hand, his eyes scanning the terrain below for any sign of danger.

A break in the foliage caught Granier's eye, and he tapped Scott on the shoulder. "There!" he shouted over the roar of the engine. "That clearing up ahead. Put us down there."

Scott nodded, bringing the Huey around in a tight arc as he prepared to land. The clearing was small, barely wide enough to accommodate the chopper's blades, but it would have to do.

As the Huey touched down, Granier and his team leapt from the doors, their boots sinking into the soft earth as they fanned out in a defensive perimeter. The jungle pressed in on all sides, a wall of green that seemed to swallow them whole.

Granier signaled for the team to move out, and they set off into the undergrowth, their senses heightened and their weapons at the ready. They had studied the aerial photos of the abandoned airfield closely, committing every detail to memory, but there was no substitute for seeing it with their own eyes.

As they pushed deeper into the jungle, the vegetation grew thicker and more tangled, the vines and creepers wrapping around their legs like grasping fingers. But Granier and his men were undeterred, their machetes flashing in the dappled sunlight as they hacked their way forward.

After what felt like an eternity, they finally broke through the treeline and found themselves standing at the edge of the old runway. The concrete was cracked and overgrown, the tarmac nearly lost beneath a sea of green.

Granier felt a surge of excitement as he surveyed the scene. This was exactly what they had been hoping for - a place that was remote, isolated, and utterly invisible to the prying eyes of the outside world.

He signaled for the team to spread out, And check the hangar and maintenance buildings. Satisfied they were alone they set to work clearing the runway of the worst of the vegetation. It was tough, sweaty work, but they attacked it with purpose, knowing that every vine and creeper they removed brought them one step closer to their goal.

As they worked, Granier and one of his men broke off to explore the nearby maintenance hangar. The structure was dilapidated and sagging, its metal walls rusted and its windows shattered, but it was still standing and would be of use.

Inside, they found a treasure trove of abandoned equipment and spare parts - old generators, fuel drums, and even a few decrepit jeeps that looked like they might still be salvageable. With a little ingenuity and a lot of hard work, they might just be able to turn this forgotten corner of the jungle into a functioning base of operations.

After several hours of backbreaking labor, the team regrouped at the edge of the runway. They were exhausted and drenched in sweat. They had accomplished their mission, had found a place where they could regroup and plan their next move.

Granier looked around at his men. "Good work, boys," he said, his voice hoarse with fatigue. "This is just the beginning, but it's a damned good start."

With that, Granier radioed Scott to pick them up at the airfield. As the Huey lifted off into the gathering dusk, the abandoned airfield receded beneath them like a half-forgotten dream.

As the Huey banked towards Da Nang, Granier felt relieved. They had found their sanctuary, their refuge from the gathering storm.

Da Nang Airbase, South Vietnam

Granier and his recon team could feel the adrenaline pumping through their veins as the Huey touched down on the tarmac at Da Nang. They had found the perfect location for their new base of operations, and now all that remained was to regroup with the rest of the Ghost Warriors and plan their next move.

But as they leapt from the chopper and raced towards the waiting aircraft, they could sense that something was wrong. The rest of the team was moving with a frantic urgency as they hustled to load up the Chinooks and the Spectre.

Coyle caught sight of Granier and waved him over, his expression grim. "We've got trouble," he said, his voice tense. "Our lookout just spotted a team of CIA entering the airfield, and they've got a company of South Vietnamese Marines with them. We're outnumbered and outgunned."

Granier's mind raced as he tried to process the news. They had come so far, had risked so much to get to this point. They couldn't let it all be for nothing.

"Dao, grab your rifle and follow me," he said unshouldering his own sniper rifle. "Coyle, get everything in the air. We'll catch up."

Coyle knew what Granier and Dao were going to do without saying it – buy time.

As the rest of the team scrambled to finish loading

the aircraft, Granier and Dao sprinted towards the edge of the tarmac, their sniper rifles held at the ready. They could see the CIA team approaching in the distance, their unmarked sedans kicking up clouds of dust as they raced towards the airfield. The ARVN Marines followed close behind.

Granier and Dao dropped to the ground, their rifles already finding their targets. With a burst of superhuman speed and precision, they began to pick off the tires of the approaching vehicles, sending them careening out of control and forcing them to stop, their occupants taking cover behind them.

Behind them, the Spectre's engines roared to life, the massive gunship lumbering down the runway like a wounded beast. The Chinooks followed close behind, their rotors churning the air as they strained to lift off.

But the CIA team was not so easily deterred. Even as their vehicles were useless, they pushed forward on foot, their weapons spitting fire as they tried to close the distance to their prey.

Granier and Dao kept up their relentless barrage, their rifles cracking with each shot as they worked to take out more vehicles. They did not shoot at the CIA officers or the Marines. But they knew they couldn't hold out forever just shooting the vehicles' tires. Sooner or later, the CIA team and the Marines would flank them, would overwhelm them with sheer numbers and firepower.

Just as all seemed lost, a familiar sound filled the air - the whipping thrum of rotor blades, the roar of an engine pushed to its limits. Granier looked up to see Scott's Huey screaming towards them, its door gunners laying down a withering hail of suppressive fire, churning up the tarmac in front of the CIA officers and

Marines, keeping them back.

Granier and Dao leapt to their feet and sprinted towards the waiting chopper. They could hear the crack of bullets whistling past their ears as the CIA team tried desperately to bring them down.

But they were too fast, too determined. With a flying leap, they hurled themselves into the open doors of the Huey, their rifles clattering to the deck as they scrambled to safety.

As the chopper lifted off, the Spectre and the Chinooks in close formation, Granier and Dao allowed himself a moment to catch their breath, to savor the rush of adrenaline that still coursed through their veins.

But even as the elation of the moment washed over him, Granier knew that the CIA and the South Vietnamese authorities would not rest until they had brought the Ghost Warriors to heel, until they had crushed the rebellion that threatened to unravel the very fabric of the war effort.

And so, as the small fleet of aircraft banked towards the distant horizon, the sun sinking low over the war-torn landscape of Vietnam, Granier steeled himself for the battles yet to come.

Hidden Airfield, South Vietnam

The sound of an approaching helicopter filled the air as Coyle and the rest of the Ghost Warriors looked up from their work. They had been busy transforming the abandoned airfield into a functional base of operations, and the sudden arrival of a visitor put them all on high alert. They relaxed and went back to work once they saw that it was Scott's gunship approaching.

As the chopper touched down, kicking up a swirling

cloud of dust and debris, Coyle squinted against the glare of the sun, trying to make out the identity of their guest. But when the door slid open and the familiar figure of Harmon stepped out, Coyle felt a surge of relief wash over him.

Harmon strode towards the waiting team as he clutched a battered leather satchel to his chest. Coyle stepped forward to greet him, his curiosity piqued by the intelligence officer's unexpected appearance.

"Harmon," Coyle called out. "Where in the hell have you been? We thought you may have jumped ship."

"Me? Never," said Harmon. "I've been confirming details about our next target. Then, when I returned to Bien Hoa, I saw that you guys had bugged out."

"Yeah. Things got a little heated."

"Well, this place seems a lot safer."

"Unless the NVA attack. Then we're screwed."

"All the more reason to get on with the next mission. Where's Granier?"

"In the jungle, making sure nobody sneaks up on us. He should be back soon."

"Good. I've got a lot to show you."

"Grab yourself some chow. I'll let you know when he gets back."

"Good. I haven't eaten since yesterday."

"I can't promise the quality of the food, but it'll fill you up."

"…and the coffee?"

"Coffee's good. Vietnamese with sweet condensed milk."

"First class."

"There are just certain sacrifices we are just

unwilling to make and good coffee is one of them."

Harmon laughed as he moved off to the makeshift grub tent.

An hour later, Granier and Dao emerged from the jungle with their sniper rifles in hand. "You find anything?" said Coyle.

"No. We're good for the moment," said Granier. "There's a VC patrol moving South, but they seemed uninterested in the airfield. We'll keep an eye on them anyway."

"Harmon's back."

"Bought time. Where'd he say he's been?"

"Confirming details on the next target."

"And?"

"He's got some stuff he wants us to look at."

"Let's see it."

"Don't you want to grab some chow first?"

"I'll eat later."

"Suit yourself. I'll get him."

Coyle, Granier, and Harmon gathered in a small office in a corner of the hangar. Several windows were broken forcing them to keep their voices down so the guys working on repairing the Spectre couldn't hear them. Maps and aerial photos are spread out on a desk rotted by termites, an empty gallon of paint taking the place of a missing leg.

Harmon shook his head, "It's not at the Memot Plantation, like everyone thinks. That's just a decoy, a red herring to throw us off the scent. No, the real COSVN is to the southeast, at a small plantation that nobody's even heard of."

Coyle's mind was racing, the implications of Harmon's revelation sinking in. "How do you know this, Harmon? How can we be sure?"

Harmon's expression turned serious. "My operatives, Coyle. The ones I've spent years cultivating, the ones who have risked everything to bring us the truth. They've confirmed it, beyond a shadow of a doubt."

Coyle nodded, "If you are absolutely sure of your intel, then we need to act on this, and fast."

Harmon pulled out another set of aerial photographs from his satchel, spreading them across the table. Coyle and Granier's eyes scanned the grainy black and white images with intense focus.

"This is the place," Harmon said, his finger tapping a small, nondescript plantation nestled in a sea of dense jungle. "Tan Lap Plantation, about forty kilometers southeast of the Memot Plantation. That's where COSVN is hiding."

Granier leaned in closer as he studied the photograph. "It doesn't look like much."

Harmon nodded, "That's the point. They've chosen this location precisely because it's so unassuming, so easily overlooked. But my sources are rock solid. This is the nerve center of the communist command structure in the South."

"What kind of defenses are we looking at?"

“Fewer than you would think. Mostly well-camouflaged anti-aircraft emplacements. Their main ground defense is a battalion of armor vehicles. They keep everything mobile, so if they are discovered and need move, they can do it quickly.”

“Makes sense. It's why it has been so hard to find them. No infrastructure,” said Granier.

“They keep the workers on the plantation to keep up appearances. My guess is they also act as a reserve guard if there is an attack. They're using the plantation's warehouse as their headquarters and there is a long-range radio antenna next to one of the outbuildings."

"A communication bunker," said Coyle.

"That's my thinking," said Harmon placed a hand drawn map of the compound on the desk. "All their defensive trenches and machine gun emplacements are well-camouflaged. We can't see much from the aerial photos, but they are there. My recon team drew a layout of the defensive positions. Even without concrete bunkers, it's not going to be an easy nut to crack."

"What about approach routes? Any way we can get close without being spotted?" said Granier.

Harmon traced his finger along a winding river that snaked through the jungle near the plantation. "This waterway here, it runs right up to the edge of the compound. If we can infiltrate along the river, use it to mask our approach, we might be able to get the jump on them."

Coyle nodded, his mind already racing with possibilities. "It's a good start. But we're going to need more than just a way in. We need to know exactly what we're up against, what kind of force they have garrisoned there."

"Way ahead of you, Coyle. My operatives have been watching the place for weeks, gathering intel on troop movements, supply shipments, everything. I've got a pretty good idea of what we're facing."

He pulled out a sheaf of notes and handed them to Coyle. "Take a look. It's not going to be a cakewalk, but if we plan this right, if we hit them hard and fast, we might just have a shot at taking COSVN out of the game for good."

As Coyle and Granier pored over Harmon's intelligence, they knew that they were on the cusp of something big. They also knew that the risks were enormous, that they would be going up against the very heart of the enemy's power structure.

But they would not rest until COSVN was a smoking ruin and the enemy was thrown back. Without COSVN the North's offensive would be a shambles. The leaders in Hanoi would have few options but to delay the offensive a year or more while they reorganized their leadership in the South. And that was exactly what the South needed – breathing room.

A True Son

Tan Lap Plantation, South Vietnam

The Tan Lap Plantation sat nestled in a sea of dense jungle, its neatly ordered rows of rubber trees standing in stark contrast to the wild, untamed foliage that surrounded it. Located just twenty-one kilometers from the Cambodian border, the plantation had an air of isolation about it, a sense of being cut off from the rest of the world.

But for all its seeming tranquility, the plantation was anything but peaceful. Beneath the canopy of leaves and the façade of normalcy, a deadly secret lurked - the Central Office for South Vietnam, the nerve center of the communist insurgency.

The compound was heavily fortified, its perimeter guarded by a series of well-camouflaged trenches and machine gun nests manned by battle-hardened North Vietnamese regulars. Anti-aircraft emplacements were strategically positioned to provide overlapping fields of fire, their crews ever-vigilant for the telltale signs of an impending attack.

Patrols of soldiers moved through the plantation with a wary alertness, their eyes scanning the treeline for any hint of danger. They were the best the NVA has to offer, handpicked for their loyalty and their skill, and they knew that the fate of the revolution rested on their shoulders.

The plantation itself was a hive of activity, with supply trucks and troop transports constantly coming and going. The buildings that dotted the compound - the processing plant, the storage sheds, the barracks - all hummed with a sense of purpose, a feeling that something momentous was afoot as the North prepared for what it hoped would be its final offensive.

And yet, for all the signs of life and activity within the compound, there was an air of unease that hung over the place like a shroud. The soldiers who guarded COSVN knew that they were at the very heart of the storm, that they were the last line of defense against the forces that sought to destroy them.

They had heard the rumors, the whispers of a group of elite fighters who struck like ghosts in the night, leaving chaos and destruction in their wake. They knew that these phantom warriors were out there somewhere, plotting and planning, waiting for the perfect moment to strike. The North's hope lied in secrecy. After all these years of war, the ARVN, even with the American's help, had been unable to locate COSVN. But just because it hadn't happened yet, didn't mean it couldn't happen.

And so, the soldiers of COSVN remained ever-vigilant, their weapons always at the ready, their senses honed to a razor's edge. They knew that they could not afford to let their guard down, not even for a moment, lest the enemy slip through their defenses and strike a fatal blow.

Far beyond the perimeter of the plantation, the dense jungle stretched out in all directions, a vast expanse of green that seemed to swallow up the horizon. It was a world unto itself, a labyrinth of tangled foliage and winding waterways that could confuse and disorient even the most experienced navigator.

But for the Ghost Warriors, the jungle was a second home, a place where they moved with a preternatural grace and agility. They had spent weeks studying the terrain, mapping out every stream and gully, every game trail and natural chokepoint.

And now, as they made their final preparations for the assault on COSVN, they felt a sense of calm descend over them, a quiet confidence that came from the knowledge that they had left nothing to chance. They knew every inch of the ground they would be fighting on, every twist and turn of the river that would carry them to their target.

Hidden Airfield, South Vietnam

As the sun began to dip below the horizon, painting the sky in hues of orange and red, the sound of rotor blades filled the air. The two Chinook transport helicopters lifted off from the Ghost Warriors' base, their engines straining as they clawed for altitude.

Beside them, the Huey gunship rose like an guardian angel, its sleek form bristling with weapons. At the controls, Scott Dickson guided the aircraft into formation, his eyes scanning the jungle below for any sign of trouble.

In the lead Chinook, Granier and his team sat in tense silence, their minds focused on the mission ahead. The entire Ghost Warrior team participated in the operation against COSVN. It was a heavy commitment that demonstrated the gravity of the mission. Even the Spectre's maintenance crew had pick arms and joined their comrades in the assault. There were no reserves.

Beside Granier, Karen with her camera cradled in her lap. She had insisted on going knowing the historic importance of the assault on COSVN. These photographs wouldn't be for the generals in Saigon. They would be hers to share with the world. They would document the brave renegades of the Ghost Warriors in their desperate battle to slow the coming wave of the North Vietnamese offensive.

Beneath the helicopters, suspended in the underbelly slings, were the rafts that would carry the team up the river to their objective. The plan was daring, risky, but it was the only way to approach the Tan Lap Plantation undetected.

At the team's base, Coyle and his aircrew sat in the repaired Spectre at the end of the runway, waiting for Granier's signal. Even with the sun setting, it was deathly hot inside the aircraft as evidenced by the sweat dripping down Coyle's face in rivulets. He knew that timing would be everything. They would have to strike hard and fast once the anti-aircraft emplacements were taken out. He and his aircrew would be ready even if they were roasting like Thanksgiving turkeys in the sheet metal oven called "Spectre."

As the helicopters banked towards the northwest, hugging the contours of the terrain to avoid detection,

Granier reviewed the plan one last time with his team. They would be inserting a few kilometers from the Tan Lap Plantation, using the cover of darkness to make their approach by river.

The Huey would provide overwatch at the landing site, its fearsome array of weapons ready to rain down hell on any enemy forces that dared to challenge them. Scott would be their eyes in the sky, keeping watch for any sign of trouble and directing the fire of his door gunners as needed when the team landed.

It was the ground team's assignment to take out the air defenses allowing Spectre to make its air assault on the armored vehicles and trenches. Once the enemy's defenses were defeated, Granier and his team would hunt down the NVA and VC leaders inside COSVN. Undermanned, there were no plans to take prisoners. No quarter would be given the enemy and none was expected in return. It would be a bloody battle.

Tan Lap Plantation, South Vietnam

The sun had set as the landing zone came into view, a small clearing next to a river snaking its way through the jungle. Scott brought the Huey in low, the downdraft from its rotors whipping the foliage into a frenzy. The Chinooks followed suit, flaring as they hovered over the river. Tossing thick ropes through the open doorway, two team members rappelled into the river. With a loud clank, the rafts were released from their slings, dropping into the shallow water below. The two men in the water quickly corralled the rafts to keep them from floating down river with the current.

The Chinooks moved sideways to the landing site

next to the river and dropped to the uneven ground covered in long grass. The Ghost Warriors were out of their seats in an instant, exiting off the rear ramp, fanning out into a defensive perimeter as they secured the landing zone. They moved with a fluid grace, their weapons at the ready, their senses honed to a razor's edge.

With a final nod to the Chinook crews, Granier led his team to the rafts, the men clambering aboard and taking up their positions. Karen settled into the lead raft, her camera at the ready, her eyes scanning the riverbanks for any sign of trouble.

As the Ghost Warriors pushed off into the river, each raft was armed and ready for any potential threats. In the front of each vessel, a SAW gunner sat at the ready, their M249 Squad Automatic Weapon trained on the jungle banks.

The SAW was a formidable weapon, capable of laying down a withering hail of fire at a moment's notice. Its distinctive sound, a rapid staccato of thumps, could shatter the stillness of the jungle like a thunderclap.

For the men tasked with manning these guns, it was a heavy responsibility. They knew that they were the first line of defense for their comrades, that their vigilance and quick reactions could mean the difference between life and death.

As the rafts glided silently through the water, the SAW gunners scanned the riverbanks with a sharp intensity, their eyes probing the shadows for any sign of movement. They knew that the enemy could be anywhere, that an ambush could come at any moment.

The rest of the team, paddling hard against the current, took comfort in the presence of the SAWs.

They knew that they had the best in the business watching their backs, men who had honed their skills in countless battles and firefights.

But even with the SAWs at the ready, the journey upriver was a tense and nerve-wracking affair. The jungle pressed in on either side, the darkness broken only by the ghostly green glow of their night vision goggles.

Every sound, every rustle of leaves or snap of a twig, was a potential threat, a sign that the enemy was closing in. As they pushed deeper into enemy territory, the tension only mounted. The knowledge that they were drawing ever closer to their objective, to the heart of the communist insurgency, weighed heavy on their minds.

The journey upriver was a test of their endurance. Their muscles straining with the effort, their eyes scanning the darkness for any hint of danger. With each paddle stroke, each yard gained against the current, they drew closer to their destiny, to the moment that would define their lives and their legacy.

As they pushed upstream, Granier held up a closed fist, bringing the rafts to a halt. He had spotted something up ahead, a glint of metal in the moonlight. As the team edged closer, they could see the outlines of a river block, a series of steel cables and concrete pillars stretched across the water. They knew that at least one machine gun nest would be hidden along the river's shore. They had no desire to tangle with the machine gun as a firefight would be sure to give away their mission.

Granier knew that they were close now, that the Tan Lap Plantation lay just beyond the river block. He signaled for the team to paddle to the shore, the rafts gliding silently through the water until they bumped against the muddy banks.

The team disembarked quickly, hauling the rafts up onto the shore and concealing them in the undergrowth. From here, they would go in on foot, slinking their way through the jungle until they reached the perimeter of the plantation.

Not taking any chances, Granier led the way. Behind him, the rest of the team followed in a staggered column, their movements synchronized and their spacing carefully maintained. They had drilled this formation countless times, until it had become second nature, a choreography of deadly precision.

As they pushed deeper into the jungle, the darkness grew thicker, the canopy overhead blotting out the last vestiges of moonlight. They relied on their night vision goggles now, the ghostly green glow casting an eerie pallor over the landscape.

Suddenly, Granier held up a closed fist, bringing the column to a halt. He had spotted something up ahead, a flicker of movement in the shadows. The team dropped to a crouch, their weapons trained on the potential threat.

But it was just a bird, startled from its roost by their passing. Granier allowed himself a small chuckle, then signaled for the team to move out again. That was the problem with Southeast Asia. There were so many false alarms while trekking through the jungle, it was easy for soldiers to become complacent, drop their guard and give their enemy the advantage.

As they closed in on the Tan Lap Plantation, they could feel the presence of the enemy all around them, a sense of being watched, of being hunted. They knew that the next few hours would be critical, that the fate of the mission and the future of Vietnam hung in the balance.

The jungle began to thin, giving way to orderly rows of rubber trees that stretched out like silent sentinels. A mist clung to the leaves, casting a ghostly pall over the landscape.

The plantation had an eerie, almost surreal quality to it. The trees were spaced with mathematical precision, their trunks scored with neat, diagonal scars from years of harvesting the sticky white fluid. The air was heavy with the pungent scent of rubber sap, mixed with the earthy aroma of damp soil.

But beneath the veneer of order and efficiency, there was a sense of menace, of hidden danger lurking just out of sight. Granier knew that somewhere within this maze of trees and shadows, COSVN lay waiting.

He signaled for Dao to move up, the sniper sliding into position beside him. Together, they scanned the plantation with a practiced eye, looking for any sign of the enemy patrols that surely guarded the vital installation.

For long minutes, they waited, barely daring to breathe. The only sound was the soft rustle of leaves in the breeze and the distant call of a bird. It was as if the plantation itself was holding its breath, waiting for the storm to break.

And then, just as the tension was becoming almost unbearable, Granier spotted movement in the trees ahead. A flash of green, a glint of metal - an NVA patrol, moving with a casual arrogance that spoke of long familiarity with the terrain.

Granier and Dao watched the enemy soldiers draw closer, their rifles slung carelessly over their shoulders.

The patrol passed by without incident, their voices fading into the distance as they moved deeper into the plantation.

Granier waited a full five minutes, an eternity in the world of covert operations, before he signaled for the team to move out. They rose from their hiding spots, their movements fluid and silent as they slipped into the plantation.

As they picked their way through the orderly rows of trees, Granier couldn't shake the feeling that they were being watched, that unseen eyes were tracking their every move. The plantation seemed to press in around them, a living, breathing entity that resented their intrusion.

Each step took them closer to their objective, to the heart of the communist insurgency. Each moment brought them nearer to the final, decisive battle that would determine the fate of a nation. And yet, even as they pushed deeper into the plantation, into the very maw of the beast, Granier could not escape the sense of unease that prickled at the back of his neck. Granier did not spook easily and he had learned through experience to trust his instincts. But there was no turning back. Not now. Not when they were this close to COSVN and a moment of reckoning so long in the making.

They pressed on, deeper into the plantation, deeper into the unknown. The rubber trees closed in around them like a living wall, but they pushed forward, their eyes fixed on the objective that lay ahead.

A mile in, Granier, once again, held up a closed fist, bringing the team to a halt. He had spotted something up ahead, a structural silhouette through the trees. He signaled for Dao to move up, the sniper sliding into position beside him. Granier trusted Dao's skill. He had trained Dao himself. What Dao lacked in experience, he easily made up with his natural skill in the bush.

Together, they crept forward, their movements slow and deliberate. As they reached the edge of the treeline, they dropped to their bellies, crawling the last few meters until they had a clear view of the plantation.

The sight that greeted them was sobering. The compound was ringed by a series of anti-aircraft emplacements, each one manned by a crew of alert and watchful soldiers. The guns were positioned to provide overlapping fields of fire, a deadly curtain of lead and shrapnel that could shred an attacking force in seconds.

But it wasn't just the anti-aircraft guns that worried Granier. As he scanned the compound, he could see the telltale signs of a formidable ground defense as well. Armored vehicles were scattered throughout the plantation, their heavy machine guns and cannons pointing outward, ready to repel any assault. Harmon's intelligence had revealed the presence of armor around COSVN, but seeing it in a photo and now in real life as his team prepared to attack were two different things.

Granier reassured himself that as long as Coyle and the Spectre's aircrew did their part in taking out the armor and strafing the trenches, the team could handle the rest of the enemy defenses… with some luck.

Granier sent a radio signal to Harmon and his recon team to rendezvous at the designated point. Harmon had agreed to go ahead of the Ghost Warriors main assault group. He and his men would warn Granier and Coyle of any changes in the enemy's posture. They had not heard anything back from Harmon beyond a cursory check-in to make sure the field radio was working properly. No news was good news. Now, as Granier sent the rendezvous code, the radio operator heard nothing in reply. Granier was concerned, but not overly. There could be many reasons that Harmon did not reply including atmospheric interference or the dense plantation canopy that prevented him from getting the radio message. It could also be that Harmon's radio was damaged or low on batteries. They would try again once they moved their position as the assault began.

Gathering the team leaders, Granier gave the assignments with hand signals and pointing to each unit's target – the anti-aircraft guns. They all had been through this type of assault during the armored vehicle staging area assault several weeks earlier. They knew what was involved and how to complete their mission. Battlefield experience always tipped the scales in the veteran soldier's favor.

As Granier gave the final order to move out, the team units disappeared into the plantation's trees to maneuver into their assault positions. As he repositioned his tiny command group closer to the battlefield so he could observe the assaults, Granier ordered the radio operator to send the coded signal to Coyle, then try Harmon again.

Hidden Airfield, South Vietnam

Receiving the coded signal, Coyle responded with the counter coded signal, then started the Spectre's engines. He and his aircrew were in the air and banking toward the plantation's location within three minutes.

With time of the essence, it would be a full-throttle journey the whole way.

Tan Lap Plantation, South Vietnam

The radio operator informed Granier the Spectre was on its way, but he had been unable to contact Harmon and his recon team. Granier was concerned. Had the NVA found Harmon's recon team? Were they prisoners? Had they revealed the Ghost Warrior's mission under torture? There was no way to know for sure what had taken place.

Knowing that the team would never have the chance to assault COSVN again, Granier made the decision to force his doubts out of his mind and carry on with the assault. Granier waited the predetermined amount of time after the radio message had been sent to Coyle before ordering the ground assault to begin. His hope was that the anti-aircraft defenses would be destroyed just moments before Coyle and the Spectre arrived onsite.

As the team units drew closer, the enemy soldiers began to stir, alerted by some sixth sense that danger was near. Granier could see them reaching for their weapons, their faces taut.

And then, with a roar that shattered the stillness of the plantation, the Ghost Warriors opened fire. The air erupted with the chatter of automatic weapons, the whoosh of LAW rockets, and the blast of grenades.

The enemy soldiers fought back with a fury born of desperation, their bullets whipping through the trees like angry hornets. Granier saw one of his men go down, his chest torn open by a burst of fire.

But the Ghost Warriors pressed on, their weapons

spitting death. They moved from cover to cover, leapfrogging each other as they closed in on the emplacements.

It was a bloody, brutal affair, a close-quarters battle that tested their courage and their skill to the limit. The ground was slick with blood and littered with spent casings, the air thick with the stench of cordite and death.

One by one, the anti-aircraft emplacements fell silent, their crews cut down by the relentless onslaught of the Ghost Warriors. Granier could feel the tide turning, the enemy's resistance crumbling.

As the Spectre approached the plantation, Coyle sent a second coded signal to Granier telling him that they had arrived and were ready to attack the armor and trenches. The timing had been perfect.

But as the last gun fell silent and the smoke began to clear, Granier felt a sinking sensation in the pit of his stomach. Something was wrong, something was out of place.

He moved closer to one of the emplacements, his rifle at the ready. And then he saw it - the gun was ruined, its barrel warped and its mount shattered. It had been damaged long before the battle had even begun.

A cold realization washed over him, a sickening sense of dread. He ran to the next emplacement and saw the same – an unserviceable weapon. They had been tricked, lured into a trap by an enemy that had anticipated their every move.

Motioned for his operator, Granier reached for his radio. "Phantom Six, this is Ghost Lead," he said, his voice hoarse with emotion. "Abort mission, I repeat, abort mission. It's a trap."

Miles away, in the cockpit of the Spectre gunship, Coyle heard Granier's words and felt a chill run down his spine. But he couldn't abandon the mission, couldn't leave Karen and the others to face the enemy alone.

"Negative, Ghost Lead," he replied, his voice steady despite the fear that gnawed at his gut. "We're going in. We'll take out the armor and cover your retreat. Get Karen out."

As the Spectre roared over the plantation, its engines screaming like the wrath of a vengeful god, Coyle could see the enemy armor below, the armor's hulking forms spread out across the landscape, closing in on Granier and the ground team's position.

Determined, Coyle entered a pylon turn and brought the gunship's weapons to bear, the 20mm cannon and 40mm Bofors spitting fire and death. The tanks and APCs thin steel tops penetrated by armor piercing shells, erupted in gouts of flame, their crews incinerated in an instant.

But even as the Ghost Warriors cheered and the enemy reeled in confusion, a new threat emerged from the horizon. A flight of MiG jets, their sleek forms glinting in the sun, streaked towards the Spectre. Phase II of the enemy's trap had begun.

Coyle felt his blood run cold as he saw the enemy fighters bearing down on them. The Spectre was a formidable weapon, but it was no match for the speed and agility of the MiGs.

He threw the gunship into a desperate series of evasive maneuvers, the airframe groaning under the strain. But the MiGs were relentless, their cannons spitting fire as they closed in for the kill.

The Spectre shuddered as rounds ripped through its

fuselage, alarms blaring and warning lights flashing. Gunners and loaders were ripped to shreds by the large caliber shells, blood flowed across the deck.

In the cockpit of the Spectre, Coyle gripped the controls with white-knuckled intensity, his eyes scanning the skies for the telltale glint of enemy jets. The red lights casting an eerie glow across the instrument panel.

"Incoming, three o'clock high!" shouted the co-pilot, his voice taut with fear and adrenaline.

Coyle wrenched the control yoke, sending the Spectre into a sharp bank as a MiG screamed past, its cannons spitting fire. The gunship shuddered as rounds tore through the fuselage, the sound of rending metal filling the air.

"Damage report!" Coyle barked, his eyes never leaving the skies.

"Port engine's hit, losing power," replied the flight engineer, his hands flying across the controls. "Hydraulics are leaking, losing pressure, and we've got a fire in the cargo hold."

Coyle's mind raced as he tried to formulate a plan. The Spectre was a formidable weapon, but it was never designed to go toe-to-toe with fighter jets. They were outmatched and outgunned, and he knew it.

But he also knew that he couldn't just give up, couldn't let his crew and the Ghost Warriors on the ground down. He had to fight, had to give them a chance.

"Bring the 20mm Vulcans online," he ordered, his voice steady despite the chaos around him. "We'll target those MiGs and give 'em hell."

The surviving crew leapt into action, the weapons systems humming to life. Using all his skill, Coyle maneuvered the heavily damaged aircraft to track the enemy jets. The 20mm cannon roared, its tracers arcing through the sky like furious fireflies.

For a moment, it seemed to work. One of the MiGs erupted in flames, spinning out of control as it plummeted towards the jungle below. The crew of the Spectre cheered, a fleeting moment of triumph in the midst of the maelstrom.

But their elation was short-lived. More MiGs appeared on the horizon, their sleek forms cutting through the air like sharks through water. They swarmed around the Spectre, their cannons and missiles seeking out the vulnerable points of the aging gunship.

Coyle threw the aircraft into a series of wild evasive maneuvers, the airframe groaning under the strain. He climbed and dove, twisted and turned, using every trick in his considerable arsenal to try and shake the pursuers.

But it was no use. The MiGs were too fast, too agile. They danced around the Spectre like wolves around a wounded elk, darting in to deliver lethal blows before streaking away again.

The gunship shuddered as more rounds found their mark, alarms blaring and warning lights flashing. Coyle could smell the acrid stench of burning wires, could feel the aircraft losing power and responsiveness with each passing second.

"We're losing hydraulics!" shouted the co-pilot, his face ashen. "Controls are going slack!"

Coyle fought with the yoke, his muscles straining as he tried to keep the aircraft level. But it was a losing battle. The Spectre was dying, its lifeblood leaking out through a hundred wounds.

And then, with a final, shuddering gasp, the burning engines cut out entirely. The gunship hung in the air for a moment, suspended in a sickening moment of stillness, before it began to plummet towards the earth.

In the crew compartment, the men braced themselves with the knowledge of what was to come. They had given their all, had fought to the last bullet and the last breath.

But it hadn't been enough. The enemy had been too strong, too determined. And now, as the jungle rushed up to meet them and the wind screamed through the shattered canopy, they could only hope that their sacrifice had not been in vain.

Coyle closed his eyes, his thoughts turning to Karen and Scott, then to Granier and the Ghost Warriors on the ground. He had failed them, had let them down when they needed him most.

But even as despair threatened to consume him, he felt a flicker of defiance, a stubborn refusal to give in to the inevitable. He reached for the controls one last time, his hands steady and sure.

If this was to be his end, then he would meet it on his own terms, with courage and dignity. He would not let the enemy have the satisfaction of seeing him broken and defeated.

And so, with a final, anguished cry of defiance, Tom Coyle fought the dying Spectre with every ounce of skill and strength he possessed, determined to give his crew and his friends on the ground every last chance at survival.

It was a futile gesture, a last, desperate stand against the pitiless reality of war. But it was a gesture that spoke volumes about the man himself, about the unbreakable spirit that had driven him through the long, dark years of the conflict.

And as the Spectre plunged into the jungle, trailing smoke and flame like a falling star, that spirit shone bright and true, a beacon of hope and courage in a world consumed by darkness and despair.

In the plantation below, Granier and Karen watched in horror as the Spectre lurched and spun, trailing smoke and flame.

And then, with a final, agonized scream of metal, the Spectre dove into the jungle, disappearing from view in a huge fireball as the ammunition onboard and ruptured fuel tanks exploded, followed by a roiling cloud of smoke and debris.

Karen screamed. Granier grabbed her and pulled her close, trying to comfort a girl that had just lost her father. He too felt a wave of grief and rage wash over him, a searing pain that threatened to consume him entirely. Coyle was gone. The Spectre, their ace in the hole was no more, and the Ghost Warriors were alone, trapped in the heart of the enemy's stronghold.

From a distant landing zone where the helicopters crews were waiting for orders and listening to the radio as the battle unfolded, Scott too had seen the tragic crash of the Spectre and the death of his father. He fought back the tears. He had to. He was in the middle of a fight that they were losing. The team needed him. He would mourn Coyle later.

As Scott watched helpless the triumphant enemy jets moved away from the crash site and strafed Granier and the team's position. Scott's helicopters were no match for the enemy jets. He and his crew were grounded for the moment, waiting for a chance to affect the battle for COSVN and exact revenge for his father's death.

Granier ducked instinctively as the MiGs roared overhead, their cannons stitching the ground with lines of deadly fire. The air was filled with the stench of cordite and burning rubber, the jungle reverberating with the echoes of the attack.

As the jets broke off their ground assault, Granier surveyed the carnage around him. Several of his men lay still and silent, their bodies twisted and broken by the brutal onslaught. The sight of their lifeless forms, men he had trained and fought beside for so long, filled him with a searing rage and an aching sense of loss.

He knew there was no time for grief, no time for mourning. The enemy armor was closing in, the sound of their engines and the clatter of their treads growing louder with each passing second.

"Consolidate positions!" Granier barked, his voice cutting through the chaos like a knife. "Form a defensive perimeter, now!"

The Ghost Warriors sprang into action, their movements swift and precise despite the shock and the horror of the attack. They dragged their wounded behind cover, then took up positions behind fallen trees and mounds of earth, their weapons trained on the approaching enemy.

As the MiGs disappeared over the horizon, Scott ordered his helicopter crews to attack in hopes of giving Granier and the team some breathing room, then executing a rescue. Three minutes later, they were in the air and headed into the plantation.

Granier did a head count and ammunition check. The

team was low on both. If they could retrieve some of the fallen enemy's weapons and ammunition, they could increase their own supply and have a fighting chance. But it was too late…

With a roar of engines and a blast of cannon fire, the enemy armor burst through the treeline. The hulking tanks and APCs advanced relentlessly, their metal hides glinting in the dappled sunlight that filtered through the canopy.

Granier tried to formulate a plan. He didn't have much to work with. Even if they had more ammunition the M16s bullets were no match for armor. The team was outmatched and outgunned, facing an enemy that had every advantage in terms of firepower and numbers.

And yet the Ghost Warriors were not so easily cowed. With a defiant cry, they let loose with a barrage of LAW rockets, the anti-tank weapons streaking through the air.

The rockets found their marks, exploding against the armor of the enemy vehicles in bursts of flame and shrapnel. For a moment, the advance faltered, the tanks and APCs reeling under the unexpected onslaught.

But it was only a momentary respite. The enemy infantry, hidden behind the bulk of the armor, surged forward, their weapons chattering as they sought to close the distance and engage the Ghost Warriors in close combat.

The firefight that followed was fierce and bloody, a desperate struggle for survival. The Ghost Warriors fought with every ounce of skill and courage they possessed, their rifles and machine guns firing into the ranks of the advancing enemy.

The enemy was relentless, their numbers seemingly inexhaustible. For every soldier that fell, two more seemed to take their place, pressing forward with a fanatical determination that bordered on madness.

Granier saw his men falling around him, cut down by the hail of bullets and blasts from enemy mortars. He fought on, his own weapon bucking and kicking in his hands as he poured fire into the charging enemy.

And then, a bugle sounded and just as suddenly as it had begun, the gunfire died away. The enemy soldiers, those that remained, took cover behind the shell-pocked earth and the smoldering wrecks of their vehicles.

An eerie silence descended over the battlefield, broken only by the distant idling of engines and the groans of the wounded and dying. Granier looked around, his mind reeling from the sudden turn of events.

It was a strange and surreal moment, a brief island of calm in the midst of the storm of violence. The Ghost Warriors, those that remained, hunkered down in their positions, their eyes scanning the plantation for any sign of movement.

But for now, there was only stillness, a strange and unsettling peace that seemed to mock the horror and the carnage that had come before. Granier knew that it couldn't last, that the enemy was merely regrouping and preparing for another assault.

Granier made his way through the carnage, his heart heavy with the weight of the losses they had suffered. So many brave men, friends and comrades, had fallen in the desperate struggle against the enemy onslaught. The sight of their lifeless bodies, twisted and broken amidst the shattered landscape, filled him with a grief that threatened to overwhelm him.

Another quick headcount and Granier realized that over half of the team was dead and the other half was wounded but still fighting. They had come this far, had fought and bled and sacrificed for a cause that they believed in. And though the odds were stacked against them, though the enemy seemed to hold every advantage, Granier knew that they would not surrender. Victory or death were the only options.

Granier heard Karen weeping. He had forgotten about her during the battle. He knew she was hurting and yet, he didn't know what to do. He was hurting too from the loss of his best friend. He had no words of comfort to offer her.

A thick, swirling mist had crept in from the jungle mixing with the smoke, shrouding the plantation in an otherworldly haze that seemed to muffle sound and distort perception.

As he approached Karen, huddled behind a fallen tree with her camera clutched to her chest, he could see the raw, unfiltered anguish etched across her face. Seeing her father's fate had struck her like a physical blow.

Granier knelt beside her, his hand reaching out to offer what little comfort he could. But before he could speak, a flicker of movement caught his eye. A figure, silhouetted against the mist, was walking slowly and deliberately between the battle lines.

For a moment, Granier thought it was the beginning of another enemy assault, his hand instinctively reaching for his weapon. But as the figure drew closer, his eyes widening in disbelief, he realized that it was no enemy soldier that approached, but a ghost from their own ranks.

It was Harmon, walking upright, seemingly oblivious to the carnage that surrounded him. The enemy soldiers, hidden in their positions, made no move to stop him, their weapons lowered as if in silent acknowledgment of his passage.

Granier rose to his feet, his mind reeling with confusion and suspicion. As Harmon drew near, his eyes downcast and his shoulders slumped, Granier could see the shame and the guilt that radiated from every line of his body.

"What the hell is going on, Harmon?" Granier demanded, his voice tight with barely controlled anger. "Where is your recon team?"

Harmon looked up, his eyes meeting Granier's for a brief, agonizing moment before darting away again. "I'm sorry, Granier," he said, his voice barely above a whisper. "I never wanted it to come to this."

And then, in halting, painful words, the truth came spilling out. Harmon's son, captured by the NVA during a battle in the Mekong Delta, had become a pawn in a twisted game of espionage and treason. To ensure his son's safety and secure his release, Harmon had been forced to betray his own comrades, to lure them into a trap of the enemy's devising.

The aerial photos, the recon images, all of it had been a lie, a carefully crafted deception designed to draw the Ghost Warriors into the open. The real COSVN, the true nerve center of the communist insurgency, lay elsewhere, hidden and protected. This place, this plantation, was nothing more than a snare meant to bleed them dry.

Granier felt a wave of nausea wash over him, a sickening sense of betrayal that left him reeling. He had trusted Harmon, had relied on his intel and his expertise. And now, to learn that it had all been a lie, that they had been led like lambs to the slaughter...

But even as the anger and the disgust threatened to consume him, Harmon pressed on, his voice taking on a desperate, pleading edge. "The commander, he's agreed to accept your surrender," he said, his eyes flickering nervously between Granier and the mist-shrouded jungle beyond. "He'll treat you as prisoners of war, not renegades. It's the best chance you have. The only chance."

Granier's lip curled in a snarl of contempt. "And you believe him?" he spat, his voice dripping with scorn. "You think they'll just let us walk away, after all we've done? They'll torture us for information, break us down until there's nothing left. And then, when they're finished, they'll put a bullet in our heads or a noose around our necks."

Harmon shook his head, his expression a mask of anguish. "No, Granier, it won't be like that. I've secured guarantees, assurances. They'll honor the agreement, I swear it."

But Granier was beyond listening, beyond reason. The betrayal cut too deep, the wound too raw. He turned away, his hand clenching into a fist at his side.

And then, in a moment that seemed to stretch into eternity, Karen stepped forward, a strange calmness in her face. In her hand, glinting dully in the mist-filtered light, was her revolver, the weapon that had been her constant companion through all the long years of the war.

"You killed my father," she said, her voice flat and emotionless, her eyes locked on Harmon's face.

Harmon's mouth opened, a desperate plea forming on his lips. But before he could speak, before he could utter a word in his own defense, Karen's finger tightened on the trigger.

The shot rang out like a thunderclap, the sound echoing through the mist-shrouded plantation like the tolling of a funeral bell. Harmon's head snapped back, a neat, red hole appearing just to the right of his nose bridge. He stood there for a moment, swaying gently, before crumpling to the ground like a puppet with its strings cut.

Granier stared at the fallen form of his former friend and comrade, his mind reeling with the enormity of what had just happened. The betrayal, the loss, the sheer, unrelenting horror of it all threatened to drag him down.

But then, just as the darkness threatened to close in, a flicker of light caught his eye. A flare, arcing through the sky from the direction of the crashed Spectre, a burning trail of red that stood out starkly against the swirling mist.

A sudden, desperate hope kindling in Granier's soul. He pointed to the flare, his voice ragged with emotion. "Karen, look!"

She turned, her eyes widening as she saw the signal, the unmistakable sign of life amidst the carnage and the destruction. "Could it be...?" she breathed, her voice trembling with a mixture of fear and longing.

Granier shook his head, his mind racing with possibilities. "I don't know. The NVA, they're not searching the crash site. The smoke is enough to guide them. But this..."

He trailed off, his eyes locked on the fading trail of light. "Could there be survivors?" Karen asked, her voice barely above a whisper.

Granier felt a grim smile tug at the corners of his

mouth, a flicker of the old, indomitable spirit that had carried them through so many trials and tribulations. "This is Coyle we're talking about," he said, his voice filled with a fierce, unshakable pride. "The man knows how to crash a plane."

He reached for his radio, his fingers trembling slightly as he keyed the mic. "Scott, did you see that flare?"

There was a moment of silence, a pause that seemed to stretch into eternity. And then, crackling through the static, came the voice of their comrade, their brother-in-arms. "Yeah. I'm turning the birds around now. We're going to check it out."

Granier felt a surge of relief wash over him, a flicker of hope that cut through the darkness like a beacon in the night. They had lost so much, had suffered so many defeats and setbacks. But even now, even in the face of overwhelming odds and the betrayal of one of their own, Granier and his team refused to give up.

Spectre Crash Site

The jungle was a cacophony of sound and fury as the mangled remains of the Spectre gunship lay strewn across the scarred earth. The once-mighty aircraft had been torn asunder by the force of the impact, its fuselage shattered into twisted fragments of metal and composites.

At the rear of the wreckage, the shattered remnants of the cargo hold burned with a fierce intensity, the flames licking hungrily at the ruptured fuel tanks and the spilled ordnance. The heat was unbearable, the air shimmering with a sickly, wavering haze that made it difficult to breathe or see.

But it was the sound that was the most jarring, the most unsettling. The staccato popping of ammunition cooking off in the inferno, the hissing of pressurized hydraulic lines venting their contents, the groaning and creaking of metal as it cooled and contracted in the tropical heat.

Twenty yards away, the cockpit lay in a crumpled heap, its once-sleek lines crushed and deformed by the force of the crash. The canopy was shattered, the instruments a tangled mess of sparking wires and shattered gauges.

At the base of the wreckage, four figures huddled together, their faces streaked with soot and blood, their eyes haunted by what they had witnessed. Coyle sat with his back against the twisted metal, his collar bone and arm broken, his face filled with pain and grim determination.

Beside him, the co-pilot, flight engineer, and radar operator lay in a semicircle, their bodies broken and battered, their breathing shallow and labored. They were the lucky ones, the survivors of a crash that should have claimed all their lives. Coyle had pulled them from the wreckage.

But even as they clung to life, to the faint hope of rescue and salvation, they knew that their ordeal was far from over. The enemy was coming, drawn by the smoke and the flames, the promise of easy prey and valuable intelligence.

Coyle could hear them now, the distant shouts and cries, the crashing of bodies through the dense underbrush. His hand tightened on the grip of his M16, the bandolier of ammunition slung across his chest a comforting weight in the face of the impending onslaught.

They had already made their decision, he and his men. They would not be taken alive, would not allow themselves to be captured and tortured for information. They would fight to the last ounce of strength in their battered bodies.

With a grunt of pain, Coyle lowered himself to the ground, using the shattered remains of the cockpit as cover. He sighted down the barrel of his rifle, his finger resting lightly on the trigger, his eyes scanning the jungle for any sign of movement.

And then, with a roar of gunfire and a blur of motion, the enemy was upon them. NVA soldiers burst from the treeline, their weapons firing, their faces contorted in snarls of hatred and bloodlust. The NVA hated the American gunships and their crews. They wanted revenge for their fallen comrades and the fear they felt when they heard the dragon flying in the night sky.

Coyle opened fire, his rifle bucking and kicking in his hands as he poured round after round into the advancing enemy. Beside him, his men added their own fire to the barrage, their weapons chattering and stuttering as they fought with every ounce of strength they possessed.

But it was a losing battle, and they all knew it. The enemy was too many, too well-armed and well-equipped, pressing forward with a relentless, implacable resolve.

Coyle's rifle clicked empty, the last round expended. With a curse, he fumbled for a fresh magazine, his fingers slick with sweat and blood. He could hear the enemy moving to his flank, trying to outmaneuver and surround them, to cut off any chance of escape or resistance.

But he would not leave his men, would not abandon them to the mercies of the enemy. They had fought together, bled together, and now, if necessary, they would die together.

As he slammed the fresh magazine into place and prepared to make his final stand, Coyle's thoughts turned to Karen and Scott, to the family he had found amidst the chaos and the carnage of the war. He was grateful to have known them, to have loved them, even if only for a little while.

And then, just as the enemy soldiers burst from the underbrush, their weapons leveled and their fingers tightening on the triggers, the sky above erupted with the roar of rotor blades and the chatter of machine gun fire.

Scott's gunship tore through the canopy, its door minigun dealing death into the ranks of the advancing NVA. The enemy soldiers scattered, some cut down in mid-stride, others diving for cover behind the shattered trunks of fallen trees.

And then the Chinooks were there, their rotors kicking up a maelstrom of dust and debris as they hovered over the crash site. Ropes snaked down from the open doors, and a team of medics and soldiers fast-roped to the ground, their weapons at the ready.

Coyle felt a surge of relief wash over him, a flicker of hope that cut through the pain and the despair like a beacon in the night. They were saved, snatched from the jaws of death by the skill and the courage of their comrades.

As the medics tended to the wounded and the soldiers secured the perimeter, Coyle and his men were hoisted up into the waiting Chinooks, their battered bodies strapped securely to stretchers.

And then they were airborne, the jungle receding beneath them like a half-remembered nightmare, the roar of the rotors and the rush of the wind drowning out the sounds of the battle below.

Coyle lay back against the stretcher, his eyes closed and his breath coming in ragged gasps. He had survived, had cheated death once again. But the cost had been high, the sacrifice almost more than he could bear.

Plantation

The battle raged on with renewed ferocity, the NVA armor advancing relentlessly, their cannons and machine guns firing. The Ghost Warriors fought back with everything they had, their LAW rockets and grenades seeking out the vulnerable points in the enemy's defenses.

But it was a losing battle, and they all knew it. The NVA's numbers and firepower were simply too great, their tactics too well-honed and their resolve too strong. One by one, the Ghost Warriors fell, their bodies torn and shattered by the merciless onslaught.

Granier fired his rifle, the weapon bucking and kicking in his hands as he poured round after round into the advancing enemy. Beside him, Karen crouched behind a fallen tree, her camera forgotten as she added her own fire to the barrage.

And then, like a miracle from above, Scott's voice crackled over the radio, the words cutting through the chaos and the carnage like a beam of pure, unbridled hope.

"Coyle's alive," he said, his voice tight with urgency and excitement. "He's a little banged up, but we got him and three more survivors in a Chinook. We're heading back to pick you up now."

Granier felt a surge of relief wash over him, a flicker of hope that cut through the despair like a beacon in the night. Coyle was alive, and help was on the way. They just had to hold out a little longer, had to buy enough time for the choppers to arrive.

He keyed his radio, his voice steady and calm despite the urgency of the moment. "Great news. We're going to need a landing zone, somewhere relatively safe where you can set down. The area's crawling with NVA, and we're running low on ammo and supplies."

There was a moment of silence on the other end of the line, a pause that seemed to stretch into eternity. And then Scott's voice came back, "Understood. We're scanning the area now, looking for a spot that's defensible and clear enough for the birds to touch down. But you're going to have to fight your way clear of the enemy first. We can't risk setting down in the middle of a firefight. We'll get chewed to bits and that doesn't help anyone."

Granier knew they would need to break contact with the NVA, would need to punch through their lines and find a position that they could defend until the Chinooks arrived.

He turned to his team, his eyes scanning their faces. They were battered and bloodied, their ranks thinned by the relentless onslaught of the enemy. But in their eyes, he saw a fire that could not be extinguished, a fierce, unquenchable fortitude that would carry them through to the end.

"Alright, listen up," he said. "We've got a ride out of here, but we need to fight our way clear of the enemy first. That means we push forward, we punch through their lines and find a position that we can defend until the choppers arrive. Understood?"

A chorus of nods and grunts greeted his words. They knew the stakes, knew the price they might have to pay to once again win their freedom.

Granier turned to Dao, the silent sniper he had personally trained. "Dao, you and I will form the rear guard," he said. "We'll hold the enemy back, buy the others the time they need to break through and find a landing zone."

Granier didn't ask Dao to volunteer. He knew Dao's answer and didn't waste time with a meaningless gesture. He also knew that there was no one he would rather have at his side in this moment than Dao, the man who had become his brother, his comrade-in-arms. He trusted Dao with his life. Dao was one hell of a shot.

Granier turned to Karen and said, "You did well, Karen. Real well. Tell your dad, we did our best. Even though we fell short, we did the right thing. I wouldn't have it any other way."

Tears of gratitude in her eyes, Karen nodded.

As the Ghost Warriors gathered their wounded, Granier gave them the order, "Go."

They surged forward, their weapons blazing, filled with an unquenchable fire.

The NVA were shocked by the fierceness of an enemy they thought was spent and on the verge of surrender. They recoiled from the Ghost Warriors' charge into their lines.

Granier and Dao took up position at the rear, their sniper rifles at the ready and their eyes scanning the jungle for any sign of the enemy.

They knew that they were the final bulwark against the darkness that threatened to engulf them all. But they were ready, their minds and bodies honed to a razor's edge by the long years of war and sacrifice.

And as the enemy closed in, Granier and Dao opened fire, each bullet dropping a soldier charging toward the Ghost Warriors, trying to stop their prey from escaping.

Granier and Dao fought with a fierce intensity, their sniper rifles cracking as they poured fire into the ranks of the advancing NVA.

Watching their comrades fall from the deadly duo of snipers, the NVA broke their charge and hit the ground scrambling for cover.

Granier and Dao didn't let up. They kept the faith their men had in them and held the rear.

But even as they took a heavy toll on the enemy, picking off unit commanders with ruthless efficiency, they knew that they could not hold out forever. The NVA were too many, too well-armed and too determined.

Granier turned back to see the Chinooks landing somewhere in the jungle. The Ghost Warriors had made.

Helicopter Landing Site

As the Chinooks' rotors kicked up a maelstrom of dust and debris, Karen and the surviving Ghost Warriors raced across the blood-soaked earth. The jungle behind them filled with gunfire and explosions, a cacophony of violence that threatened to engulf them at any moment.

Karen leapt into the nearest chopper, her eyes

scanning the faces of the wounded and exhausted men around her. She searched desperately for the one face she longed to see above all others, the face of her father, Tom Coyle.

But he was nowhere to be found, and for a moment, Karen felt a sickening sense of dread wash over her. Had she come this far, fought so hard, only to lose him now, at the very end?

Unwilling to give up, she pushed her way through the crowded cabin, ignoring the cries of pain and the moans of the injured. She jumped out the doorway back into the maelstrom and ran to the second chopper. She had to find her father, had to know that he was safe.

And then she saw him, sitting in the back of the second Chinook, his face pale and drawn, his arm wrapped in a blood-soaked bandage. But he was alive, gloriously, miraculously alive.

"Dad!" Karen cried out, her voice cracking with emotion as she flung herself into his arms. Coyle held her tight, his good arm wrapped around her shoulders, his breath warm against her ear.

"Karen," he whispered, his voice hoarse with exhaustion and relief. "I thought I'd lost you. I thought I'd never see you again."

Karen pulled back, her eyes shining with tears as she looked up at her father's battered face. "I'm here, Dad. I'm here, and I'm not going anywhere."

For a long moment, they simply held each other, their tears mingling on their cheeks. The world around them faded away, the chaos and the carnage and the horror of the battlefield disappearing into nothingness.

But then Coyle stirred, his eyes searching the cabin, his brow furrowed with concern. "Granier," he said, his voice tight with worry. "Where's Granier? Did he make it out?"

Karen felt a lump form in her throat, a heavy weight settling in the pit of her stomach. She took a deep breath, steeling herself for the words she knew she had to say.

"Granier stayed behind with Dao," she said, her voice trembling slightly. "They bought us the time we needed to escape, held off the enemy so we could make it to the choppers. They saved our lives, Dad. They saved us all."

Coyle's face crumpled, his eyes squeezing shut as the weight of Karen's words sank in. Granier, his friend, his brother-in-arms, had sacrificed himself so that they could live, had given his life so that they could have a chance at a future.

For a long moment, the two of them sat in silence, the roar of the Chinook's engines filling the cabin, the wind whipping through the open doors. They clung to each other, father and daughter, united in their grief and their gratitude, their hearts heavy with the knowledge of what had been lost, and what had been saved.

Plantation

Granier and Dao fought on, waiting for the right moment to abandon their position, their ammunition getting dangerously low. Even under their withering fire, the enemy advanced. It was hopeless. Only moments remained before they were overrun by the angry wave.

He turned to Dao, "Dao, you need to make a run for it," he said, his words cutting through the chaos and the carnage like a knife. "Get to that Chinook, now!"

Dao hesitated for a moment, his eyes flickering between Granier and the distant chopper. He knew what his friend was asking, knew the price that would be paid.

But he also knew that there was no other choice, no other way to ensure that at least one of them made it out alive. And so, with a final nod of understanding, he turned and sprinted towards the waiting helicopters, his rifle clutched tightly in his hands. If he could make it to the edge of the jungle, he could cover Granier's retreat.

Granier poured fire into the trees in front of Dao, trying to keep the enemy at bay. But even as he fought with every ounce of strength and skill he possessed, he saw the NVA soldiers closing on Dao's position, their weapons leveled and their fingers tightening on the triggers.

And then, in a moment that seemed to stretch into eternity, he saw Dao stumble, saw him fall to the ground as a spray of bullets tore through his body.

Granier's breath caught in his throat as he watched his friend crumple to the earth like a puppet with its strings cut. And then, without a second thought, he was running towards Dao's fallen form, enemy bullets whizzing past him.

He reached him in seconds, his hands already searching for a pulse, for any sign of life. But as he cradled Dao's head in his lap, as he saw the blood pooling beneath his body, he knew that the wounds were fatal, that there was little he could do.

And yet, even in that moment of despair, Granier refused to give up, refused to let his friend die alone on the battlefield. He hoisted Dao onto his shoulders, his muscles straining with the effort as he began to run once more toward the waiting helicopters.

The enemy was all around them now, their bullets whipping past Granier's head and tearing into the ground at his feet. He could hear their shouts, their cries of triumph as they closed in for the kill.

Granier felt a thump in his thigh and a sharp pain. He was hit. His leg gave out and he tumbled to the ground dropping Dao. Dao groaned. Granier was bleeding heavily from the bullet wound.

But he would not stop. He would stand by his friend, his comrade, until the bitter end. Using his rifle as a crutch, Granier climbed to his feet, the wound in his leg feeling like hot branding iron. He pick up Dao once again, hoisting over his shoulder and continued their desperate journey to the Chinook.

A mortar shell exploded next to them. Granier and Dao went down again, both hit by shrapnel. Granier tried to climb to his knees, but the pain was too much, his strength sapped from blood loss. He looked toward the Chinook in the distance, then on the NVA closing in on them. Too far, too late. Seeing the two snipers on the ground unable to continue, the Chinook pilots took off with the remaining Ghost Warriors. They would save those they could. It was over.

Granier chambered a round into his rifle, knowing the dirt clogged barrel would probably blow up in his face. At least he would die by his own had and not the enemy's. That gave him some satisfaction in his final moments.

And then, just as all seemed lost, just as the enemy's fingers tightened on their triggers and their bayonets gleamed in the moonlight, Scott's gunship appeared overhead, its rotors whipping the air into a frenzy as it descended like an avenging angel.

The door gunner opened up with his minigun, the weapon spitting fire and death into the ranks of the advancing NVA. Granier watched in awe as the enemy soldiers were cut down like wheat before the scythe, their bodies torn and shattered by the relentless onslaught.

And then the chopper was down, its skids sinking into the soft earth as Granier pulled himself and Dao across the ground toward the open doorway, brass from the minigun clinking on the deck. It seemed miles away as he inched forward.

Scott leapt from the pilot's seat and ran toward them. He grabbed Dao and threw him through the doorway like a duffle bag. Granier was next, Scott sparing any tenderness in the name of expediency. Granier grunted as he landed on the deck. Scott climbed back in the pilot seat and they took off as the minigun ran out of ammunition.

"Out," called the door gunner as he abandoned his weapon and grabbed the medical kit from the aircraft's wall. The gunner turned to Granier and went to work on stemming the bleeding from his wounds. Granier reached out and stopped him. "Him first," he said nodding toward Dao.

"He's lost too much blood," said the gunner.

"Him first," said Granier again.

The gunner slid across the deck and went to work on Dao. Granier put pressure on his own wounds, wrapping his belt above the wound in his thigh, using it as a torniquet.

The gunner looked down at Dao's lifeless eyes and the blood no longer pulsing from his wounds. He felt for a pulse in his neck. There was none. He turned to

Granier and said, "I'm sorry. Your friend's dead."

Granier was crestfallen. He didn't stop the gunner as he again switched back to tending Granier's wounds.

Staring at Dao's lifeless body, Granier felt the weight of his friend's sacrifice settling on his shoulders like a mantle of grief and loss.

They had made it out, had escaped the jaws of death by the narrowest of margins. But the price had been high, the cost almost more than he could bear.

And as the helicopters banked towards the distant horizon, the sun rising over the war-torn landscape of Vietnam, Granier wept, his tears mingling with the blood and the sweat on his face.

Dao was gone, his life given in service to a cause greater than himself, a cause that had consumed him. Granier knew that his friend would not have had it any other way, that he had died as he had lived - a true son of Vietnam.

Saigon, South Vietnam

The sterile white walls of the military hospital room seemed to close in around Coyle and Granier as they sat on their beds, their hands handcuffed to the metal frames. The soft beeping of the monitors and the distant chatter of nurses and doctors drifted in from the hallway, a stark contrast to the tense silence that hung between the two men.

Coyle winced as he shifted in his bed, the movement sending a sharp pain shooting through his broken collarbone and arm. Beside him, Granier sat stoically, his eyes fixed on the cards in his hand, his expression unreadable.

At the door, two US Marine guards from the

embassy stood watch, their rifles held at the ready, their faces impassive. They were there to ensure that the two rogue CIA officers didn't try anything foolish, that they remained under close supervision until their fate could be decided.

Coyle glanced up from his cards, his eyes meeting Granier's across the small table that had been set up between their beds. "So," he said, "what do you think they're going to do with us?"

Granier shrugged, his gaze never leaving his cards. "Hard to say," he replied, his tone equally guarded. "We broke a lot of rules, went against a lot of orders. They could throw the book at us, if they wanted to."

Coyle nodded, a grim smile tugging at the corners of his mouth. "Yeah, but we also did a lot of good out there. We showed the enemy that they're not invincible."

Granier looked up, his eyes flickering with a hint of amusement. "You really think that's going to matter to the brass? To the politicians back in Washington?"

Coyle sighed, his gaze dropping back to his cards. "No, probably not. But it should. We risked everything, gave everything, to try and make a difference. That should count for something."

Granier was silent for a moment. "Maybe," he said at last, his voice barely above a whisper. "But even if it does, even if they acknowledge what we did, it's not going to change the fact that we went rogue. We operated outside the chain of command, took matters into our own hands."

Coyle's fingers tightening on his cards. "We did what we had to do," he said. "We saw an opportunity to strike at the heart of the enemy, to give the South a fighting chance."

Granier nodded, his expression softening slightly. "I know, Coyle. And I don't regret it, not for a second. But we have to be realistic. We're in a tight spot here, and it's not going to be easy to get out of it."

The soft knock on the door startled Coyle and Granier from their conversation, their eyes darting to the entrance of the hospital room. The ARVN guards snapped to attention, their rifles held at the ready as the door swung open to reveal the stern, unsmiling face of Thomas Polgar, the CIA's top man in Saigon.

Polgar strode into the room, his eyes shifting to the two men with a mixture of anger and exasperation. He dismissed the guards with a curt nod, waiting until they had filed out of the room before turning his attention back to Coyle and Granier.

"You two have really stepped in it this time," he said, his voice barely containing his fury. "Do you have any idea the shitstorm you've unleashed?"

"We did what we had to do, sir," Coyle said, his voice steady and calm despite the gravity of the situation. "We saw an opportunity to strike a blow against the enemy, to give the South a fighting chance. We couldn't just sit back and let that slip away."

Polgar's eyes narrowed, "And in doing so, you went against every protocol, every chain of command. You operated outside the bounds of your authority, and now you expect me to clean up your mess."

Granier leaned forward, his expression serious. "Sir, with all due respect, we were trying to make a difference out there. We saw the writing on the wall, saw the way the war was going. We had to act, had to do something to try and turn the tide."

"I understand your intentions," Polgar said, his voice measured. "And on some level, I even admire your dedication to the cause. But the reality is, you've put me in a very difficult position. The South Vietnamese are howling for your heads, and I'm half inclined to give them what they want."

Coyle and Granier exchanged a glance. "Only half inclined…?" said Coyle.

"The South Vietnamese want to prosecute you, to make an example of you. And if I let that happen, it sets a dangerous precedent for the future."

"So, what do we do, sir?" Coyle asked, his voice hesitant and unsure.

Polgar fixed them with a hard stare, his expression unyielding. "You stick to your story, and you don't deviate from it for a second," he said, his words clipped and precise.

Uncertainty crossing Granier's face. "And what is our story, sir?"

Polgar's lips twitched in a humorless smile. "That you were acting under orders from me, from the CIA. That everything you did, every mission you carried out, was sanctioned and approved by the highest levels of our government."

"But sir, that's not true." Said Coyle.

Polgar's smile widened, a glint of something dark and dangerous in his eyes. "And that's the beauty of it, gentlemen. The truth doesn't matter, not in this game. All that matters is what we can make them believe, what we can convince them to accept. The South Vietnamese need us, need our support and our resources. They can't afford to alienate us, not now, not with the enemy closing in on all sides. So, we give them a story they can live with, a version of events that doesn't make them look weak or ineffectual."

Anger sparked in Granier's eyes. "What about the

sacrifices our men made, the lives we lost? Are we just supposed to pretend that none of that happened, that it was all just some elaborate charade?"

“The truth is, the world doesn't always reward the righteous, doesn't always acknowledge the sacrifices of the brave."

He straightened up, his voice taking on a note of finality. "We do what we have to do, what we need to do to survive. We play the game as best we can. And in the end, when the dust settles and the smoke clears, we'll still be standing, ready to fight another day. While you may have fallen short of your ultimate goal of getting the South Vietnamese military to defend its borders, your operation was not a total loss. You hurt our enemy and that is never a bad thing. Our analysis shows that may have even slowed them down. Their fuel reserves were greatly reduced and your assault on their airfield and armored vehicle staging area cost them equipment that is not easily replaced. It will take them time to make up for the losses and they won’t want to begin their final offensive with those replacements. While I don’t approve of how you went about it, I think you did something that the South Vietnamese weren’t doing and they should have. You and your team made a difference. That’s to be commended."

Coyle and Granier were silent for a long moment, their minds racing with the implications of Polgar's words. They had always known that the world of covert operations was a murky one, filled with shades of gray and moral ambiguities. As CIA officers they were part of that world.

As they looked into Polgar's eyes, as they saw the steely determination and unwavering resolve that burned within, they knew that they had no choice, that they would have to play the game, to follow the script that had been written for them.

"This war is drawing to a close whether we like it or not," said Polgar. "We have other wars to fight in other countries. If America is to survive, we must stop the communist revolution wherever it raises its ugly head. We need men like you to do that. You do as we say and we'll get you out of this. And then… NEVER DO IT AGAIN unless so ordered."

Granier and Coyle thought for a long moment. They knew that they were skirting the hangman's noose or at least a long prison sentence. Neither relished the thought of covering up what they had done. It seemed cowardly. But Polgar was right. There would be other wars to fight and they were both warriors at heart. It was hard to let Vietnam go. They, like many others, had fought so hard to win, made so many sacrifices, lost so many friends. It didn't seem right to just move on to the next war. There were still things that needed to be done. People that helped them that needed to get out.

The one thing they were both sure of was they were no help to anyone if they were behind bars or dead. And so, with heavy hearts and a bucket full of misgivings, they agreed to take Polgar's lead and let him get them out of the mess they have created. If only it had worked, but it wasn't in the cards.

"I'm leaving the guards, but I'll have the handcuffs removed," said Polgar as moved to leave. "It's not that I don't trust you. I'm just not a fool. You keep your noses clean and get better. We've got a rough year ahead of us."

And with that, Polgar left.

"So, now what?" said Coyle.

"The beast is coming and nobody is going to stop it. We need to get our people out as fast as possible."

"Our people?"

"Anyone that helped us during the war will be considered a traitor by the communists. The final offensive will be a death sentence to anyone that stays. We can't let that happen."

"How are we going to do that?"

"We still have a team. We'll use them."

"And what if Polgar disagrees?"

"He plays his game, we play ours," said Granier.

Moments later, one of the guards removed their handcuffs.

Letter to Reader

Dear Reader:

I hope you enjoyed *Twilight of War*. Unlike most of my previous novels in the series, Twilight of War was more about the characters than the history. I enjoy writing about Coyle and Granier. This was a chance to unleash them in a way I have not done before. Anyway, I hope you liked it. The next novel in the Airmen Series is ***The Beast Cometh*** – Book 21. Here's a quick snapshot:

Coyle, Granier, and their team of elite warriors have one final mission that must be completed before the communist capture Saigon and the war ends. There will be a final battle for the country, but Vietnam's fate seems to have already been decided… or has it?
I can't tell you anything more or I will spoil it.

Oh, and there're lots of historical battles and suspense. And of course, we find out the final fate of our heroes. I hope you like it.

Sharing my work with your friends and reviews are always welcome. Thank you for supporting The Airmen Series.

Regards,

David Lee Corley, Author

TWILIGHT OF WAR

Author's Biography

Born in 1958, David grew up on a horse ranch in Northern California, breeding and training appaloosas. He has had all his toes broken at least once and survived numerous falls and kicks from ornery colts and fillies. David started writing professionally as a copywriter in his early 20's. At thirty-two, he packed up his family and moved to Malibu, California, to live his dream of writing and directing motion pictures. He has four motion picture screenwriting credits and two directing credits. His movies have been viewed by over fifty million movie-goers worldwide and won a multitude of awards, including the Malibu, Palm Springs, and San Jose Film Festivals. In addition to his twenty-four screenplays, he has written fourteen novels. He developed his simplistic writing style after rereading his two favorite books, Ernest Hemingway's *The Old Man and the Sea* and Cormac McCarthy's *No Country For Old Men* An avid student of world culture, David lived as an expat in both Thailand and Mexico. At fifty-six, he sold all his possessions and became a nomad for four years. He circumnavigated the globe three times and visited fifty-six countries. Known for his detailed descriptions, his stories often include actual experiences and characters from his journeys.

www.ingramcontent.com/pod-product-compliance
Lightning Source LLC
Chambersburg PA
CBHW030623310726
48979CB00003B/857

* 9 7 8 1 9 5 9 5 3 4 3 1 0 *